Thomas A. Janvier, Félix Gras, Catharine A. Janvier

The Reds of the Midi

An episode of the French revolution

Thomas A. Janvier, Félix Gras, Catharine A. Janvier

The Reds of the Midi
An episode of the French revolution

ISBN/EAN: 9783337227470

Printed in Europe, USA, Canada, Australia, Japan

Cover: Foto ©Andreas Hilbeck / pixelio.de

More available books at **www.hansebooks.com**

AN EPISODE
OF THE FRENCH REVOLUTION

TRANSLATED FROM THE PROVENÇAL OF

FÉLIX GRAS

BY

CATHARINE A. JANVIER

WITH AN INTRODUCTION BY

THOMAS A. JANVIER

NEW YORK

D APPLETON AND COMPANY

1896

CONTENTS.

INTRODUCTION.

In all French history there is no more inspiring episode than that with which M. Gras deals in this story: the march to Paris, and the doings in Paris, of that Marseilles Battalion made up of men who were sworn to cast down "the tyrant" and who "knew how to die." And he has been as happy, I think, in his choice of method as in his choice of subject. Had his hero been a grown man, or other than a peasant, there would have been more reasoning in the story and less directness. But this delightful peasant-boy Pascalet—so simple and brave and honest and altogether lovable— knows very little about reasoning. To him the French Revolution is but the opportunity that he has longed for to avenge the wrongs done to his peasant father; and he is eager to capture "the King's Castle" and to overthrow "the tyrant" because he understands—though vaguely: for the Castle he believes to be only a day's march across the mountains from Avignon, and the tyrant is a very hazy concept in his little mind—that somewhere along these lines of spirited action harm will come to the particular Marquis against whom his grievance lies. And so he joins the Marseilles Battalion and goes with it on its conquering way; and through his uninstructed, but very wide open, eyes we see all that happens on, and all that flows from, that heroic march. Nor are the standards and convictions which accompanied the action changed in the narration. Pascalet has become old Pascal; but he still is a peasant, and he still regards the events which he tells about from the peasant's point of view.

It is this point of view, with its necessarily highly objective scheme of treatment, which gives to M. Gras's story a place entirely apart from all the fiction of the French Revolution with which I am acquainted. Ordinarily—because it is so much easier to do—writers of stories of this period prefer to make them with Aristocrats for heroes and heroines; and, done that way, it certainly is very easy indeed to excite sympathy and to achieve lurid dramatic effect. But the more difficult way that M. Gras has chosen, and in choosing has cast aside deliberately so much of the easily-manipulated machinery of ordinary romance, seems to me to lead to far more realistic and also to far more artistic results. His epitome of the motive-power of the Revolution in the feelings of one of its individual peasant parts is the very essence of simplicity and directness; and equally simple and direct is his method of presentment. Old Pascal goes straight ahead with his recital of personal incident and of the scraps of historic fact which have come, more or less accurately, to his personal knowledge because he was a part of them himself; and his rare attempts at explanation of the undermeaning of events is but the echo of the popular sentiment of the time in which he lived. The author always is out of sight in the background. Even in the instances when a side-light is necessary it comes with an absolute naturalness in the shape of question or comment from the chorus—from one or another of the delightful little company in the Shoemaker's shop to which the story is told. This method has the largeness and the clearness of the Greek drama. The motives are distinct. The action is free and bold. The climax is inevitable. Even allowing for my natural prejudice in favour of the work of a very dear friend, I think that I am right in holding this story in high esteem as an unusual and excellent work of art.

A leading motive with the author has been to do justice to a body of men that history has treated very unfairly. For more than a century the Battalion that marched from Marseilles to Paris, and there took so large a part in precipitating the French Revolution, has been very generally slandered. French and English historians, with few exceptions, have united in describing it as a band of cut-throats and thieves: in part made up of runaway galley-slaves from Toulon, and in part of international scrapings from the slums of Marseilles. Carlyle, in his time, was almost alone in doing partial justice to this company of hot patriots. "Forçats they were not, neither was there plunder nor danger of it," he wrote; but added, hedgingly: "Men of regular life or the best filled purse, they could hardly be." Yet, lacking full knowledge in the premises, his Scotch shrewdness withheld him from committing himself. "These Marseillese," he concluded, "remain inarticulate, undistinguishable in feature; a black-browed mass, full of grim fire, who wend there in the hot sultry weather: very singular to contemplate. They

wend; amid the infinitude of doubt and dim
peril; they not doubtful: Fate and Feudal Europe, having decided, come girdling in from
without; they, having also decided, do march
within. Dusty of face, with frugal refresh-
ment, they plod onwards; unweariable, not to
be turned aside. Such march shall become famous. They must . . . strike and be struck;
and on the whole prosper, and know how to
die." But he felt that he had not uncovered
all the truth, and that what remained hidden
was worth digging for. Before parting with
these vaguely-defined heroes he offered the
suggestion: "If enlightened·Curiosity ever get
sight of the Marseilles Council-Books, will it
not perhaps explore this strangest of Municipal
procedures; and feel called to fish up what of
the Biographies, creditable or discreditable, of
these Five hundred and Seventeen (*sic*), the
stream of Time has not irrevocably swallowed."

Nearly fifty years passed before Carlyle's
suggestion was carried out in its entirety; and
the two men who then completely cleared up
this obscure passage in history, Messieurs Joseph Pollio and Adrien Marcel, did much more
than explore the Marseilles Council-Books.
They carried their search for facts deep and far;
and the result of their investigations was the

documentary history, "Le Bataillon du 10
Août" (Paris. Charpentier. 1881), that has
placed the Marseilles Battalion honourably before the world.   As the records show, the five
hundred and sixteen men composing it, drawn
almost wholly from the National Guard of Marseilles, "were carefully chosen as being those
whose civicism and probity were guaranteed
by the twelve Commissioners named by the
Conseil Général"; and the few volunteers from
neighbouring towns—including, in the Third
Company, Louis Vauclair from Avignon—were
accepted under the same conditions.   In the
end, having accomplished the purpose for
which it went to Paris, the Battalion returned
to Marseilles; where it was received with civic
honours (October 22, 1792), and subsequently
was incorporated into the Army of the Pyrénées.   Other battalions were despatched from
Marseilles, at later dates, which were less carefully chosen and which had records by no
means so good.   With these the first Battalion
has been confounded, either by accident or in-
tention, and ever since has suffered for their
sins.   But the men of Marseilles with whom
Pascalet marched, chanting the Republican An-
them that ever since has been known by their
name because they first gave it currency in

France, were precisely the simple and honest patriots—stern only in the discharge of the great duty which they believed was theirs—whom M. Gras has described.

The loving touch that is so evident in the setting of the story comes naturally, for there the author is writing of his own people and his own home. It was in the little town of Malemort, a year worse than half a century ago, that Félix Gras was born. His charming Prologue—even his lament that Fate forbade him to be a shoemaker, and so cut him off from hearing any more of old Pascal's stories—is pure autobiography; and the lightly, and so delightfully, touched-in portraits—the Grandfather, Lou Materoun, the Shoemaker and the rest, including old Pascal himself—are all direct from life.

I am confident that M. Gras would have become a very good shoemaker, had he been permitted to follow the inclination that was so strong upon him when he was ten years old. Assuredly, he would have given to the practice of that gentle and philosophic craft the same energy (though differently applied) that has won for him success in law and in literature. But as the Department of Vaucluse would have lost an excellent Juge de Paix, and as the world would have lost a rare poet, it is fortunate that his shoemaking aspirations were sapped by the judicious interposition of the colour-box and the cornet-à-pistons and the five little blue volumes telling about the War of Troy.

When his schooling was ended he came back to his father's farm at Malemort; but as his passion for hunting (quite as strong now as then) led him most outrageously to neglect his farm-work in order to go off with his dog and gun into the fastnesses of Mont Ventour, he presently was despatched—being then twenty years old—to Avignon to begin the study of the law: from which study farther escapades into the mountains were not practicable.

In his case the ways of the law led into the ways of literature very directly. The Avignon notary to whom he was articled, Maître Jules Giéra, was himself a writer of merit and was the brother of Paul Giéra, one of the seven founders of the Félibrige: the society of Provençal men of letters, having for its leaders Frédéric Mistral and Joseph Roumanille, which has developed in the past thirty years so noble a literary and moral renascence not only in Provence but throughout the whole of Southern France. With one of these leaders, Roumanille—who had married Rose Anaïs Gras, his sister, the winner of the prize for poetry at the Floral Games at Apt in 1862—he already was intimate; and his coming to Avignon, and entry into the lawyer's office, therefore, was his entry into the most inspiring artistic society that has existed in modern times—that has had, indeed, no modern parallel in its vigour and hopes and enthusiasms save perhaps in the Pre-Raphaelite Brotherhood; and that has had no modern parallel whatever in its far-reaching results. His association with such companions, with whose aspirations he was in close sympathy, quickly produced its natural consequences: he accepted law as his profession, but he made literature his career.

He has justified his choice. His first important work, an epic poem in twelve cantos, "Li Carbouniè" (1876), treating of the mountain life for which his affection was so profound, placed him at the head of the younger generation of Félibres; and his succeeding epic, "Toloza" (1882), with his shorter poems collected under the title "Lou Roumancero Prouvençau" (1887), placed him second only to the master of all Provençal poetry, Mistral.

The theme of " Toloza " is the crusade of Simon de Montfort against the Albigenses—treated with a fervent strength that is in keeping with the author's own fervent love of liberty in person and in conscience, and with the beauty that comes of a poetic temperament equipped with easy command of poetic form. It vibrates with a very lofty patriotism and with strong martial spirit and with a great tenderness, this *geste provençale* in which the gleaming flitting figures of the two dames and the four troubadours at once enlighten the sombre narrative and stand out with a clear brightness against the black back-ground of that unholy war.

His shorter poems have a different and, as it seems to me, a still richer flavour. But perhaps I like them best because it was through them that I first knew him. Of the volume in which they are in part collected, " Lou Roumancero Prouvençau," I wrote five years ago: " We had read no farther than 'Lou Papo d'Avignoun' and 'Lou Baroun de Magalouno' when our minds were made up that here was a singer of ballads whose tongue was tipped with fire. They whirled upon us, these ballads and conquered our admiration at a blow. We knew by instinct—what time and greater knowledge have shown to be the truth—that

of all the Provençal poets whom we soon were
to encounter none would set our heart-strings
more keenly a-thrilling than did this fiery bal-
lad-maker, Monsieur Gras." And after our
meeting had taken place I added: "Our ideal
had not exceeded the reality. As fine and as
sympathetic as his poems is Félix Gras himself.
The graciousness of his person, his gentle nature that is also a most vigorously manly nature, his quick play of wit, his smile, his voice
—all were in keeping with, even exceeded,
what we had hoped to find." That was five
years ago. My appreciation of his work is
fuller, my feeling toward himself is deeper,
now.

His prose is the prose of a poet, yet racy
and strong. As a leading contributor to the
Armana Prouvençau—of which annual, the
most important of the periodic publications of
the Félibres, he has been the editor since Roumanille's death—he long since won popu-
larity with a public that judges by high standards and that by nature is nicely critical. But
his finest prose work is included in a volume
of Avignon stories, "Li Papalino" (1891) which
have the ring of the *novella* of Boccaccio's
time. In these stories his delicate firmness of
touch is combined with a brilliancy and clear-

ness of style that presents his dramatic subjects with the sparkle and vivacity of the Italian tale-tellers of the Thirteenth and Fourteenth centuries —but always with a flavour distinctly his own. The Papal Court of Avignon is alive again before our eyes: with its gallantries, its tragedies, its gay loves and deadly hates, its curious veneering of religious forms upon Mediæval tenderness and ferocity. With this period, which appeals so strongly to poetic instinct, he long has been on terms of commanding familiarity; as not only these stories but many of his most fiery shorter poems show. And it seems to me, therefore, that not least to be commended of the qualities included in his literary equipment is the flexibility that has enabled him, in the present work, so entirely to change his method in order to adapt it to the vivid treatment of a subject taken from modern times.

Finally, this prophet is honoured in his own country. Since August, 1891—in succession to Roumanille, who succeeded Mistral—Félix Gras has been the Capoulié, the official head, of the Félibrige. In his election to this office he received the highest honour that can be bestowed upon a poet by his brother poets of the South of France.

The present translation has been made directly from the Provençal manuscript, under the author's supervision and with the benefit of his advice. The only changes from the original are a few modifications of expression which, while proper enough in the case of country-folk speaking a language of Latin origin, would jar a little on ears tolerant only of the nicety of English speech; and these changes the author has approved. Otherwise the translation has preserved the letter, and I think somewhat of the spirit of the original; and I can venture to say for it, at least, that it has been made with a faithful and a loving care.

THOMAS A. JANVIER.

SAINT REMY DE PROVENCE,
September 1, 1895.

THE REDS OF THE MIDI.

PROLOGUE.

WHEN our neighbour Pascal, the son of La Patine, had grown so very, very old that he had begun to nibble into his ninetieth year, his dotage came upon him. He, who in the long winter evenings had told us from thread to finished seam how he marched with the Marseilles Battalion up to Paris to besiege King Capet in his castle; Pascal, who had told us of all the battles of the Empire, from the famous fight at the Pyramids to the end of all at Mont-Saint-Jean; good old Pascal de la Patine was certainly in his dotage.

Over and over again he kept saying: "I shall die soon; I certainly am going to die; and when I die my brother Lange will die too—and then who will take care of the mule?"

Poor Pascal! It was sad to see in such a plight the man who had dazzled us with his

epic tales, lasting the winter long. Sometimes,
even, he would improvise in verse in a slow
rhythm, with only here and there a rhyme.
Through a whole evening he would chant us
an episode of the Revolution; or of some
grand killing of English or Germans or Rus-
sians in the time gone by.

· I still can see him: always seated in the
same place, on the middle of the bench that
ran across the whole width of the wall at the
back of the shoemaker's shop—the meeting
place to which all the neighbours came to
spend their evenings.

The shoemaker and his apprentice used between them a single lamp; but each had his
separate *vihole*, hanging before him by a
leather thong, and the reddish lamp-light passing through the globe of clear water cast upon
the sole or shoe on which he was working a
brilliant streak of light as clear as sunlight.
The good stove, as red as a poppy, made the
room oven-hot. We all sweltered there comfortably, simmering like a stew in an earthen
tian. And when old Pascal, passing into one
of his bard-like moods, fell to chanting his
story, then even the shoemaker and his apprentice, braving the angry looks of the shoemaker's wife, turned their backs to the work-

table and for that evening stopped tap-tapping on their soles and like the rest of us listened open-mouthed with eyes as big as barn-doors and ears like dish-covers.

I know now that the supreme joy of my life came to me then, when I was nine years old: when as each evening ended and bed-time came I longed and longed for the morrow —that I might hear, as I sat in my corner, on my little bench with the cat, the end of the battle left half-fought the night before.

Therefore was it a mortal blow to me when, being come to ten years, I was sent to the little seminary of La Sainte Garde to begin my school-ing. I even now can plainly see my father's cart harnessed to our old sorrel horse—who in all his long life never once had kicked. I see it plainly as it bumps over the stony road through the *garrigues*, carrying my mattrass in a blue-and-white checked cover, and my pig-skin trunk with stiff silky bristles standing out all over it. I see our pretty blue cart—in which, in our stable, I often had played see-saw—standing at last in the seminary court-yard; while two men, dressed like gentlemen in frock coats, take out its load.

It was then that my sorrow sharply began. My father took me up in his arms and gave me

two big kisses (even to-day I can feel his rough
beard against my soft cheeks); he put a great
handful of sous into my hand—and then he left
me! Victor the door-keeper, who had a little
pointed beard on his chin that made him look
like a good-natured goat, came with his great
bunch of keys and, cric-crac, locked the door!

As long as daylight lasted, things went on
pretty well. I counted and recounted my sous,
letting them drop one by one so as to show
them off. I made the acquaintance of a dozen
little fellows shut in like myself that morning.
But after supper, when night fell, when I—alas,
poor me!—had to go to bed all alone, I thought
of my dear mother who when I came home
dead with sleep from the shoemaker's always
helped me untie my shoes; and I thought of old
Pascal de la Patine, whom I could plainly see
sitting on the bench telling his beautiful stories.
The tears burst forth, pouring down my cheeks
to my pillow. I cried and cried; until at last
sleep, the childish sleep that nothing disturbs,
took possession of me and held me softly in
her arms.

When I awoke, the idea that all day long
I could not see my mother, and that again,
when night-fall came, I could not spend the
evening with old Pascal, tormented me and

made me dull and unhappy. The next night I cried still more, and the next day I was still more dull.

At the end of a week my father and mother came to see if I had eaten and slept as I should, and if I were getting used to my new life. How I dismayed them when I told them that I could not eat, and that I wanted to go home!

"But, my boy, surely you see that you must study. You must learn arithmetic and all the rest, otherwise what will become of you when you grow up?" said my father.

"I say I want to go home. I know quite enough."

"What do you know, child? You know just nothing at all!"

"I know how to read."

"You can read, yes. Well, what then?"

"I know how to cipher."

"That's all very well, as far as it goes; but you must learn latin, greek—how do I know what more!"

"I don't want to—I want to go home with you!"

"Now see here, what do you want to be —a doctor, a priest, or a lawyer?"

"None of them."

"You want to be a farmer? That's a

poor trade, son. You must get rid of that notion."

"No, I don't want to be a farmer—I want to go home!"

All this time my mother said nothing. She merely nodded her head, while she kept on peeling chestnuts for me—which I munched while contradicting my father. Until at last, fairly out of all patience, my father cried : "Speak out then! If you don't want to be doctor, priest, lawyer nor farmer, what do you want to be ?"

"Well, if really you wish me to tell," said I, looking down, "I want—I want to be a shoemaker!"

"Oh plague take you!" said my father, clapping his rough hands together, "a shoemaker! That beats all! Don't you know that shoemakers always smell of shoemaker's wax ? Come, come, I think the blood in your veins must be dying out. What could have put it into your head to be a shoemaker ?"

But I, ashamed of having betrayed my inmost thoughts, did not dare to answer. I dared not say that it was because I longed to listen forever to the stories old Pascal de la Patine would tell during all the long evenings to come. What would I not have been willing to become, so that I might ever hear such stories!

Well, my father, knowing that time would settle all, persuaded me to remain a few days longer at the school; and promised me that if I could not get used to the school-life he would come for me at the end of the month, and that if then I still was absolutely determined to become a shoemaker I should be apprenticed to our neighbour, in whose house I had passed so many happy evenings. But in order to reconcile me to my new school he said that I might study painting—which at that time was my great passion—and also music; and then and there he ordered for me a colour-box and a cornet-à-pistons: Mr. Trouchet, the steward, was to have them brought from Carpentras the very next day.

Dazzled by the promise of these delights, I felt as if a great weight were lifted off my heart; and, rising on tip-toe, I whispered in my mother's ear: "Please send me the five little blue books that I read three years ago when I had the whooping-cough—the books that tell about Ulysses and Achilles."

"Yes, yes, I know" said my mother, "the War of Troy. I will send them to-morrow."

Then my dear people gave me another handful of sous, and filled my pockets with boiled chestnuts. They kissed me; and then, cric-crac, Victor the door-keeper with the kind goat's face barred the door behind them—and thoughtfully I returned to my lessons.

Nevertheless, the paint-box, the cornet-à-pistons, and my promised five little blue books, filled my heart with joy: and it is to those three things that I owe my escape from having become a cobbler for the rest of my days. Naturally, I grew accustomed to the seminary; and great Homer with his War of Troy drove old Pascal out of my mind.

And yet—often I ask myself: Would it not have been better to have persisted? Had I become a shoemaker, how many good stories might I not have told! And now I can tell you only one: the one that I heard in the happy year which ended when I put on trowsers with suspenders and began my schooling—and so left shoemaking forever behind!

CHAPTER I.

IN THE BAD OLD TIMES.

THAT evening the party was complete. I, in my corner on the little bench with the cat, said not a word; but I thought to myself: "If only some one would ask old Pascal to tell a story! Yesterday he finished telling us the battle of Mont Saint-Jean; to-day, perhaps, he will tell us nothing."

Just then Lou Materoun, as he pressed with his thumb into his clay pipe a piece of amadou that smelt sweet as it burned, said: "I've always wanted to ask you, Pascal, how it was that you, a peasant from Malemort, happened to be in the Battalion from Marseilles that went up to Paris the year of the Revolution? That always has puzzled me."

"It was poverty, young fellow," old Pascal answered in his rich clear voice; "it was just poverty. But if you have the patience to listen I'll tell you about it from first to last."

We knew then that a story was coming;

and so we all settled ourselves comfortably to listen, and old Pascal began:

Why are people always grunting, now-a-days? They actually grunt because of over-plenty! Now-a-days each peasant has his own corner of earth. He who has earth has bread, and he who has bread has blood. I, who am speaking to you, was twelve years old before ever I had seen either kneading-trough, bread-hutch, oil-jar or wine-keg; things owned now-a-days by the poorest peasant in the land. In the one room of my father's hut—it was more a hut than a cottage—were two cradle-like boxes filled with oat-straw in which we slept, the cooking-pot in the middle of the room hanging from a roof-beam, and a big chopping-block—and that was all! That was just all!

We were lodged in this hut, which stood a little above the village of Malemort and close to the Château de la Garde, because we belonged—with the other farm animals—to the estate of La Garde, owned by the Marquis d'Ambrun. My father gathered the acorns from the oaks of the Marquis, and was allowed to keep the half of them for his pay; and we also had the right to till two scraps of land, from which we got enough beans and vetches and herbs to keep us from actually starving to death —we three and all our fleas. You will know how we lived when I tell you that not until I got away from La Garde altogether did I taste anything as good as a bit of fresh-baked soft bread dipped in soup made of rancid pork.

My people baked bread but once a year. When the day for making it came my father and mother went down to the village and there, husks and all, kneaded the coarse flour made of the rye and beans and acorns we had managed to collect in the course of the year. It was on the very block that you can see in front of our stable, the one on which I cut fodder for the mule, that each morning my father with his big axe chopped up our food for the day. By the end of the year the bread was so hard that it nicked the edge of the axe.

The first bit of white bread that ever I tasted was given me one day as I passed in front of the Château by Mademoiselle Adeline, who was of the same age as myself. And for giving it to me she got a round scolding from her mother, the Marquise.

"Adeline, Adeline!" cried the Marquise, "Why do you give your white bread to that little wretch? You must not teach him what white bread is, or the day may come when he will snatch it out of your mouth!" and then turning to me, she went on: "Get out of here, little beast! Get out! Hurry—or I will set the dogs on you!" And I, gripping fast my bit of bread, scampered off to our hut as fast as I could go. That piece of bread was the most delicious thing I have eaten in all my life. And yet the cruel words of the Marquise made it bitter with a drop of gall.

Another time I was worse served. I was coming home from a hunt for some magpies' nests that I knew of in the poplars in the valley of the Nesque. It was ten o'clock; and, as I had eaten nothing that day, hunger was twisting my empty insides. As I passed behind the Château, skirting the stables and sheep-folds, I saw in the gutter a fine cabbage-stalk. My mouth watered and I ran to pick it up; but the Marquis's sow with her litter also saw it at the same time, and ran as quick as I did. The swine-herd, a cruel fellow, when he saw me stretch out my arm gave me such a whack with his stick that he took away my breath. I left the cabbage-stalk to the pigs and ran as hard as I could run, for the brute would have beaten me to a jelly; and as I made off I heard the Marquis calling from his window: "Well done! Well done! What is that little rascal doing there? Does he want to take the food out of the mouths of my pigs? Vermin that they are, those peasants! If they could but get at us, they would eat us up alive!"

That day another great drop of bitterness fell into my heart.

So, too, when Monsieur le Marquis, Madame le Marquise and Monsieur Robert, their son—who was Cavalier du Roy—chanced one day to pass before our hut and I saw my old father and my old mother kneel down on the threshold, just as if the Host were going by, shame devoured me; and it seemed as if a red hot iron were pressing into the pit of my stomach—it hurt me so to keep back my rage.

"You wretched boy," called out my father as he rose from his knees, "the next time I'll take good care that you kneel to our kind master!"; and to know how good and how simple my father was made the fire, not of God, burn the more fiercely within me.

The only one of those living in the Château whom I could look upon with pleasure and salute with respect was little Adeline, the young lady who gave me the piece of white bread. She had gentle eyes, and smiled at me each time that we chanced to meet. But as she grew up it seemed to me that little by little her smiles grew fainter. Her eyes, I know, were just as gentle, only I dared not look at her any more.

One November evening during All Saint's week, while we were in our hut around a pot of dried beans—the last left from our store for the year—my father said: "To-morrow, son, we must begin to gather our acorns in the Nesque for the winter. Times are going to be hard with us. I don't know all that is taking place, but I have been told that in Avignon people are killing each other off like flies; and there is the Revolution in Paris, and Monsieur le Marquis and all the family are going to help the King of France, who is in great danger."

This was the first time I had heard of the King of France, but instantly the thought came to me: "If I could only fight him, this King of France whom the Marquis is going to defend!" How old was I then? I don't know. I never knew exactly—the records of baptism, you see, were burned; but I must have been thirteen, perhaps fourteen years old. Certainly, my father's words astonished me—but as much, perhaps, by their number as by what he told. He always had a short tongue, poor man.

The next morning I had forgotten all about the King of France when, before day-break, we started to gather our harvest of acorns.   It was fearful weather.   The ground was frozen two spans deep; a cutting wind was blowing; from time to time snow-squalls burst out of the sullen sky.   The dawn was just breaking when we reached the ravine of the Nesque, bordered by great oaks: through which the wind blew sharply and tossed hither and thither their leaves—that looked as if they had been turned into red copper by the cold.   Excepting the red oak-leaves, everything on the earth and above it was grey.   The sky was one mass of even grey cloud, stretching from east to west just like a piece of grey felt. Flocks of linnets, red-breasts, yellow-hammers, and other little birds came down from the mountains—flying close to the ground or, with feathers all fluffed up, huddling together in the stubble or bushes.   When the poor little things act that way, it always is bitter cold.

Let any one try to gather acorns in cold weather with numb hands!   Among the pebbles in the dry bed of the river the shining acorns, no bigger than olives, so slide and slip through your fingers that it takes a whole big half day to gather two pecks of them.   My

3

poor father, I can see him now! As he crouched down and leaned forward he left between his skimpy greenish stuff-jacket and his buckled breeches a great gap, where the sharp edge of his lean spine showed plainly through his coarse worn-out shirt; and his rough woollen stockings were full of holes, and so worn off at the heels that his feet were naked in his wooden shoes stuffed with dry grass.

The furious cold wind, which whipped about and whirled the copper-red leaves, whistled in the osiers; and in the hollows of the rocks it howled and roared like some great fearful horn. I hugged myself close, my skin all cracked with the cold, and thought of the good time to come when, sheltered behind a rock, we could eat, with our hunger for a sauce, the hard nubbin of black bread which my father that morning had chopped off for us on the block with the big axe.

We were working hard in silence—for the very poor never have much to say—when all of a sudden I heard the hounds of the Marquis in full cry. They were at the other end of the ravine, on the slope of the mountain. I jumped up and stared with all my might. When one is young there is nothing so delightful as to see a hare chased by a pack of dogs. I saw them a long, long way off: the hare, light as smoke, was far ahead. From time to time she would squat on her haunches, listening, and then would be off again; and at last I saw her run down toward the dry bed of the stream. The hounds, in full cry, came tearing after her. When they over-ran the scent, they quickly tried back and found it again. Where the hare had stopped to listen, they snuffed around and yelped the louder. The pack was spread all across the slope. In front were the large black-and-tan hounds, their ears a span long, who easily over-leapt bushes and openings in the ground. Then came the smaller and heavier dogs, slower but surer. Then, away behind the rest, the beagles with their short sharp cry—good beasts for taking the hare in her form, but slow-going, because their little twisted legs are no good for jumping and they have to go round even the bunches of wild thyme.

I held my breath, for the hare was almost on us and was going to pass right in front of me. But just as I picked up a stone—sbisto! she saw me! She doubled like a flash, with one spring she was over the Nesque, and with another she was up the mountain side and safe in the woods—so good-bye to my hare! The dogs came on quickly, overrunning the scent at the point where she had doubled, but picking it up again in no time. And then the whole pack in full cry swept on down the hillside until they were lost in the forest far off among the ravines, and only their cry came ringing back to us faintly from the distance.

My father had not noticed any part of all this. Without even lifting his head he had kept on gathering the acorns with his stiff fingers. As I still stood there, open-mouthed, all of a sudden on the slope of the mountain behind me I heard a noise of rolling stones. I turned and saw Monsieur Robert, the Cavalier du Roy, running down toward us; holding in one hand his dog-whip and in the other his gun. He rushed down on us like a wounded wild boar—it is the only thing I can think of as savage as he was then! My poor father at once dropped down on his knees to him, as was the peasant habit of those times; but the brute, without a word, gave him such a blow across the face with his dog-whip that he knocked him to the ground. Seeing this, I ran to the side of the ravine and, kicking off my sabots, began to climb up the rocks —clinging with my hands and with my feet too. I heard every blow that lashed my poor father, and I heard the brute calling out to him: "Dirty beast of a peasant! I'll teach you to spoil my hunting!"—and then more blows.

In the mean time the game-keeper had come up: a huge man who could only speak very bad French. Folks said he was a German. He had a name no one could say—a Dutch name fit to drive you out of the house—and, as he had to be called something, we called him Surto. This beast also began to hammer my poor father, who was writhing on the ground like a half crushed worm.

I had stopped on a high rock from which I could see the two monsters at their cruel work. I picked up a stone as big as my head and threw it. The stone whistled through the air, just brushing against the game-keeper's ear, and fell hard and heavy on Monsieur Robert's toes.

"Aïe!" he yelled, and turning saw me. Off went both barrels of his gun. The shot whizzed round me, but I plunged into the wood—and then it was: Catch me who can!

I was only a child—but I understood my danger. I hid myself in the depths of the woods and did not dare go back home. Shivering, almost dead with the cold, I ate my bit of bread crouching in a thicket and a little sheltered behind a rock. The bread was so hard that I had to break it with a stone. I softened it with my tears; for while eating it I was thinking of my father as I had seen him with his face all covered with blood, and dreading that he had been killed. And my mother, what would she think when I did not come back to the hut? And when she saw her poor man, her Pascal, crushed and bleeding? "Ah!" sighed I, looking at the stone I held, "Ah, how happy this stone is. How I would like to be this stone, for then I would not suffer any more"—and my heart hurt me as if it was cut with a knife.

Twilight was coming on. In winter it does not last long; the night comes all at once. The wind blew sharper and sharper. Far off on the edge of the sky a long red line streaked the grey clouds and showed that the sun was setting. Then the sky and plains and mountains, which all day long had been dull grey, turned to a violet; while the trees and the naked bushes and the rocks took on a reddish tone. The wind dropped a moment, paying honour to the setting sun; a fox barked on the opposite slope—and then suddenly all was dark.

I ventured out of my lair and climbed the

bushy side of the ravine.   Just as I reached the top, brrrou! a covey of partridges flew off from right under my feet with a sound like a load of cobblestones tumbling out of a cart.   The start they gave me was soon over; and then, shivering and blue with the cold, I went down into the plain.

At almost every step I halted and looked around.   The smallest rock, a tuft of thyme, a live-oak bush, seemed a crouching man on the outlook—perhaps Surto with his gun! I was more afraid of that man than of all the wolves on the mountains put together.   Although the wind still roared and howled, the stones rattling under my feet seemed to me to make a tremendous noise.   The night was very dark—not a star to be seen; the dull grey sky still spread over everything.   Yet I could see pretty well around me.   We the poor, the very poor, can see in the dark.   The flocks were all in their folds, it was so cold.   But as I went along the slope above the Nesque, not far above the Château, it seemed to me that I could hear the pigs grunting; and I certainly could see the light carried by the swine-herd—so it must have been about pig-feeding time.

I had but a few steps more to take in order to reach the high rock from which I had thrown the stone at Monsieur Robert. I was burning to get there, that I might know whether or not my father was lying dead at the bottom of the ravine, beaten to death by those two beasts. I walked softly along, but the little stones still made too much noise under my feet and I got down and crawled silently on all fours. I reached the overhang of the rock and craned over into the ravine. I stared and stared until I could see no more, but all that I could make out was a long black line and a long white line coasting the foot of the mountain. The giant oaks which bordered the Nesque made the black line, and the white line was the dry bed of the watercourse with its smooth white stones.

When I was quite certain that my father was not lying there, to be food for the wolves, I drew softly back on hands and knees. Still filled with dread, I went down into the ravine through the holly and thorny scrub-oak bushes; pushing through the thickets, for I did not want to follow any beaten path to the Nesque. I was afraid of that great monster of a game-keeper who somewhere, I was sure, was watching for me as if I had been a fox—and I thought that the whistling of the wind and the rattling of the whirling leaves would keep any one from hearing the noise of the holly and the thorny oak bushes which caught hold of me, and of the stones which rattled down under my feet.

When I reached the border of the Nesque I looked out between two tufts of bushes to right and to left, but neither saw nor heard anything out of the way. And, what gave me still more comfort, lying there where I had kicked them off, so that I might run the faster, were my sabots! Then—believe me or no as best pleases you—in order to give myself courage, I made the sign of the cross upon my breast and said the only prayer my mother had taught me:

> Great Saint John of the golden mouth
> Watch over the sleeping child.
> From harm protect him should he go
> To play around the pond.
> In forests, too, take care of him
> Against the tooth of wolf.
> Forever and ever be it so,
> Fair Saint John who hast all my heart.

—and then I felt that I would be cared for and was safe!

With one spring I reached and put on my sabots, and then flew like lightning through the stubble and brush and climbed steep slopes

like a lizard. I slipped through the olive-
orchards; carefully keeping away from the
paths, and as far as I could from the Château—
the gleaming windows of which I could see
on the heights above. Suddenly all the dogs
at the Château began to bark together, and as I
feared that they had heard or scented me I
went off still farther over the hills of the En-
garrouïnes—so that I might be quite safe from
the game-keeper, outside the lines of the estate.

But our hut still was far away, and I knew
that if I went there I should be caught; if not
that night, certainly the next day. Still I longed
to see my father, to comfort my mother. It
seemed as if I could hear her calling me—
"Pascalet! Pascalet!"

In spite of the dark night, my eyes could
make out far off on the hill of La Garde something black between the woods and the olive-
orchards; something that looked like a heap of
stones. It was our forlorn hut—laid up of
stones without mortar and roofed with stone
slabs. In my heart I seemed to see inside of it
our one room, our oat-straw beds, the pot
hanging by its pot-hooks and chain from the
beam, the big block behind the door on which
my father chopped the bread and which also
was our table. I longed for our little hut and

all in it; but fear, my great fear of the game-keeper, for a long while held me still.

At last I was able to screw up my courage and go on. Keeping out of the path, and taking a big stone in each hand, I went forward slowly and step by step. Now and then I stopped and listened. Feeling my way, dodging from one stone wall to another, I got at last behind the hut. Softly I crept up to the hole stuffed with grass that served us for a window, and pushing in the grass and leaning my head forward I called: "Mother! mother!"

No one answered—there was no one there!

Then my blood grew cold within me. I thought that both my father and my mother had been killed. I ran round to the door of the hut. It was wide open. The game-keeper was nothing to me then! I called out at the top of my voice: "Mother! Father! Where are you? It is your Pascalet!"—and my sorrow so hurt me that I rolled on the ground in such a passion of crying as I never before had known.

For more than an hour I lay there while I sobbed and groaned. At last, tired out, desperate, raging because I was too weak to revenge myself against those who had caused my bitter pain, I got on my feet again—while a dark thought came into my mind. The pond,

the big pond that watered all the fields of the
Château, was before me among the olive trees.
Only a month before I had seen the body of
pretty Agatha of Malemort drawn out of its
waters—a girl, not twenty years old, who had
drowned herself there because of some trouble
I could not understand. I ran off as if crazy,
my arms spread wide open as though to embrace some one; and when, through the trees,
I saw the pond glittering I thought I saw Paradise. As I came within a few steps of the
edge I closed my eyes, took three jumps, one
after the other and—pataflou! I was in the
middle of the pond!

Pascal stopped, yawned, and stretched himself. "Well, it's getting late—and I haven't
yet watered the mule. I'll tell you the rest to-
morrow. Right about face! March!"—and
he was off.

As I walked home beside my grandfather,
holding his hand, I asked him: "But Pascal
didn't really drown himself, did he?"

"Have patience, little one," my grandfather
answered. "To-morrow we shall know."

CHAPTER II

DEATH OR SLAVERY.

THE next night I ate my supper on both sides of my mouth at once—bolting my chestnuts and porridge, and all the while in fear that I might be late at the cobbler's shop and so lose even a single one of Pascal's words. And while I was gobbling I kept saying to myself: "Suppose Pascal should choose this evening to take his olives to the mill, and should leave us all gaping with no story at all!"

With my mouth still full, I got up from the table and went to the cupboard where my grandfather's lantern was kept and brought it to him ready lighted for our start. "Well," said he, "you are in a hurry, mankin."

"Oh, do come grandfather. Perhaps Pascal already has begun!" I cried beseechingly, and at the same time pulled him by the hand. But there was no need for beseeching, the good old man would have let me drag him anywhere; he refused me nothing. When I think of him, the tears come into my eyes. In a moment we were off, and we reached the cobbler's just as Pascal was stepping over the threshold.

The three of us went in together. Already the shop was nearly full. Pipes were getting loaded, ready to be balanced in turn for lighting over the smoky lamp: beside which, like two little golden suns, hung the shining *viholes*. The lively heat of the stove in the close room—tight shut all day long—with its smell of stale tobacco-smoke mingled with the smells of shoemaker's wax and wet leather, made an atmosphere so pungent that it fairly hurt one's nose; but it grew better when Lou Materoun and the rest lighted their pipes—each charged at the top with a scrap of fragrant amadou, that the fire might catch easily—and so gave us a fresh smell of burning that drowned out all the old smells of dead tobacco-smoke and wax and tan-bark and greasy leather thongs.

The shoemaker and his apprentice were hammering away at a pair of soles. They were hurrying: it was easy to see that they wanted to get done with their noisy lap-stone work and so clear the way for the story to go on. Under the blows of the mushroom-headed hammers the soles curled up and became dark and shiny. With his big black thumb, all dotted with pricks from his awl, the shoemaker turned and returned the leather on his lapstone; and presently the work was done. I was getting very· restless. I looked in the bucket under the table to see if there were any more soles to be pounded; but in the bucket, full of dark water, there were only a few stray scraps of leather—the pounding was at an end.

I couldn't hold my tongue any longer; and I, who always kept quiet, said quite boldly: " Pascal, how did you get out of the pond ? "

And Pascal, who was only waiting to be started, leaned forward a little and immediately began :

Well, my big jump ended in my sitting down in the middle of the pond with a smack that made me tingle with pain, and with a shock that went all up through me to the very roots of my hair—for the pond was frozen as hard as a stone! Hurt and half stunned, I crawled as well as I could toward the frozen bank; and there, in a sort of dazed misery, I sat down on the cold ground. What would become of me, what could I do ? I was fatherless, motherless, homeless, left all alone in the fields of a cold winter night. The only idea in my poor little head was that the one road out of my trouble was to die. I might go to the wolves in the mountains, or to Surto and the wicked Monsieur Robert at the Château—in either way the wild beasts would kill me, and I would be quit of my sorrow and pain.

But suddenly a good thought came to me. I remembered that the only time I had gone to be catechised Monsieur le Curé had said to us: "My children, never forget that God is your father. When you are in trouble or pain or poverty, or when you are nigh unto death, pray to him and he will listen unto you. And go often and see him in his own house, which is the church. Go there just as you would to some kind and charitable neighbour's house. You will see that he will help you."

The remembrance of these promises came back to me, though for three years I had never thought of them; and I got up, greatly comforted. I had often met Monsieur le Curé —or Monsieur le Prieur, as we called him in my day—on the road to the Château de la Garde. But because he went there to visit the Marquis d'Ambrun that did not make him at all the same sort of man as the Marquis. He spoke kindly to every one. He even shook

my father's hand when he met him, and would
ask after his wife La Patine and after little Pascalet. He laughed, he joked with the poorest
of us. Oh, he was good dough well baked,
that man—good all the way through.

As I went down toward the village of
Malemort in the cold darkness, whipped cruelly
by the freezing wind, I seemed to see quite
plainly our good Monsieur Randoulet: his kind
face, his grey eyes, his long white hair curling
on his shoulders, his fine delicate hands, his
gown so long that the hem always was hitting
against his heels, his black stockings, and his
shoes with their silver buckles; and in my ears
seemed to sound kind words spoken in his
womanly-gentle voice. Of all the people who
came to the Château he was the only one who
did not frighten me. He was the only one
who, when I saluted him took off his hat to
me, saying: "Good-day, little man."

It must have been about midnight when I
entered the village. No one was in the streets,
no lights were in the windows; and the only
noises were the roaring of the wind, and now
and then the banging of a badly fastened shutter, and the endless murmur of water spirting
from the fountain into the shell-shaped trough
all hung with icicles.

I went on quickly through the lonely streets, straight to the Curacy beside the church. But when I found myself in front of Monsieur Randoulet's door I began to get frightened again. Would he speak harshly to me? Would he take me back to the Château? Would he give me again to Surto? No (I answered back to myself, reassuringly), he would not do these things. Monsieur Randoulet always had smiled when he spoke to me. Kindness always shone upon his face. He was good, he could not do evil. Surely he would protect me instead of betraying me: and I raised the knocker thrice and let it fall again—one! two! three!

And then I began to tremble, in dread that I had knocked too hard. I waited, listening. Nothing stirred in the Curacy. I went back along the church wall and peered up at all the windows, but all were tightly closed and dark. I went again to the door, again lifted up the knocker, waited again a moment and then— one! two! I did not dare knock the third time. In a minute I heard the voice of Monsieur Randoulet calling: "Janetoun! Janetoun! I think I hear some one knocking;" and of Janetoun answering him from the upper story: "Monsieur is mistaken—it is only a shutter rattling in the wind." Then I knocked three times, boldly; and straightway I heard Monsieur le Curé calling: "I told you so—go see what it is."

Presently I saw a light in a window far up under the tiles; and then I heard the click-clack of Janetoun's wooden shoes as she came down the stairs. I heard her hand on the lock; but before she opened the door she called: "Who's there?"

"It's me," I answered.

"But who are you?" she called again; and I answered her: "It's Pascalet de la Patine."

Hardly had I finished saying my name when the door opened and my eyes were dazzled by the flash of light from the lamp which Janetoun carried in her hand; and as I stepped into the doorway she said crossly: "Monsieur le Curé is abed and asleep—and if he wasn't he couldn't go running through the streets in all this cold. What do you want with him? Speak up! What do you want here at this time of night, anyway?"

She shut the door behind me, for it truly was bitter cold, and went up around the turn of the spiral stairs so as to get out of the draught; and there stood facing me, waiting

for my answer. But her sharp words had so
upset me that I did not know what to say.
At last, shaking with cold and fear, I managed
to stammer out: "I want to see him."

"You want to see him! You want to see
him! Good gracious, what a box of impu-
dence! Don't you know better than to come
routing people up at two o'clock in the morning in winter weather like this? And don't
you know that it is only a death-call that would
take Monsieur le Curé out on such a night and
at such an hour? Aren't the days long enough
for you? Come when it is day."

As she spoke, Janetoun came down the
stairs—up which I had crept a step or two—to
send me into the street again. But Monsieur
le Curé had heard all our talk, luckily, and from
above called out to her: "Let little Pascalet
come up—and start a fire in the kitchen so that
he may warm himself. I wish it so."

Janetoun stopped grumbling, and her sabots
went clattering up the stair-case and I followed
her. We entered the kitchen, still warm from
the fire of the night before, and still full of the
smell of the sauces of Monsieur le Curé's supper. This alone was enough to comfort my
poor stomach—as empty as a clapperless bell!
How good Monsieur le Curé's stews must be!

I thought—for the smells were like those which came to me when I passed by the kitchen at the Château. And it was still better when Janetoun, with her face nearly an extra span long for vexation, broke some light wood across her knee and filled the fire-place with it and soon had a fine white crackling blaze. It seemed as if I had got into Paradise!

Presently I heard the soft flip-flop of Monsieur Randoulet's slippers. But when he came into the kitchen, muffled up in his long wrapper and with a blue-checked handkerchief tied around his head, I did not know him—until he spoke to me with his gentle womanly voice. Then there was no mistaking him. It was indeed good kind Monsieur Randoulet himself.

"Is it thou, Pascalet?" he said. "Thou art a good boy, and thou hast done exactly right in coming here. Do not be afraid, I will take thee to see thy father. He is badly hurt, but he will get over it." And as he spoke he stroked my cheeks with his soft hand and drew me gently to his side.

I was filled with wonder. I had not even opened my mouth, and yet Monsieur le Curé knew all that I desired.

"Where is my father, monsieur?" I ventured to ask.

"He is in the hospital, where your mother is caring for him. I will take you to them in the morning—this is not the time. I am sure you have not eaten anything to-day. Janetoun, isn't there something in the cupboard?"

"What can there be?" Janetoun answered sulkily; and as she opened the cupboard she added: "There is nothing at all but a stuffed tomato."

As she said this she put on the table a little stew-pan in which was a tomato as big as my fist and browned like a pie. Just to look at it made my mouth water!

"Would you like that?" asked Monsieur Randoulet. "Go ahead, then, and eat it. Don't be afraid. Eat it out of the pan—here is a good piece of bread—and afterwards you shall have a good cup of wine and go to bed. When day-time comes I will take you to see your father in the hospital."

To know that my father was not dead, that my mother was taking care of him, that Monsieur Randoulet would stand between me and Surto—to know all that made me so happy that I felt sick. When I tried to eat I could not manage it. My gullet was all drawn together, my mouth was dry; and my heart still was so full of the dismal fear of that dreadful day that there was no room in it for my joy. I felt queer in my inside, and my legs got weak under me and my head swam. Monsieur le Curé saw what was the matter.

"Here," said he, "start your appetite with this glass of wine," and he poured two fingers of red wine into a beautiful glass cup that tinkled like a bell and that had a foot like the chalice used in the mass. You may be sure I made no bones about swallowing it down. Friends, that was wine! In an instant I no longer was the same boy. I bit into my bread and began to cram my hollow inside—my jaws going like a sausage-chopper.

And I no longer was afraid. I talked to Monsieur le Curé as I would have talked to a boy of my own age. I told him all that had happened that day—the coming of the hare, my poor father's beating, the flinging of the stone, my day in hiding, and at last of my leap into the pond. As he listened to me, Monsieur le Curé sat down in front of the fire and warmed himself, his arms half raised and his hands out-spread to the flames as he used to hold them at mass when, standing in front of the missal, he sang the Præfatio. When I had finished he got up, poured for me another full glass of wine and said: "You are a good boy. You have done right in coming here."

Then he turned his back to me to hide his tearful eyes; and lifting his arms above his head, his hands clasped as when he raised on high the Host at the elevation, he exclaimed: "Oh wicked master! Oh false Christian! The Son of God shed his blood for great and small, for marquis and for serf. Wicked master! False Christian! To-day art thou master, but to-morrow thou mayst be cast down! Thy hand is raised against thy God, and thou makest Jesus his Son to weep: for he sees his people starve. Oh master accursed! Oh false Christian! Saint Roch will take from thee the bread thou ravishest from those who are crying for food! Thou wilt see the gleaming sword of great Saint John the Baptist, and thou shalt feel its sharp edge! Thy stronghold shall fall down before thee, the tocsin will forever ring for thee, and thou shalt see thy fountain run with blood! Oh wicked lord! Oh wicked Christian! On thee rests heavily the curse of God!"

In repeating these words old Pascal had risen to his feet and, unconsciously imitating the gestures of the good curé, had raised his hands above his head in denunciation—while we all, overcome by his fervour, listened breathlessly and gaped at him with wide open eyes.

For a moment he was silent; and then, re-seating himself, he continued:

Presently Monsieur Randoulet turned toward me, took me gently by the hand, and led me away; Janetoun following with the lamp. We went through a beautiful parlour that smelt of incense like a sacristy; and at the end of it was a double door which Monsieur le Curé opened, and there inside, in the alcove, was a big bed.

"Now then," said he, "you shall sleep here, in the bed of the Bishop of Carpentras!" He stroked my cheeks once more with his soft hand, and again pressed my head against his side, and then left me alone with Janetoun.

I did not know what to do with my hands, I dared not touch anything. Janetoun, as soon as her master had left us, seized me by the arm and in her rough voice cried: "What are you gaping at! Get off your rags and go to bed!" And turning her back on me she clattered off with the light—leaving me in the alcove alone in the dark.

Poor little me! I soon got off my coarse

wool jacket and breeches and rough stockings. Feeling my way carefully, I climbed into the big bed—as soft as feathers could make it. I buried myself in it, I burrowed down in it. In the twinkling of an eye I was as warm as a chick under the hen; and in another twinkling I was as sound asleep as a top! The bed was so soft, the white sheets smelt so clean, that as I dropped off I felt myself among the angels— I who all my life had gone to sleep hungry and whose bed had been always a truss of straw.

In my sleep I dreamed that I was floating in the air on a cloud, and that nothing could reach me to do me harm. I was in the midst of this wonderful dream when all of a sudden I heard loud shrill cries, such as you hear when a pig is being stuck; and then came a rumbling and squeaking like a rusty well-wheel, and the clatter that the bucket makes banging against the sides of the well; and then, right over my head, bom! bom! bom! three great claps of a bell! My blood turned cold within me and, before I had time to remember where I was, again came the screaming and the rumbling and the squeaking and the banging—and again bom! bom! bom!

And then suddenly I remembered that I was in the Bishop's bed in the Curacy, and my fright left me as I understood the meaning of all these strange sounds: that the bell-tower of the church was right above me, and that the bell-rope ran up through the alcove and rubbed against the tester of my bed. It was the morning Angelus that was ringing; the same Angelus that sounded so clearly and so beautifully in the early morning far off in our hut of La Garde.

Just as the last stroke of the Angelus rang I heard Janetoun's sabots clattering; and then the alcove door opened creakingly and I saw her standing in the grey morning light. She put a bundle on my bed and said in her rough voice: "Get up, little boy! Here, put on this shirt, these breeches, this jacket, these shoes and this cap. Do you understand?" and so saying she spread out the clothes on the bed.

I gazed, gaping like a clam, at all this brand-new outfit; but before I had time to say a word Janetoun had turned on her heel, and from the parlour door was calling back to me that I must get up at once or I would keep Monsieur le Curé waiting.

That warning was enough. I jumped out of my high bed with a single bound; and in no time I had scrambled into the white shirt, the new breeches, the warm jacket, the hole-less stockings, the pretty little buckled shoes, and the little three-cornered hat. When I saw myself in my fine clothes, I did not know what to do with my hands—and indeed could scarcely walk! But I would not for the world have kept Monsieur le Curé waiting; and so, timidly tip-toing along, taking care not to slip on the shining tiles, I went down to the kitchen.

Monsieur Randoulet already was seated at the table, and before him was a steaming cup of something black. When he saw me, he could not help laughing. "Oh look at the little scamp of a Pascalet, why he might be the consul's son! Sit down here and get your breakfast.

"Do you like this?" he added, and gave me a cup of black steaming stuff, just like his. He took a spoonful of brown sugar from a dish and stirred it into my cup. "There, that will warm up your little stomach," he said—and gave me a big fougasse with its crusty horns.

He ate and drank; and then, doing just as he did, I sipped at my cup of black water and dipped in it a horn of my fougasse. Not until seven years later did I know that that black stuff was coffee—for the next time I tasted it was at Jaffa, after the battle of the Pyramids, when Bonaparte gave us coffee to keep us from the plague.

"Well," said Monsieur Randoulet, wiping his lips, "did you like it?"

"Yes, Monsieur le Curé."

"And now do you want to see your father?"

"Yes, Monsieur le Curé."

"Up then, and we'll be off. Button your jacket, it is cold." And we went down into the street.

By that time it was broad day; and as we passed by the church we saw before it, on the pavement, a big pool of blood. Monsieur Randoulet stopped short. "Ah, the wicked ones," he cried, "to fight, to knife each other in this way! Children of the people—eating the same black bread, dragging the same chain after them, tanning their skins at the same work, burning in the same hell, slaves of the same master! Ah poor people, poor people! They unite their strength and they sweat blood only for the profit of their executioners!"

We kept on to the hospital, but a few steps away, and entered without knocking—for the doors of the House of Charity always are wide open—and so passed up the stairs. At the stair-head, to the left hand, was the room for the sick, into which Monsieur Randoulet led me; and as we entered Sister Lucy, who was the sister in charge, came forward to meet him with a reverent greeting. On each side of the room were narrow white beds. In the first four to the right were four wounded men whose wives were taking care of them. But at the far end of the room, to the left, I saw my poor mother at the head of a bed; and I made but one jump to her and threw myself into her arms. And my mother, weeping, gave me a kiss! The poor do not kiss often— their children not at all. I cannot recollect that any one had ever kissed me before. When my mother kissed me it seemed as if in that moment I lived over all the days of my life, while my heart within me swelled with joy. And then, turning, and leaning over the bed, I covered my old father's wounded face with tears; while he kept saying, over and over: "Pascalet! Pascalet! Art thou indeed Pascalet, my son Pascalet?"

But when I stood up again and saw my father's face; when I saw the red swollen welts, a finger thick, that Monsieur Robert's and Surto's whips had raised on his cheeks and forehead; when I saw his poor swollen

eye, almost starting out of his head—then I
began to tremble with a burning rage. My
face was on fire and my ears rang. My teeth
were eager to bite, my nails to rend. I longed
to burn the Château, to poison the wells!

But I was so helpless! All that I could do
was to weep. I clinched my hands and said
within me: "Oh, when I am big!"

My old father began to move about rest-
lessly; and then to push down the coverings
with his thin hairy hands.

"Why art thou moving about that way?"
my mother asked, covering him again with the
white sheets.

"I want to say something, La Patine.
Come forward, thou and Pascalet. Listen.
You are not in the way, Monsieur le Curé.
Now that Pascalet is here, I want to say this
to you: You must both go, toward mid-day,
to the Château to see our lord Monsieur le Marquis, and our lady Madame le Marquise, and
Monsieur Robert; and you must tell them that
as soon as I am well I will go and ask their
pardon. You will fall at their knees, at their
feet, and you will beg them to have pity on
you and on me. Tell them that our lives are
in their hands. Dost thou hear, wife? Pascalet, dost thou hear? You must not fail."

Here Monsieur Randoulet cut him short:
"No, no, Pascal, this is not the moment for
that; when you are well, we will see about it.
Believe me, I know."

"Mon Dieu! Mon Dieu!" said my old
father. "What will ever our good master the
Marquis think of us, and Monsieur Robert also,
if we do not ask their forgiveness? But, Monsieur le Curé, if you think it is not suitable—
not suitable now?"

"No, no, this is not the moment. I will
look after it all, do not be uneasy. And now
good-bye, Pascalet. Come this evening and
sleep at the Curacy. You understand, Pascalet?"

"Yes, Monsieur le Curé," said I, looking
at him with reverence—for it seemed to me
that in him I really saw the good God.

But when he turned to leave us my father's
words came back to me: "You must go and
ask forgiveness!" *I* ask forgiveness! I was
red with shame, the blood boiled in my veins
—and the wicked thought came to me: Why
have I such a father? I was ashamed of him.
Not only would I disobey him, but I did
not know what I would do if he tried to
force me.

I was drawn away from these bitter thoughts

by hearing Monsieur le Curé, as he passed beside the other beds, speaking to the poor
women who, weeping, were taking care of
their wounded men. One had his cheek laid
open by the bottom of a bottle so that all his
teeth showed; another had both legs broken
at the knees by a blow from an iron bar; into
the back of the third a knife had been plunged
up to the hilt; and the fourth had been almost
disembowelled by a blow with a ploughshare.
This last, though so frightfully wounded, had left
the tavern and had managed to stagger as far
as the church before he fell. It was his blood
we had seen.

"But how has this happened? Who are
the wretches who have wrought this misery?"
Monsieur le Curé asked again and again.

"They will not speak out," cried the four
women together. "They will not tell. They
will only say that it was the Papalists—who
called them Liberals and then fell on them and
wounded them as you see!"

"Ah, if *I* dared but speak out!" said one
of the women.

"What good would speaking out do?"
said another. "The rich are always the rich
—they never are in the wrong."

"Come, come, this has nothing to do with

the rich," said Monsieur le Curé.   "Rich people don't kill off poor people like flies."

"When you go up to the Château, monsieur," said one of the women, turning her head away and speaking in a low voice, "just ask big Surto what took place.   He knows all about it.   Could stones speak out and tell all, that man wouldn't keep his head on his shoulders for long!"

"Then all this has come from a quarrel between Liberals and Papalists?"

"That is all, Monsieur le Curé.   Are we the kind of people to do harm?"

Monsieur Randoulet turned away from them for a moment, while his eyes filled with tears. When he spoke again he said gently: "Take good care of these poor fellows.   I will not forget you and your children—you shall not want."

Before he left the hospital he tried to get a word from the wounded men.   But their hurts, and the fever that was beginning to come on, kept them from answering—and so he went away.

Surto's name, spoken by one of the women, gave me goose-flesh.   To my mind that man, that monster, that German, was ready for any crime.   He frightened me more than wolves or tigers, or the very devil himself! I was sure that he was looking for me; that he wanted to kill me in some dreadful way to revenge his master, Monsieur Robert, whose foot I had mashed with the stone—and I saw myself torn to pieces with the whip, and then strung up to one of the oaks on the avenue of the Château.

And so I stayed close-hidden all day long in the hospital; where—with my father and my mother and the Sisters—I thought that I was as safe as in the Curacy itself. And yet it was in the hospital that the danger was to come.

I waited until black night shut down close upon the village—until not a light showed in a single window and I was sure that everybody was in bed—before I dared to stir toward the Curacy. But in the very moment that I turned to go we heard faintly the sound of men's voices singing the "Pange Lingua," and with this the tinkling of a little bell. Sister Lucy opened the window and looked out, and said as she closed it again: "They are the White Penitents. They must be escorting the Holy Sacrament to some sick man. But where can they be going? Who can it be?"

The tinkling of the bell and the singing came nearer and nearer, and at last reached the hospital; then they stopped, and we heard the sound of heavy footsteps on the stairs. The door opened, and in came six White Penitents: spectre-like creatures in long white gowns, with their heads hidden in pointed cowls— *cagoules*, as the Penitents call them—which came down to their shoulders and had two staring round holes for their eyes.

When I saw these six ghosts with their stretched-out heads pointed above and below, without any mouth and without any nose, with only two black holes where the eyes ought to be—and still more when I saw the biggest of them glancing at me fiercely with his hollow eyes—I trembled with fright and, holding my breath to make myself smaller, squeezed down in hiding between my father's bed and the wall.

In that very instant the six Penitents drew each a great knife out from his long hanging sleeve, and without a word they went up to the four wounded Liberals and so larded them with thrusts and cuts that their blood soaked through the straw mattresses and streamed upon the floor! The women screamed for help, and Sister Lucy ran beseechingly from one executioner to the other—until a sidewise kick in her ribs sent her reeling against my father's bed, breathless and sick. My mother fell over against me, in a swound from fear.

All this happened quicker than I am telling it you. When the Liberals were dead, stabbed through and through, five of the Penitents, all bloody, ran four steps at a time down the stairs. But one, the biggest one, stayed behind. He came straight to my father's bed and stooped and looked under it—so that I saw his eyes flashing through the holes of his *cagoule.* Then, stooping, he reached out his arm and caught my wrist and so dragged me out.

I screamed at the top of my voice. But no good came of screaming. There was no one to help me. Only my poor old father and the weak women and the dead were there—and the monstrous great Penitent, dragging me with him from the room, hustled me down the stairs and so into the street. Whether or no, I had to follow him. He held me like a vice. When I called for help he turned and cuffed me; and by the time that a window opened—as happened once or twice—we were far away. So we passed beyond the skirts of the village; and at last, tired of struggling, more dead than alive, I followed him quietly— as an unhappy dog follows one who drags him at the end of a thong to throw him over a bridge.

What could that murderous wretch want with me? From the moment that he had come into the hospital I had guessed who it was; but when we turned, after leaving the village, into the road leading to the Château there was no room left for hoping that my guess might be wrong. I knew for certain that this man who was dragging me after him, who held me with his big strong hand—red with the blood of murdered men—was Surto; and I felt that since it was Surto who had me fast—there in the darkness of night, and on that lonely road through the fields where there was no chance for me of rescue—I was as good as lost.

Pascal, who was a born story-teller, paused at his climax; while we, greedily listening, bent forward open-mouthed and eager for him to go on. And just at that very moment the shop door flew open with a bang, and in rushed La Mie, the shoemaker's wife, like a malicious whirlwind!

"What are you all doing? What are you thinking about?" she cried angrily. "Here it is eleven o'clock—in another moment it will be midnight. And you have been chattering about nothing for a good two hours! The oil is wasting, and my miserable cobbler of a husband is losing his time like a child. And as for you, you lazy dog," she added, turning to the apprentice, "not a stitch have you set the whole night long. It is enough to drive a saint crazy. Begone, all of you!" And La Mie, in a towering passion, blew out the lamp.

"You hard-tongued slut," cried the shoemaker through the darkness, grinding his teeth, "I'll serve you out for this!"

As for the rest of us, we groped our way along the walls to the door, got out into the street, and set off for our homes and beds. But we hardly had taken ten steps when we heard the sound of the shoemaker's strap whacking La Mie's back with sounding blows.

CHAPTER III.

· DURING the whole of the next day the one thing that was talked about in our village—at olive-mill, washing-place and bake-oven—was La Mie's tremendous whacking; which had lasted, it was rumoured, until well on toward morning. And when I heard all this gossip I wondered if that evening the shoemaker's shop would be open for the meeting.

But I felt reassured when my grandfather, as he swallowed his last mouthful of supper, snapped his knife together, put it in his pocket, and said: "Come on, little man, light the lantern. You will see she has had enough to make her behave herself for a fortnight!"

Well, he was right. The shop was open just the same as usual; shoemaker and apprentice were tapping away as cheerily as ever; and what was more, there was La Mie in person, smiling and agreeable, seated close to the light knitting her stocking. She talked of va-

rious things and made herself pleasant to everybody. "Good evening, Dominic" (that was
to my grandfather). "Pray take this chair.
And you, my dear, put down that saucy cat
who has jumped up on your little bench."
And then, turning to her husband, she added:
"Why, see there, your lamp is burning badly,"
and so saying she took her scissors and
trimmed the lamp. And in the tone of her
voice, all the while, there was a ring of supreme satisfaction and content.

I did not understand her good humour. But
all the neighbours smiled, and then La Mie
smiled too—for every one knew that after the
shoemaker and his wife had quarrelled and
made up again they always were the best of
friends. And so, when Pascal came, she said
with all possible cordiality: "Ah, we have
been waiting for you. Draw up to the stove.
I heard that you were telling a story, and I
said to myself that I would come and listen
with the rest—because your stories always are
so good. Begin right away."

And I, fearful that Pascal might have forgotten just where he left off, and that we might
lose a part of the story, ventured to strike in:
"You know, Pascal, you stopped where the
big White Penitent was dragging you through

the black night along the road to the Château."

"Yes, yes, I remember," Pascal answered. And then, after waiting a minute or two until we all were comfortably settled, he went on:

I certainly thought that I was lost. Every time that I hung back, or tried to break away, Surto gave me a buffet; and when he changed me from one hand to the other he swung me around so rapidly that it seemed as if he would jerk loose my arms. All this time he was walking fast—and never for an instant did he let me go free.

Up on the heights, at the end of the road, I could begin to make out the black row of oaks in front of the Château—and I knew that once beyond those oaks it was all up with me. Yet if only I could get loose for so much as a second I felt sure that I would be all right—for a single spring aside would take me out of the road and into safety. I knew every hand's breadth of the country thereabouts—the steep hill-sides, the tufts of bushes, the ditches, the walls, the paths; and then, too, in the blackness of night a start of two steps is worth more than a long run by day. But the first thing to do was to get my start by making him let go of my hand.

At first I thought of biting him—of biting off his finger, perhaps; but I saw that wouldn't do, for I couldn't bite him at once in both hands. And then my great danger sharpened my wits and gave me a better notion: making me remember the trick that often had been put upon me by the little wild creatures—crickets, beetles, cigales, the praying-mantis—which sometimes I caught in the fields. As I touched them they would always—either from fear or by cunning—gather themselves into a little heap, moving neither foot nor leg, so that they seemed quite dead. I could turn them as I pleased; blow on them; shout at them—yet they never stirred. But did I for a single moment look aside—off would scuttle my crickets, and my cigales and beetles instantly would fly away! It always was a fresh surprise to me, this trick; and the good thought that came to me was that I should play it in my own behalf. There was no time to be wasted, and the very minute that I had this notion I acted upon it— dropping like a dead creature and hanging limp from Surto's huge hand.

"Vat, you vont valk any more?" he cried. "Vell, take that then!"—and he gave me a

kick in the ribs that seemed to crack every one
of them and that knocked all the wind out of
me.   But I set my jaws hard and made no
sound; nor did I give any sign of life when he
followed up the kick by a cuff with his great
paw that made my teeth chatter.   He seemed
to suspect a trick, for all this while he never
let loose his grip on my wrist; and when he
found that neither kicks nor cuffs could make
me walk he dragged me along behind him, my
body bumping on the rough ground.   This
was not good going for me; but it also was
bothersome for him.   He had not taken ten
steps—to every one of which he swore a big
German oath—before he stopped again.   By
that time he must have begun to believe in my
trick, for I heard him mutter: "I'll haf you
any vay, tead or alife!"—and then he tried to
swing me up on his shoulders.

Luckily for me, his Penitent's dress was in
the way and he couldn't manage it.   The big
sleeves caught him in his arms, and the *cagoule*
flapped about so that the holes no longer were
before his eyes.   It was as though he had his
head in a bag.   Still holding me, he tried to
throw off the *cagoule* with one hand. · But it
would not come loose; and at last, entirely
tricked by my limp deadness, he let me drop

on the ground while he went at it with both hands. My chance had come! In an instant, while he still was fumbling at the *cagoule*, I was on my feet; and before his head was clear of it I had jumped the ditch by the roadside and had bounded in among the brushwood— and so was well away!

"Te tevil! Ten tousand tevils! I'll haf you yet, you little peast!" he cried out after me; and I heard him crashing into the brush- wood as he leaped the ditch and then came pounding along heavily in my wake. But he might as well have been chasing thistledown! I had the start of him; I knew my way; the darkness covered me. Presently, when I was a long way ahead, I heard him whistling for the dogs at the Château. Dogs were another matter. They could get along even better than I could in the dark. I ran harder than ever. But the dogs were slow in coming. I am not sure that they came at all. Faintly, far behind me, I heard Surto's strong Dutch curses as I came in sight of the outlying houses of Malemort. I was saved!

It was after midnight when I entered the village; yet the streets were full of people and all the houses were alight. The kniving of the four Liberals had turned the whole place upside

down.   As I crossed the Rue Basse I heard
the cries and moans of the women, up in the
hospital, wailing over their dead; and the
murmurs and curses of the crowd standing
about the hospital door.   Still all of a tremble
with fear, I dared not enter the crowd.   It
seemed to me that only with Monsieur le Curé
would I be safe—and I went to the Curacy
without a halt.   Janetoun had not gone to bed,
and at my first little knock I heard the clatter
of her wooden shoes.

"Who is there?" she called out.

"I, Pascalet."

Then Janetoun quickly swung the door
open.   "Well, I never!" she cried.   "It *is*
Pascalet, sure enough.   Where did you get
away from the White Penitent?"

"Up by the Château.   I played him a trick
that made him let me go—and then I ran off
from him in the dark."

"But what did he want with you?"

"He wanted to kill me."

"Kill you!   Kill *you*—little Pascalet!   The
monster!   Do you know who it was?"

"Oh yes, I know very well.   It was Surto."

"The game-keeper of Monsieur le Marquis?   That fine handsome big man?   What
are you talking about?   It is impossible!"

"No, it is not impossible. I know him very well. It was he."

"You are crazy, child. Be careful not to speak that wild thought to any one else. Have you had your supper?"

"Yes—Sister Lucy gave it to me."

"Very well. Then you shall go to bed. Monsieur le Curé has not come home yet. They sent for him to bring the holy oil to the hospital—but the men there are past holy oiling, from what I hear. When he comes back I'll tell him you're here. But you'd better get to bed, so come on."

Janetoun led me to the big parlour, opened the doors of the alcove, and showed me again the great soft bed of the Bishop of Carpentras; and as she was closing the doors of the alcove upon me she said: "At least make the sign of the cross before you go to sleep."

I groped my way to bed. But when I was between the sheets, in among the soft feathers, I could not sleep. I had one shivering fit after another; and the White Penitent, with his *cagoule* that made his head seem like a kite, always was before my eyes. I would see him standing up straight and tall at the foot of the bed; then his long arms would reach out over me; his grasp would settle tight on my foot; and when I tried to cry out for help he would clutch my throat with his blood-stained hands. When sleep did come to me he still kept with me and lashed me in my dreams; until at last he brought out his long knife and was making ready to pin me with it to the bed, as he had done with the men at the hospital. And then, suddenly, there was a loud creaking noise; the door of the alcove opened; a blinding light shone upon me—and there, beside my bed, was Monsieur le Curé with a lamp in his hand.

"Don't be afraid, Pascalet," he said. "It is I—Monsieur Randoulet. You must get up now. Day will soon be breaking. You must go."

"Monsieur," I said, "I cannot go back to the hospital. I am afraid."

"You are not to go to the hospital, Pascalet. You are to go quite away from here, to a place where you will be in safety. And now you must get up quickly. Before the daylight comes you must be off."

Without another word I was out of bed and sliding into my clothes. But when I looked for my cocked hat it was not to be found.

"Ah, it is your little hat you are looking

for," said Monsieur Randoulet. "Here it is. You left it at the hospital;" and then he led me quickly to the kitchen, where Janetoun already had a glowing fire. Janetoun was greatly excited. She was going to and fro in a hurry exclaiming: "Oh Heaven! Oh Heaven!" and between whiles heaving great sighs.

Monsieur Randoulet brought out a blue cloth wallet into which she put two double-handfuls of figs, two more' of almonds, some apples, and a loaf of bread. Then, with a comfortable gurgling sound, she filled for me a little brown flask made out of a brown gourd —so polished that it shone like a chestnut— from the great jar of wine.

When all was finished, Monsieur Randoulet took my hand in both of his and said to me: "My child, we are fallen on evil times. The men about us, worse than wolves, seek to devour their own kind. Our streets run red with blood. Even thou, my child, even thou, they seek in order to make thee perish—and, withal, thou art a good boy. Therefore it is well that thou shouldst go far from here, even to the city of Avignon; so far away that they no longer can do thee harm. In the flask and wallet which Janetoun has filled are food and drink enough to suffice thee for two days—double

the time that thou needst to be upon the road.
Here is a letter which thou must keep by thee
carefully until thou art come to Avignon, where
thou art to present it to Monsieur le Chanoine
Jusserand. He will find honest work for thee
to do, so that thou mayst gain thy livelihood
with clean hands. And remember always, my
child, that no man ever regrets the good that
he has done; and that to every man, sooner or
later, comes retribution for his evil deeds.
Kiss me and promise me that thou wilt never
render evil for evil; but for evil, good—even as
our blessed Lord has taught us from the height
of his cross."

And I, my heart hurting me because of
Monsieur le Curé's goodness and the pain of
going out alone from my home, answered:
"Yes, Monsieur le Curé, I promise. But——"

"What is it?"

"My mother—who will take care of her?"

"Do not trouble thyself, my child. Neither
thy father nor thy mother shall suffer want."

He hung the bag full of victuals about my
neck, and thrust into the pocket of my coat
the shining flask filled with good wine. "Come
now," he said, "I will start thee in the right
road"—and he led the way down the stairs,
and so to the outer door.

The stars were still in the sky when we reached the street. No one was stirring. The only noise was the gurgling of the fountain. We went on together in silence until we were outside the village and fairly upon the high road to Avignon. Then Monsieur Randoulet took me in his arms, kissed me, and said: "Remember, Pascalet, all that I have told thee. I will take care of thy father and thy mother; and as for thee, so thou be a good boy, Monsieur Jusserand, the Canon, will see to it that thou hast a chance to gain thy bread. Do not lose the letter. By sunrise thou wilt be half way on thy journey. Ask the first people whom thou meetest if thou art on the road to Avignon. Walk on like a man—and at mid-day thou wilt sight the Palace of the Popes."

Again he embraced me, and I felt him slip something into the pocket of my jacket; but I could not guess what it was, nor could I think much about it, because just then my heart was so full. "Thank you very, *very* much, Monsieur Randoulet" was all that I could find to say. And then I started on the road to Avignon.

I walked and I walked—on and on over the white road and through the black night. The farmhouse dogs came out barking from as far off as they could scent me. Some even tried to bite me. And I, poor little miserable boy, made myself as small as I could and walked on and on! Once I almost turned back. I was frightened not less by the darkness than by the silence—which every now and then was made keener by the hooting in some elm or willow by the roadside of a screech-owl: a dismal bird.

But at last, as I walked on steadily, daybreak came; and all of a sudden the beautiful clear sun sprang up over Mount Crespihoun—sending my shadow far ahead of me on the white road and cheering and comforting me with his warm rays. My long shadow amazed and delighted me. "It is not possible," I said to myself, "that you are as big as that; that you are so well dressed; that you have a cocked hat! Why, you look like a man!" And I grew almost happy to feel myself suddenly so grown up, and free, and my own master out in the world. Just then I remembered that when Monsieur Randoulet had left me he had slipped something into the pocket of my jacket; and when I fetched it out to look at it, behold! wrapped tight in a blue paper I found three beautiful white silver crowns! This was too much! Three whole crowns! What could I ever do with such a sum? Then indeed I felt myself a big strong man. In that moment I do not think that even Surto would have frightened me.

I strode along the road as proud as Lucifer; and presently, looking up, I saw before me a great city with houses having many windows—quite unlike our little houses at Malemort—while rising still higher in the morning sunlight were noble towers: "What, Avignon already?" I said to myself. "Well, you have come a good pace!" But just then I met a lame old peasant on his way to hoe his vineyard, and his answer to my question if it were Avignon took a little of the conceit out of me.

"Well, my lad," he answered, "it's plain that you're not from around here. That's not Avignon—that's Carpentras. The city of Avignon, God be thanked, is far enough from here. If you keep right along your road you'll hardly get there by sunset."

The old man put down his hoe from his shoulder as he spoke; and then, leaning on its handle as shepherds lean on their crooks, he looked hard at me and added: "Tell me, my lad, is the matter very important that is taking you to Avignon just now? If it is not, you

had better turn right around and go back to
the place you came from. They say that
things are happening in Avignon fit to make
your blood run cold. And it isn't surprising,
either. They are a bad lot, down there—
jealous, envious, deceitful, cowardly—bad all
the way through. Brigands, people call them;
and that's what they are." He was silent for
a moment; and then, coming close to me and
speaking in a low voice in my ear, he went
on: "They are worse still. They are working
for what they call the 'Revolution'; for some
sort of a new government in France, and
against the Pope. They want to get rid of the
Pope's government—brigands that they are!
And, do you know, twice they have tried to
besiege our town of Carpentras? That shows
what wretches they must be. I need say no
more, my lad. Good-bye!" and off he went
up the road. When he had gone a little way
he turned again and called: "I have a piece of
good advice to give you: Go back whence you
came!" and then, his hoe on his shoulder, he
went hobbling away.

But I, having my orders from Monsieur le
Curé, was not to be put about by the chance
warnings of a lame old man. I went forward,
steadily and stoutly, as though I had not heard a

single word. The sun rose higher and higher as I walked on and on. I passed long stretches of *garrigues*, whence came to me the sweet clean smell of thyme growing wild there on the rocky hills ; and then longer stretches of meadow land dotted with *vejados*—the little sod-heaps capped each one with a stone which are set up to warn away shepherds with their flocks. And so noon-tide came and passed.

It was in the early afternoon that first I saw the Rhône, one of the biggest rivers in the world. I have seen the Rhine, the Danube, the Bérézina: they all are smaller than the Rhône. I don't know how to make you see it better than by saying that it is as wide as Monsieur Véran's twenty-acre field. Only suppose that instead of seeing the brown wheat stubble you saw a great ditch full of water running from away off down to the very sea—and then you would have the Rhône!

At last I came within sight of the Pope's City. Saints in Heaven! What a beautiful town it was! Going right up two hundred feet above the bank of the river was a bare rock, steep and straight as though cut with a stone-mason's chisel, on the very top of which was perched a castle with towers so big and high —twenty, thirty, forty times higher than the towers of our church—that they seemed to go right up out of sight into the clouds! It was the Palace built by the Popes; and around and below it was a piling up of houses—big, little, long, wide, of every size and shape, and all of cut stone—covering a space as big, I might say, as half way from here to Carpentras. When I saw all this I was thunderstruck. And though I still was far away from the city a strange buzzing came from it and sounded in my ears—but whether it were shouts or songs or the roll of drums or the crash of falling houses or the firing of cannon, I could not tell. Then the words of the lame old man with the hoe came back to me, and all of a sudden I felt a heavy weight on my heart. What was I going to see, what was going to happen to me in the midst of those revolutionary city folks? What could I do among them—I, so utterly, utterly alone?

In order to scare up a little courage I felt in my pocket to make sure that I still had the letter that Monsieur Randoulet had given me. There was the good letter, and as I touched it I seemed to feel the kind Curé's hand; and there, too, were the three beautiful white crowns, each one of them worth three francs. And then, my spirits rising until I was as light

as a bird, I marched on again until I came to
the gate of Saint-Lazare in the walls of Avignon.

Oh what sights I saw there and what a
crowd! How many shall I say? I don't
know—at least ten thousand. The people
were jumping, dancing, laughing, clapping
their hands, hugging each other, until you
might have thought they all were merry-mad.
I found myself, I scarcely know how, mixed
in with this crowd—which was spread out
along the base of the ramparts and was going
in and out of the wide open gates. All of a
sudden some one raised the cry: "The farandole! The farandole!"—and the *tambourins*
began to buzz, pipes began to squeal, and I
saw coming toward me a swaying line of
dancers hand in hand: an endless farandole
stretching as far as I could see.

And what a farandole! There in line were
bare-footed ragamuffins hand in hand with
well-to-do well-dressed citizens each with his
watch on. There were soldiers, washwomen
and hucksterwomen in their Catalan caps,
dandies with silk-tied queues, porters, ladies in
lace dresses. There was a Capuchin monk,
red as a peony, and a brace of priests; and
there were three nuns kicking up their heels

and showing their fat calves. Then followed
a long line of girls, of children, of everything.
And all these people capered and danced
and sang in time to the pipes and tabors scattered along the line. There was no end to it
all—and the crowd clapped hands and applauded and from time to time sent up a great
shout of "Vive la Nation!" Presently I too
caught the madness—and away I went with
the others in the farandole, shouting "Vive la
Nation!" at the top of my lungs.

It was so long, that farandole, that neither
beginning nor end could be seen to it. Before
the last of the dancers had come out by the
Porte Saint-Lazare the leaders had entered the
city again by the Porte du Limbert; while the
crowd pressed close behind, squeezed together
like a swarm of bees. Utterly bewildered,
gaping like an oyster, I followed my leaders;
and so entered Avignon by the Porte du Limbert and went on through the Rue des Tein-
turiers, the street of the Water Wheels.

What a queer street that is! Half of it is a
paved street and the other half is the bed of
the river Sorgue; and on the side of the river
huge black wheels, dipping down into the
swiftly-running water, stick out from the cali-
co-mills and dye-houses and turn the machin-

ery that is inside. As that day was a great festival, the weavers and dyers were not at work. Everywhere the buildings were hung from roof to ground with great pieces of party-coloured calico—red, blue, green, yellow, with big bunches of flowers all over them—and from drying lines stretched across the street there floated thousands and thousands of the pretty bright-coloured neck-kerchiefs which our girls wear: so that the whole place seemed to be ablaze with flags and festoons and banners shimmering in the sunlight as they fluttered in the cold air. And all these fluttering waving things, and the buzzing roar and the surging and swaying of the crowd, with the sparkling Sorgue water falling with a tinkling drip in the sunshine—like cascades of autumn leaves—from the great slowly turning wheels which seemed like huge snails moving backwards; all this sparkle and glitter and tumult and turmoil, I say, was enough to dazzle a man and make him mad with joy!

The press in the narrow street was so close that the farandole dancers could not caper with any comfort at all. Every now and then I could catch sight of their heads far in advance bobbing up and down above the level of the crowd—as they vainly tried to keep time to the squealing of the pipes and the quick tapping of the *tambourins*.   And so on we went —some of us lifted off our feet at times in the tight squeeze—up through the street of the dyers and the street of the hosiers, and then out through the Rue Rouge to the Place de l'Horloge in front of the Hôtel de Ville; where there was room to spread out again and the farandole dancers once more could skip it and jump it as they pleased.   Again I saw pass and repass that strangely linked human chain. There were the bearded Capuchin and the pot-bellied burghers, the nuns red as poppies, the soldiers, the priests, the washwomen, the fine ladies, the loafers, the children, the porters—in a word, there was all Avignon dancing the farandole: while up on the Rocher des Doms cannon thundered, and all the crowd, dancers and on-lookers, roared "Vive la Nation!"; and high in the clocktower of the Hôtel de Ville wooden Jacquemart and Jacquemarde, who keep the time for Avignon, beat upon the great bell and sent its loud clangour booming above us in the clear air.

From the Place de l'Horloge we went onward, the crowd keeping with us and following us, to the open square in front of the Pope's Palace: where all the merry-making was to come to a climax in a People's Festival. In the middle of the square was a platform on which already were seated the Commissioners who had arrived the evening before from Paris to make formal proclamation of the reunion of Avignon to France. The crowd soon spread over the Rocher des Doms, and increased constantly. People were squeezed and pressed together like wheat in a hopper. They were piled up everywhere—the windows, the balconies, the very roof-tiles were black with heads. The circling dancers with joined hands made a great swaying curve which took in both the square of the Pope's Palace and the Place de l'Horloge. The mass of the crowd was surrounded by this huge farandole; and in the midst of the balancing dancers the onlookers clapped their hands and stamped their feet in time to the drumtaps and shouted: "Vive la Nation! Down with the Pope's Legate! Vive la France!"

Presently one of the Commissioners stood up on the platform and made signs for quiet; and when, little by little, the drummers and pipers had stopped playing and the noise of the crowd slowly had ceased, the Chief Commissioner, the formal delegate from the National Assembly at Paris, read out the great

decree: which declared Avignon and the Comtat Venaissin severed from the dominions of
the Pope and once more united to France.
And then the crowd burst forth into such a
shouting of "Vive la Nation!" and "Down
with the Pope's Legate!" that it seemed as if
their cries never would have an end.

But quiet came suddenly when the Commissioners were seen to turn toward the Pope's
Palace and to make signs to some workmen
posted up on the roof, and as the workmen
obeyed their order a solemn silence rested on
the crowd. On top of the Palace, sticking up
above the battlements, you still may see the
little stone gable where hung for I know not
how long the silver bell that to most people
was almost the same thing as the Pope himself. It rang when the old Pope died; it rang
when the new Pope was blessed and crowned
—and people said that it rang all by itself,
without touch of human hand. In Avignon,
the ringing of that sweet-toned little silver bell
seemed to be the Pope's own voice; and to
see it gleaming in the sunshine up there in the
gable above his Palace made one understand,
somehow, his greatness and his glory and his
riches and his power.

And there before our eyes, obeying the

order of the Commissioners, the workmen
were taking that bell away forever—because
the Comtat was a part of France again, and
the power of the Popes over Avignon was
gone!

In the dead silence we could hear the click-
ing of pincers and the tapping of hammers
and the grating of files; and then a single
sharp sweet clang—which must have come
when the bell, cut loose from its fastenings,
was lifted away. Having it thus free from the
setting where it had rested for so long a while,
the workmen brought it to the battlements;
and in plain sight of all of us, down the whole
great depth of the Palace walls, lowered it by
a cord to the ground. And the poor little bell,
glittering like a jewel in the sunshine, tinkled
faintly and mournfully at every jar and jerk of
the cord as though it knew that its end had
come: now giving out, as it swayed and the
clapper struck within, a sweet clear sound;
and again, as it jarred against the wall, a sound
so harsh and so sad that to hear it cut one's
heart. All the way down those great walls it
uttered thus its sad little plaint; until we
seemed to feel as though it were a child some
one was hurting; as though it were a living
soul. And I know that the pain that was in

my heart was in the hearts of all that crowd. The silence, save for the mourning of the bell, was so deep that one could have heard the flight of a butterfly—and through it, now and then, would come from some one a growling whisper: "Liberty and the Rights of Man are all very well, but they might have left our little bell alone!" And it is certain that for an hour or more after the funeral of the little bell was ended no one shouted "Vive la Nation!" or "Down with the Pope's Legate!" or "Vive la France!"

But quickly enough *tambourins* and fifes began to play again; the farandole again got going; again there sounded the buzz and murmur of the crowd. And then the men began to bring the victuals for the Festival: great baskets of freshly baked white bread, fat jars of olives, and baskets of nuts and of golden winter grapes. All these good things were arranged in front of the platform where the Commissioners were standing, and whoever pleased was free to go up and draw a fixed portion: a loaf of bread, seven olives, six filberts or walnuts, and a bunch of grapes.

Getting to the baskets through the crush that there was around them was no easy matter. But I managed it, though pretty well banged and bruised by the way; and when my rations were secured I looked about me for a place where I could munch them in some sort of comfort and at the same time see what was going on.

The steps leading up to the portico of the Pope's Palace seemed to be just the place for me, as from there you see over the whole big square. A good many other people had had the same notion and were seated or standing on the steps eating away; but a soldier of the National Guard, who was there with his wife and little boy, moved up and made room for me so that I found myself very well fixed indeed. The soldier was a good-looking fellow —fair and rosy and with blue eyes, a kind you don't often find in these parts—and under his big fierce yellow moustache he had a very friendly smile. At first he didn't say anything to me, but when he saw me cracking my walnuts with my teeth he could not hold his tongue. "The deuce!" he cried. "You've got a pair of iron nippers in those jaws of yours, youngster, and no mistake!"

He went on cracking his own walnuts with a Rhône cobble-stone, smiling pleasantly and giving the kernels to his wife and little boy. As for me, I was both abashed and pleased by his taking notice of me. I grinned foolishly, and looked down, and did not dare to answer him. His big plumed hat, his blue coat with its red facings, his long sword—curved like a partly straightened sickle—upset me and filled me with admiration. I couldn't help thinking how splendid it would be to have such a man for a father—even for a cousin, a friend!

Suddenly he stood up and looked over the crowd. "They're tapping the barrels," he said, and held out his hand to his wife for a straw-covered bottle that was lying by her side. Then, seeing my little brown gourd, he said: "If that's empty, give it to me and I'll get it filled for you."

Empty it was, for I had drained it on the road, and without daring even to say thank you I gave it to him; and off he went through the press up toward the end of the square, where the crowd was packed close around six big wine-casks ranged beneath the wall of the Cardinal's palace in a row. The casks had just been tapped—and I can tell you the crowd went for them! For a moment we saw our soldier shouldering his way in among the people; then we saw only his hat; and at last we saw only his red feather, as it went bobbing up and down among the heads in the distance.

In ten minutes or so he got back to us—his bottle and my gourd as full as they would hold. His moustache was all wet, and little red drops of wine hung from the tip of each of its hairs.

"Father," called out the little boy as soon as he saw him, "I want some more grapes."

"There are no more grapes. You shall have some wine."

"No, I want grapes."

"But I tell you they are all gone."

"Come, darling, drink the nice wine," said his mother, holding the full bottle to his lips.

"No, no, I want grapes."

I had not yet eaten my grapes. I got up and handed my bunch to the child, saying: "There, little fellow, eat these," and I felt my cheeks getting red again.

"What, deny yourself for that little glutton! I really can't have it," said the soldier.

"Please," said I, "let him eat my grapes. He is such a dear little boy."

"You are very kind," said the mother, smiling at me. And then, taking the grapes and giving them to the child, she made him thank me for them with a little bow.

"You don't seem quite like one of our Avignon people," the soldier said as he handed me back my gourd. "I don't want to know what isn't my business, but do you belong here?"

"No," I answered, "I am from Male-mort."

"And what do you come here for?"

"I don't know exactly. But I have a letter for Monsieur le Chanoine Jusserand, who is to find me some way of getting a living. Could you tell me where he lives?"

At this my soldier frowned, and looked at me so hard that he frightened me. "What!" he cried. "A letter to Canon Jusserand! Then you must be an Aristo, a Papalist!"

"I? I don't know just what you mean. But I don't think that I'm a Papalist."

"Then what do you want with Canon Jusserand?"

"I was told he would give me some work to do."

"Why, don't you know that Canon Jusserand is an Aristo? *He* won't find work for any but Papalists, that's sure. But you seem to be a nice sort of a boy, and I'll tell you what to do if the Canon receives you badly.. Come and look for me in the guard-room in the Hôtel de Ville on the Place de l'Horloge, and I will see that you get into the National Guard. I'll take you in my own company. How old are you?"

"I must be sixteen, more or less," said I— adding on at least a year.

"That's all right. You can be enrolled if you're sixteen. Then that's settled, is it? Now I'll show you how to go. Take that narrow street over there, just in front of us. Keep down it and turn to the left and you'll be in the Rue du Limas. There you will see a house with a balcony, and that is where the old Canon lives."

As he said this he turned toward his wife and I saw him winking and making a sign to her. She answered him by laughing a little; and then, getting up and coming in front of me, she unfastened a tricolor cockade from her catalan cap as she said: "Now that you are a good Patriot and hate the Papalists, I will give you my cockade." And when she had fastened it into my hat she turned to her husband and added: "See how jaunty he looks! You are right, he will make a pretty National Guard."

And then the soldier slapped me on the back and shouted, and I shouted after him: "Vive la Nation! Down with the Legate!"

"Now," said he, "go find your Canon.

But don't forget what I said. You know where to look for me if he turns you off. Ask for Sergeant Vauclair."

"Thank you very much," I answered. "I won't forget." And, so saying, I left him— all upset, and not knowing whether it were fear or joy that made something leap so in my breast.

It was very hard work getting across the crowded square, as I had to squirm through the crowd and break the farandole. But as soon as I reached the narrow way that led to the Rue du Limas there was no one to be seen but a few old men, and in the Rue du Limas itself there was not even so much as a cat. This was the quarter of the Whites, the Aristocrats. Every door, every shutter, was tightly barred. But I knew that there were people in the houses for I could hear voices; and in some that I passed women loudly telling their beads. I went straight to the house with the balcony and knocked. In a moment a little window was opened over head; but before I could look up it was clapped to again, and I did not see any one.

Then I heard doors open and shut inside the house and the sound of footsteps in the corridor, and then the creaking of the two bolts as they were drawn back and the grating of the big key as it was turned twice in the lock. At last the latch was raised and the great door was opened the very smallest bit.

A sour-faced old woman, yellow as saffron, peeked at me through the crack and in a sharp voice asked: "What do you want?"

"I want to see Monsieur le Chanoine Jusserand," I answered.

Then she opened the door wider, and I took a step forward. But before I could cross the threshold she gave a scream as if I had been for killing her, snatched off my hat, and fell to yelling: "Help! Jesus Maria, help! A brigand in the house! Help! Help! We're all lost!"

The old fury jerked the tricolor cockade out of my hat and tore it to pieces with her crooked fingers; spit on my hat, and flung it into the street; and then, still howling for help, she trampled on the scraps of my cockade while she held up her petticoats as if she were crushing a scorpion. Finally she gave a fierce yell out of her big mouth—as big as an oven, and the single fang in it as long as the tooth of a rake; pushed me so hard that I almost fell down, and then clapped the door to with a bang. In another second the two bolts grated again as they were shot back into their places, and the big key locked and double-locked the door.

I was struck all of a heap by this outburst. I couldn't make head nor tail of it. But by this time all the windows in the neighbourhood were open and from everywhere women were screaming: "There's a brigand in the street! To the Rhône with him! To the Rhône!"—and as I stooped to pick up my hat from the gutter a shower of brickbats and tiles and stones came down around me. I was only too glad to get out of that Rue du Limas—where, without in the least meaning to, I had kicked up such a row.

I felt as silly as a soused cat as I went back to the square of the Palace; and there I mixed in with the crowd and stared at the farandole till nightfall. I turned over and over in my head all that had passed, trying to make sense of it. I had spoken politely to the lady in the Rue du Limas. Why then had she treated me as if I were a robber or a murderer? Why had she torn off my cockade? Why had all her neighbours called out: "To the Rhône with him! To the Rhône with him!" I had done no harm to anybody. Then why should I be hooted at and stoned?

I looked around me and thought bitterly:

"Here are all these people, eating, drinking, dancing, singing. Each one has a home and a bed to go to. I am the only one here who has no shelter for the night, no relations, no friends. In the only place where I had any right to go, I was treated like a robber." I found myself wanting to get back to the old times when the sow took the cabbage-stalk from me. What was I good for anyway? What would become of me?

Then I began to think of the Rhône, the great Rhône, just as I had thought of the pond at La Garde. There was, to be sure, the soldier Vauclair, who had spoken kindly to me and who seemed to be a good man. But most likely he had but made fun of me when he said I should be enrolled in his company of the National Guard.

Night was coming on fast. The Palace square was emptying rapidly, only one or two *tambourins* were left and the farandole was breaking up. I saw one of the three nuns going off arm in arm with two soldiers. A few tipplers still hung around the wine-casks, standing them up on end so as to drain out the very last drop.

I went on the Place de l'Horloge. People there were stepping out briskly, for the cold

began to nip.　Only a single lamp was lighted,
the one over the entrance to the Hôtel de Ville
—where people were coming out and going in
all the time.　I did not dare to enter to ask for
my National Guardsman.　I was afraid that I
would only be laughed at and turned away.
Up and down I walked in the dark, thinking
what I had better do.　At last I made up my
mind.　The kind-looking soldier certainly had
told me to ask for him; and, after all, if things
went wrong I still had the Rhône to fall back
on.　And so, plucking up courage, I ventured
within the entrance and peered through a glass
door into the lighted up guard-room in the
hope that I might see my friend.

As I stood there, staring, the Porter came
out of his room and clapped his hand on my
shoulder: "Now then, what are you after
here?" he asked.

"I want to see Monsieur Vauclair," I answered.　"Is he inside there?"

"There are no 'monsieurs' here; we are
all citizens," said the Porter.　"This smells of
treason," he went on.　"It must be looked
into."　And holding fast to my shoulder, so
that I felt his five fingers digging into me
like claws, he called out: "Sergeant, Sergeant
Vauclair!"

The glass door of the guard-room opened instantly and out came my handsome Guardsman—bare-headed, his moustache twirled up and his pipe in his mouth.

"What's the matter?" he asked.

"Look here," said the Porter, "do you know this sprout? To my mind he has the mug of an Aristo. Maybe he's a spy. He asked for 'Monsieur' Vauclair."

"Oh, it's you, youngster, is it? You're pretty late," said Vauclair kindly. "And so the Canon wouldn't have anything to do with you, eh? Well, you'll be better off here. Come, I'll enroll you right off. Vive la Nation!"

He took me by the hand, while the Porter said doubtfully: "Oh, you know him, do you? All the same, look out for him. I haven't any use for people who say 'monsieur'!"

The Porter went back into his quarters, still grumbling, and Vauclair led me into the guard-room. It was a long narrow room, lighted by a big lamp hung from the ceiling by a chain, and in its middle a good stove was roaring away. Along the walls were benches on which the men of the Guard were sitting, smoking and talking; and at the far end were rough wooden bunks in which they slept. Guns and swords and cocked hats were hanging on the walls; and the walls were pretty well covered with all sorts of fool-pictures of soldiers done with charcoal, and with scribblings which I suppose were writing—but I didn't know what writing was, in those days. The pipe-smoke was thick enough to cut with a knife. Everybody was smoking—except one man who had laid his head down on his arms on the table and was sound asleep.

"Comrades, here's a new recruit for the Revolution—a volunteer for our Company," said Vauclair as we entered the room. And then, turning to me, he added: "That's so, youngster, isn't it? Now then, speak out— Liberty or Death! ·Vive la Nation!"

I was beginning to get the hang of things a little by this time. Standing on the tips of my toes to make myself taller, and swinging my hat above my head, I shouted: "Vive la Nation! Liberty or Death!" and all the National Guardsmen cried after me: "Liberty or Death!"

The noise woke up the soldier who was snoring on the table. Rubbing his eyes and looking around him sleepily he called out: "Why the devil are you all making such a row?"

"Here's a new volunteer," said Vauclair, leading me up to the table. "Get the roster and we'll enroll him right off."

"Good for him!" the man answered.

By this time he was quite awake and had brought out from the drawer of the table the roster of the Company and the form of enlistment that was to be filled in. Spreading the papers out before him and dipping his pen in the ink-bottle, he turned to me and said:

"Your name, Citizen?"

"Pascalet."

"Your father's name?"

"Pascal."

"Hasn't he any other name than Pascal?"

"I never heard any."

"Your mother's name?"

"La Patine."

"La Patine? Isn't she called also Gothon or Janetoun or Babette?"

"I don't know. I never heard her called anything but La Patine."

"Well, we'll put it down La Patine, anyway. Where were you born?"

"At Malemort in the Comtat."

"That's all right. Now sign your name."

I had to tell him that I couldn't; that I didn't know how.

"No matter," said Vauclair taking my
hand. "You don't know how to write with
black ink, but we'll teach you to write with
red! Where is the quarter-master? Ah, there
you are, Bérigot. Take this man to the equip-
ment-room, and fit him out so that he may be
ready to present himself properly under arms."

An old grumbler got up from the bench,
shook out his pipe, lighted a lantern and
nodded to me to follow him. We climbed up
into Jacquemart's clock-tower by a winding
stair-case as steep as a ladder and so narrow
that only one person could pass at a time. We
went up and up and up. At last we reached
a square room crammed full of soldier-clothes
and cocked-hats and guns and swords. The
quarter-master took a careful look at me and
then, turning to the heap of clothes, rummaged
all through it and finally dragged out a coat.
"There, that will fit you," said he. "Try
it on."

Oh what a lovely coat it was! To be sure
it had been worn a good deal and was a little
thread-bare—but what difference did that make!
It was of dark green cloth with a large turned-
back red collar, and it had beautiful gilt buttons,
and fine long tails that flapped against my
calves. It certainly was very much too big

for me all over, and the sleeves were so long that they came down to the tips of my fingers. But I held my tongue about its bigness and quietly turned up the sleeves; and, as the coat was lined with red, this gave me a pair of red cuffs like my collar.

Having got my coat, I had next to get a hat; and this bothered me badly. I must have tried on between twenty and thirty—and they all came down to my ears. At last the quarter-master lost all patience and called out: "Té! Put on that red cap: then you'll be rigged like the Marseilles Federals."

I put on the pretty red cap. Its tip fell over well down to my shoulder, and on its side was stuck a full-blown cabbage of a cockade! I was delighted with it; and with the fine pair of blue breeches and the snowy white gaiters which the quarter-master tossed over to me, saying that I needn't bother about trying them on as breeches and gaiters always fitted everybody. "And now," said he, "you want a sword and a gun. Pick out what you like and let's get through."

It didn't seem possible that I really was to have a sword and a gun, and I was so upset that I took the first gun that I laid my hands on. But about the sword I was more careful.

I wanted a long curved sword, like Vauclair's; and those in the heap seemed to be all straight and short. I turned the heap topsy-turvy without finding what I wanted; and as I was fussing altogether too long over it old Bérigot called out to me: "What are you making such a to-do about? Don't you see one is as good as another? With a touch of the whetstone any of 'em 'll cut like razors. Take one and come along." And so I had to be satisfied with a short straight sword, after all.

Bérigot fastened the door behind us, and down we went. I had more than a load to carry; and my gun kept catching against the wall, and my sword all the while was sliding in between my legs and tripping me—so that two or three times I nearly pitched head over heels down the narrow stairs—and, altogether, I was as bothered as a donkey in a cane-brake. And then when we got back to the guard-room all the men came around me and every one had something to say. "The cap doesn't fit badly," said one; "He'll grow up to his sword," said another; "The coat is only a span or two too long," said a third.

"Oh, come now," Vauclair broke in, "don't bother the boy with your nonsense. He's all right. Come along, Pascalet, you shall sleep

in my quarters to-night; and before you are
up in the morning my wife will have your coat
to fit you like your skin.   All it needs is a tuck
in the sleeves and a little shortening.   Come,
we'll go now.   You must be about used up
by this time.   You shall have a bite and a sup
with us and half of my little boy's bed; and to-
morrow I'll take you to the drill outside the
ramparts—and I tell you we'll rattle the Aristos later on!"

He loaded me up with my sword and gun
and gaiters and all the rest, and together we
left the Hôtel de Ville; and then went on
through one crooked street after another to the
little Place du Grand Paradis.   Here we entered a tidy little house, at the corner of the
Rue de la Palapharnerie, and found ourselves in
the dark at the foot of a spiral stair.

"Lazuli! Lazuli!" Vauclair called, but no
one answered.   "She must be at the club,"
he said.   "No matter, we'll find the door
somehow."

We groped our way up the narrow stairs,
where my gun and sword again bothered me,
and so to the second floor and into a little
room that was kitchen and living-room and
bedroom all in one—though the bed was hidden away in an alcove at one side.

Vauclair got out the flint and steel and tinder, and when he had a spark going he started a flame on a sliver of hemp-stalk dipped in sulphur, and with that lighted the candle. All this time he was storming away at his wife.

"And so Lazuli must needs go to the club," he growled. "I should like to know if clubs are women's business! As if men were not strong enough to defend Holy Liberty and our beautiful Revolution!" This started him on another tack, and away he went on it: "We must have our Republic. We want it, and we mean to get it. We'll show King Capet, the traitor, that when we ask for figs we won't take thistles. Didn't he try to make us believe that he was on his way to get help for us when we stopped him at the frontier? And all the while, traitor that he is, he meant to put himself at the head of the nation's enemies. He is about a span too tall, that rascal King! He needs shortening—and if the stomachs of the Paris folks give out in that matter we and the Marseilles Federals will go up and do the work for them. Yes, we'll bleed him finely—just under his jowls! And as to his wife, his Austrian carrion of a wife, we'll give her a donkey-ride back-foremost—as she deserves. She's the real traitor; it's she who's always egging on the King. And then we'll attend to the tail the King drags around after him, the counts and the marquises and the court-followers, and we will shorten every one of them by the same good span!"

All the time that Vauclair was ranting away, while I was standing stiff and watching him and drinking in his words, he was busy getting the supper ready: setting the little table with three places, getting out a big loaf of bread and a jug of wine, and then bringing from the fire-place an earthen dish in which was simmering gently a most delicious-smelling stew. When all was ready he looked into the inner room and then said to me: "Clairet's asleep; and as to Lazuli, we won't wait for her. Come, sit down and eat your supper; and then get to bed and asleep as fast as you can. You'll be started out early to-morrow, you know."

But just as we were beginning on the bread and stew in came Lazuli, quite excited and very much out of breath. "You mustn't blame me for being late," she said. "Of course you know, you good Vauclair, that I've only been at the club. I've just left there. And you'll never guess what's happened, I'm sure."

"Then I won't try," said Vauclair. "What is it?"

But instead of answering him Lazuli looked toward me and said: "And so you've got a companion. Isn't it the little mountain boy who was with us on the steps of the Pope's Palace? And doesn't he make a nice-looking soldier, to be sure! His coat's a trifle too big for him—but I'll fix that in no time. Sit down now, my dear, and you too, Vauclair, and I'll tell you the news."

"Well, crack away then," said Vauclair, as he helped the stew and then cut a chunk of bread off the loaf for each of us. "What is your news, anyway?"

"It's bad news," Lazuli answered. "It's a letter from the Deputy Barbaroux up at Paris to the Federals at Marseilles, his own people. It was read out to us at the club. It says that the Aristos at Paris are having things all their own way. That the King won't allow the battalions of Federals come up from the country to camp inside Paris. That the Paris men are no better than capons and are turning around to the King's side, and that the National Guard of Paris can't be made to do anything because it is rotten to the marrow of its bones. And so Barbaroux says that it's good-bye to the Revolution unless something is done right off—and he says that the Reds of the Midi must do it; that our Federals, our sans-culottes, down here in the South, must get out their swords and their guns and come up to Paris with the war-cry of Liberty or Death!"

I had taken three or four mugs of wine—for I was very thirsty, and as fast as I emptied my rnug Vauclair filled it again—and when I heard Liberty or Death! that way, it was too much for me. "Liberty or Death!" I cried, standing up and flourishing my knife in the air. "Liberty or Death! That Barbaroux—whoever he is—is right. *I* am one of the Reds of the Midi! *I* am a sans-culotte! *I* am a Federal! *I* am one of those he wants in Paris—and I'll go! I'll get my revenge on the Marquis and on Monsieur Robert, and on that devil of a Surto; and I'll revenge the Liberals who were stabbed to death in the hospital, too. Now I understand why my father said that the Marquis and Monsieur Robert were going to Paris to help the King. But I'll go there too—now that I have a gun. We'll all go there with our guns. Liberty or Death!"

While I shouted I seemed to see ever so many lighted candles dancing on the tables. Lazuli looked lovelier than the golden angels on the altar of our church at Malemort. Vauclair seemed as tall as one of our poplars on the Nesque—and the room seemed to be tipping up on end!

"Bravo, bravo!" cried Vauclair.

"Bravo!" cried the handsome Lazuli. "Thou wilt indeed be a good Patriot! Yes, we'll all go to Paris singing the 'Carmagnole'; and all of us, all the good Patriots, will join hands together and dance around in a great *brande!*"

I don't remember well what happened after that. But I know that we three—all by ourselves—made a *brande* by joining hands and dancing around the table while we sang at the top of our voices the famous song of the free montagnards about dancing a farandole and planting the wild thyme that grows on the mountains and is the symbol of liberty.

> Plantèn la ferigoulo,
>   Arrapara.
> Fasèn la farandoulo
> E la mountagno flourira,
> E la mountagno flourira.

And when the song and our dance was ended, Lazuli led me into the inner room, to the straw bed where her little boy was sleeping, and told me to lie down there. And my head had no more than touched the pillow than I was sleeping like a log.

Old Pascal stopped short and gave La Mie a smack on the shoulder that made her jump. "You're as sleepy as a little cat, yourself," he said. "Get up and go to bed. To-morrow we'll go at the story again."

The clock in the church steeple began to strike twelve. "Gosh!" cried Lou Materoun, jumping up. "It's midnight! What will my wife say to me? I'll catch it for a week!"

"Never mind, Lou Materoun," said La Mie, as she held the light for us in the doorway. "We all know what your wife is. You have a hard road."

"Viper tongue!" muttered my grandfather as we went off together in the dark.

CHAPTER IV.

"THE MARSEILLAISE."

THE next day, being Sunday, there was no meeting at the shoemaker's; for on Sundays the neighbours spent their time elsewhere. The old and the middle-aged folk went to the Cabaret Nòu, where they played a sober game of *bourro* and drank each one his little jug of white wine. The young and gay-minded folk ostensibly went off for a stroll in the secluded valleys of our mountain, where they surreptitiously gambled away their sous in playing a new-fangled game of chance called *vendôme*. And I, who was too little for any such doings, went to bed when night came feeling as flat as a quoit; and saying to myself: "Suppose the shoemaker should take a fancy to make a holiday of Monday too and shut up his shop!"

Monday morning early I took the longest way to school, so that I might pass in front of the shop; and I was greatly reassured and heartened when, from a long way off, I saw the shutters open and heard the tap-tapping of hammer on sole. "All right!" thought I. "To-night old Pascal will go on with his story."

That evening, in good time, I was seated on my little bench in the warm little shop—which smelt as usual of shoemaker's wax and soaking leather, while overhead floated the usual bluish cloud of pipe-smoke.

Presently old Pascal stepped over the threshold, and without waiting for any one to ask him to begin he broke forth into one of his declamatory chants:

All laws are the work of the rich for the hurt of the needy;
Always the rich have too much, and always the poor have
    too little;
And I say that the man who has more than his share is a
    robber!
I say that of right belongs bread to him who is faint and
    an-hungered;
That his is the right to seize it wherever he finds it—
And the day in which bread is too scarce shall sharp knives
    be too plenty!

"What do you mean? What are you driving at with all that gabble, anyway?" spoke up Lou Materoun.

"What I am driving at," Pascal answered as he sat down, "is to tell you that I can not understand how for century after century men

went on starving and took no thought of revenge.   You can not even fancy, you who live
now-a-days, what was the lot of a poor man,
a man of the people, less than a hundred years
ago.   But I, who have felt it in my body and
who have seen it with my eyes, do know
what it was; and that is the life I am telling
you about now.   And now that you know
what I am driving at, I'll go on with my
story."

I went to bed beside Vauclair's little boy
and made but one nap of the night, sleeping
as sound as a top until morning came.   I was
tired out, my mind was easy, and I had drunk
a good deal of strong wine—and all that joined
together to give me the blessed soft sleep that
does one so much good and that is, perhaps,
the best thing in life.

My sleep had been so deep that at the first
flowering of day, when I saw the window-panes
whitening with the morning light, it was a little
while before I could tell where I was—or be
sure that all that had passed the day before
had not been a dream.   But I knew it was no
dream when, through the half-opened doorway, I saw Lazuli in the kitchen hard at work
needle in hand; a thin fine short needle that

flashed and glanced like a star-ray between her fingers as she busily made over my National Guard coat, spread out upon her knees.

Vauclair, seated beside her, was cleaning my gun and changing the flint in it; and both of them were as quiet as mice so as not to wake me. But though they said nothing, every now and then Lazuli would turn toward her husband and would show him the coatsleeve with the alterations she had made; and he, with a nod of his head, would answer: "Yes, yes, that's all right." Then Lazuli, biting short the thread with a sharp snap, would go to work again. She ended off by polishing up the buttons—the pretty gilt buttons, as bright as those on the coat of Monsieur le Marquis d'Ambrun.

I couldn't bear to let them think I was still asleep; and, as I did not venture to speak, I began to cough.

"Eh," said Vauclair, greatly pleased, "so he's awake"—and came on tip-toe to the door of the room; and when he saw the gleam of my open eyes he added: "Well, bad boy, and so you're already awake. It's a little too early; but no matter, get up and try on your coat."

Try on my coat! That made me jump out of bed and into my so longed-for coat in a flash; and I swore it fitted me like a ring fits the finger. Lazuli, smiling as she looked critically at me, smoothed down the wrinkles with her hand; for although she had taken it in everywhere it still was big enough for all out of doors! She buttoned it and unbuttoned it.

"Perhaps I had better take it in a little more under the arms," she said doubtfully.

"It fits, it fits!" I cried, afraid that she would make me take it off.

Vauclair, accepting the matter as settled, hung over my shoulders the yellow strap supporting my short straight sword—shaped exactly like the tails of those green crickets which swarm after harvest—and as the strap was a large one the sword hung pretty low and banged against my calves. I got into my blue breeches, and buckled on my gaiters—which were a little too long and too wide and so came well down over my pretty shoes. As the final touch, Vauclair took up my cap with its red white and blue cockade. He held it open with his outspread fingers and walked solemnly toward me, carrying it in front of him reverently as it had been the Host. Still holding it open he fitted it on my head, carefully arranging the tip so that it should fall over just in the

way it is represented in the busts of the Republic. Then he stepped back and gazed at
me. Delighted with his work, he clapped his
hands as he exclaimed: "There's a sans-culotte
fit to fight in the Heavenly Host! There's a
fellow to take to Paris when we go to make
the King cry mercy!"

Lazuli handed me my stuff jacket saying,
"Look and see what there is in your pockets."
I timidly drew out the letter Monsieur Randoulet
had given me for Monsieur le Chanoine Jusserand and stuffed it into my coat pocket so as to
hide it away; for the letter made me feel confused and ashamed. I did not know exactly
why, but it seemed to me as if this bit of paper,
which had been my only hope, now might
be the cause of my perdition. And yet I could
not help valuing it. I felt that I must keep it,
so as to touch it from time to time; for then it
would seem as though I touched the soft kind
friendly hand of good Monsieur Randoulet.
Out of the other pocket I took the three pretty
white crowns of three francs each. These I
did not wish to keep. I gave them to Lazuli,
saying, "Keep them for me, please." And
Lazuli, putting them in the little box that held
her ornaments and locking them safe in the
drawer of her cupboard, answered: "There,

you see where they are—when you want them,
you have only to ask for them."

From that day on I became one of the little
family in the Place du Grand Paradis.

I should tire you out were I to tell in detail
all that I saw and all that I did during the five
or six months that I spent in Avignon. Each
day at early morning I was drilled with the
others outside the city walls, with street-boys
playing tip-cat and old people sunning themselves around us. By day or by night, in all
weathers, I took my turn in mounting guard:
at the door of the Pope's Palace, in front of the
Hôtel de Ville, on the banks of the Rhône, at
the Escalier de Sainte-Anne, or—and this I
liked best of all—by the semaphore on the top
of the Rocher des Doms. Hour after hour I
gaped at that semaphore, never tired of watching its two black arms whirling about so
strangely up there in the air; arms which shut
themselves up, spread out, folded together, un-
folded again, and opened and closed like two
big razors.

And I saw good times and bad times, stab-
bings and embracings, murders and makings
up, excitement and sorrow, sad doings and
gay doings, scrimmages, farandolès, and solemn processions. Now the deep chant of the

Te Deum rang out, now the gay notes of the "Carmagnole." The *De Profundis* would be solemnly intoned while the "Ça ira" was howling out from excited throats.

Sometimes one party, sometimes the other, would get the upper hand; one day it was the Reds, the Patriots, another day the Whites, the Anti-Patriots. We often had to hurry to separate them—in one or another parish the alarm-bell was ringing all the time. And whenever we came back to barracks from drill or from guard-mount or from quieting a row, whether by day or by night, each man had his little flask of cordial-wine and his three ounces of *massopain*; and so wild were the times, so often were we out on service, that we fairly could count on getting our three flasks a day —so we were pretty well pampered with our cake and wine. And always in the evenings those of us who were off duty spent our time at the club—where we could hear the last news from Paris and Marseilles.

One day I was stationed at the Porte du Rhône on guard over the Liberty Tree planted there by the Reds, which the Whites from the streets of the Fusterie had tried to pull down. It was about the end of June, right in the midst of the harvest. I am sure of the season because the Liberty Tree was full of cigales, who were making a deafening noise—as is their custom in mid-harvest—with their song: "Sègo, sègo, sègo! Sickle, sickle, sickle!" I was watching for a chance to catch a cigale for Lazuli's little boy, when suddenly the alarm-bell rang out from the bell-tower of the Augustines; and a minute later a man pale as plaster came tearing down the Rue de la Fusterie shouting as he ran: "Save yourselves! Save yourselves! The Marseilles brigands are coming! Call home your children! Bar your doors and windows! The robbers and murderers and galley-slaves are coming! We're all lost!" and, still shouting, the pale man ran round into the Rue du Limas and disappeared in the direction of the Porte de l'Oulle.

It was a sight to see the washwomen, who were at work on the banks of the Rhône, all scamper away! They left behind them their bundles of linen, their shirts outspread to dry. They left aprons, baskets, jugs and buckets. Frightened as though a mad dog were after them, or as if a wild bull had got loose, screaming, flourishing their arms, they tore into their houses—and for a moment, in the whole quarter of the Porte du Rhône, nothing could be heard but the noise of doors and windows banging to and of clattering bolts and bars!

But from the other side, that of the Porte de la Ligne, rose up a great clamour of joyous cries and songs:

> Dansons la Carmagnole!
> Vive le son! Vive le son!

Then loud hand-clappings and exclamations of joy, and *tambourins* beginning to beat the farandole; and at the same moment the alarm-bell rang again.

"Good Heavens!" said I, when the alarm sounded, "I must be off;" and "One! Two!" up went my gun on my shoulder. "Right about, face"—and away I went at a quick-step to join the Corps de Garde at the Hôtel de Ville.

What an uproar! The whole Place de l'Horloge, blazing with sunlight, was crammed full of people, all talking and shouting and gesticulating at once; while Vauclair, in front of the Hôtel de Ville, was getting into line the men of the Garde Nationale. Drawn together by the sound of the alarm-bell, they were running in from all the streets—some of them only partly dressed, their straps thrown over their shoulders, their guns tucked under their arms, buttoning their breeches as they ran; and here and there was a running woman carrying her half-breeched husband's gun.

No one seemed to know what had happened. Some cried: "It's the Whites, the Papalists, come from Carpentras to fight us." Others answered: "No, it's the peasants from Gadagne who have risen against their lord and are bringing him here a prisoner." I could make nothing of what I heard as I pressed through the crowd to take my place in line. Vauclair, who was the sergeant on guard that day, saw me coming and called out sharply: "Why are you so behindhand? Hurry, hurry! Lord's Law, man, hurry!"

"What's it all about?" I asked as I fell in.

"What's it all about?" repeated Vauclair. "It is that the King of France is a traitor!" —and turning toward the crowd and brandishing his long sabre he cried loudly: "We are betrayed by our King!" And then, speaking to us of the Guard, he went on: "The Marseilles Battalion, on its way to Paris, passes through Avignon. We are going now to welcome these brave Federals—Vive la Nation!"

"Vive la Nation!" answered the Guard.

"Vive la Nation!" rose up the voice of the swarming crowd in a formidable shout.

And then came: "Forward, march!"—and off we started for the Porte du Limbert, all of us roaring together:

> Dance we the Carmagnole,
> Hurrah for the roar, the roar, the roar!
> Dance we the Carmagnole,
> Hurrah for the roar the cannon roar!

Men, women, children, old and young, with one voice joined in the chorus—"Dansons la Carmagnole!" The windows fairly rattled as we swept along.

In the narrow streets of the Bonneterie and of the Water-wheels there must have been at least ten thousand people packed so tight that they were fairly one on top of the other; and when those near the Porte du Limbert were at "Dansons la Carmagnole!" from the other end, up near the Rue Rouge, rang out the words "Vive le son du canon!" Mixed in with the words of the chorus were shouts of "Vive la Nation!" and "Vive les Marseillais!" The confusion and uproar were overpowering. When I looked backward I could see nothing but open mouths, and eyes starting out of heads that touched each other.

When this torrent of humanity had poured itself out of the porch of the Porte du Limbert we of the Guard ranged ourselves outside the ramparts in two lines facing inward, ready to present arms to the Marseilles Battalion when it should pass between our files; and scarcely were we halted and in line when a swarm of children came running toward us from the Chemin de la Coupe d'Or screaming: "Here they are! Here they are!"

And then around the turn of the road, brave in their red-plumed cocked-hats, appeared Commandant Moisson and Captain Garnier. On seeing us they drew their long sickle-like sabres, faced about upon the Battalion, and cried: "Vive la Nation!"—and instantly the men fell into marching-step and all together burst forth with

> Allons enfants de la Patrie,
> Le jour de gloire est arrivé!

It was the "Marseillaise" that they were singing; and that glorious hymn, heard then for the first time, stirred us down to the very marrow of our bones!

On they came—a big fellow carrying at their head a banner on which was painted in red letters: "The Rights of Man"; and if any person looked askance at that banner the big fellow seized him in a moment and made him kiss it on his knees! On they came—we presented arms and they passed between our files, still singing the "Marseillaise."

Oh what a sight it was! Five hundred men sun-burnt as locust-beans, with black eyes blazing like live coals under bushy eye-brows all white with the white dust of the road. They wore green cloth coats turned back with red, like mine; but farther than that their uniform did not go. Some had on cocked hats with waving cock's feathers, some red liberty-caps with the strings flying back over their shoulders and the tri-colour cockade perched over one ear. Each man had stuck in the barrel of his gun a willow or a poplar branch to shelter him from the sun, and all this greenery cast warm dancing shadows over their faces that made the look of them still more fantastic and strange. And when from all those red mouths—wide open as a wolf's jaws, with teeth gleaming white like a wild beast's teeth—burst forth the chorus "Aux armes, citoyens!" it fairly made a shiver run all down one's spine! Two drums marked step —Pran! rran! rran! "Allons enfants de la Pa-trie!" The whole Battalion passed onward and was swallowed up in the city gate.

As it disappeared we heard a strange noise like the clanking of chains or the rattle of loose iron; and then came four men hauling after them a rusty truck on which was a cannon. These men were harnessed to the truck as are oxen to the plough, and like oxen pulled from head and shoulders. With every muscle at full stretch, and with sweat dripping from them like rain, they bent forward with all their might to their heavy task. Rumble and bang went the truck over the cobble-stones and into the ruts, making a tremendous noise as it jolted up and down and from side to side. Following this truck came another and still another; the last having on it an immense pair of bellows, a big wooden tub full of clay, a great thing that looked like a cauldron, and pincers, hammers and tongs. This was the forge—for the repair of the guns, for the casting of balls, and for heating balls red hot before they should be fired. It took more than four men to drag this great mass—all straining forward like beasts of burden, the sinews of their calves starting and their feet so gripping the street that the nails in their shoes struck out sparks from the stones. Gasping though they were for breath, and almost spent with weariness, yet they too as they passed through our ranks raised their heads and with hoarse strangled voices shouted with the clipped Marseilles accent: " Vivo la Nacien!"

The blaze and glitter of sunshine, the whirlwinds of dust, the smell of hot human flesh, the rattle of drums, the clanking of iron, the singing and shouting—all this so dazed and transported me, so carried me away, that I, Pascal, though I knew not why, felt tears as big as filberts rolling down my cheeks as I presented arms!

When in the wake of the Battalion the cannon and forge had passed by us, we came to a shoulder, closed up, and fell in at the rear. Far off ahead the rattling drums beat the quick-step; the Marseilles men sang " Allons enfants de la Patrie"; and we and all the crowd joined in the chorus that we already had picked up: " Aux armes, citoyens!"

Our backward line of march was through the street of the Water-wheels, the Place du Change, under the walls of the Palace of the Popes, and so into the Rue de la Banasterie to the Place du Grand Paradis—where the Patriots had their club in what had been the chapel of the Violet Penitents. But as we were turning the corner by the Rue des Encans we were stopped short, and around us we heard the people exclaiming that there was a halt ahead that no one could understand. Some said that a Papalist had stabbed the Marseilles Commandant. Under Vauclair's command, a dozen of us pushed rapidly through the crowd to find out what was the matter, and to do whatever might be necessary to restore order. The trouble proved to be around the banner of The Rights of Man.

In the narrowest part of the Rue Sainte Catherine the procession had met, returning from his vesper service at the Carmelites, an old Canon followed by his old serving-woman; and when the lean old Canon saw the banner he turned up his nose at it and drew to a point his ill-natured muzzle in open contempt; and, worse than this, he actually cleared his throat and spit right at the feet of the banner-bearer! Furious at seeing the New Law so despised, its apostle had caught the poor old Canon by the nape of his neck, had forced him down to his knees on the stones and, thrusting the banner against his face, had tried to make him kiss it by force; but old skin-and-bones had struggled hard against this humiliation, and his servant had come screaming and scratching to his aid. The crowd shouted: "To the Rhône with the Papalist!" "To the Rhône with the Anti-Patriot!"

Just as we came on the ground the Federal snatched up the Canon, who was as dry as a whip-handle, and tucked him under his arm—kicking and struggling, with legs and arms outspread like a frog in a heron's beak. Then the drums took up the march, and again rang out " Allons enfants de la Patrie!" The Federal marched off in front, one arm holding up his banner, the kicking Canon gripped fast under the other like a bundle of foolishness, and after him the old servant—who hung on with all her might to her master, trying to set him free. Why that dried up old man did not snap like a pipe-stem between them, I am sure I don't know!

And who was the most astonished person of all there? Why I—for the old Canon was none other than Monsieur Jusserand, to whom Monsieur Randoulet had given me the letter; and the old serving-woman was the very woman who had torn off my cockade the day I knocked at his door in the Rue du Limas!

On we went until we entered the club-room that had been the chapel of the Violet Penitents. There the Federal dumped the Canon on what had been the steps of the main altar, and then he and Commandant Moisson and Vauclair all sat down on the altar table with their legs dangling in a row. We of the Guard, with a few Avignon Patriots, formed our line to keep the crowd back while they spoke; and there was such pushing and struggling to get into the little chapel that its walls fairly shook—and all the while the drums went on beating and thousands of voices sang, or rather howled: "Aux armes, citoyens!"

The Federal who carried the banner of The Rights of Man stood up on the altar—a great long man, as thin as Pontius Pilate—and he was a sight to behold standing there in his hobnailed shoes, his bare calves, his coat entirely too tight for him, and his bristling beard powdered white with road-dust! He took off his hat and feather and roughly stuck it on the bald pate of poor Canon Jusserand, who was crouched on the altar steps all in a heap, more dead than alive. Wiping his forehead with his coat sleeve, the Federal made a sign that he was going to read The Rights of Man. The drums stopped beating and a great silence fell over all; and then the Federal, with his mincing Marseilles accent, read out to us the New Law:

All men are born free, and the birth-rights of all men are equal.

All alike make the laws; all alike are the rulers and governed.

Broken the chains are, wide open the doors of the prisons.
Masters exist not.   No more are there slaves to be burthened.
Each man has his share of the earth that begot and will
　　claim him;
Each man sows his crop, and each sower shall garner his
　　harvest.
In all things to all men is freedom—in acts and in thoughts
　　and convictions.
Ended the day is of King and of Marquis and lordling.
Who aforetime toiled mole-like in darkness at will of his
　　masters
Stands erect in the light, and is governed alone by his
　　reason.
　　Vive la Nation!

Then the Federal got down from the altar, seized the Canon by the throat, and this time fairly forced the banner to his lips.   But the old stock-fish, who was not of the sort to stay conquered, no sooner felt himself let loose again than with a look of contempt he once more spat against the banner—and so pretty well cancelled his kiss.   At this fresh insult the big Federal was quite beside himself with rage.   Like a flash he pounced upon the Canon, held him for a moment by the scruff of his neck and the folds of his long gown, and then with a tremendous kick sent him flying over the heads of those nearest the altar into the thick of the crowd.   There was a shout of satisfaction, and then away went the Canon through the air from one pair of hands to another: now right side forward, now hind part before, now spinning around and around. And so—like a plank in the Rhône, whirling in the eddies but always going forward—he was flung hither and thither over the upturned faces until at last he was shot out of the door. And I must tell you, strange though it may seem, that seeing him thus abused hurt me in my heart—because I still had in my pocket that letter to him from good Monsieur Randoulet, and I felt as though an affront had been put upon our good Curé at Malemort.

What became of the Canon I don't know. No one paid any more attention to him; for at that moment Vauclair stood up on the altar and began to read out—in order to make the people more clearly understand how good and great was the cause of the Revolution—the laws and ordinances with which the Pope's Vice Legate so long had tied down and muzzled the people of Avignon:

The poor man may moan, but the poor man must pay,
Or he goes and he rots on the galley bench—
While he who carries or pistol or dagger
Will have a hemp necklace about his throat.
Whoso speaks of the Legate or the Legate's affairs,
If not by the Legate condemned to die,
Ten years in the galleys with robbers spends.

The man who cries "Rescue!" or "To arms!", or who
    dares
By a picture or a carving to offend the Legate,
Will lose his life and forfeit his goods!

"Oh come now, you can't mean us to believe all that," exclaimed Lou Materoun; who,
unable to keep his feelings to himself, broke
into old Pascal's chanted recital.

"Then I'm a liar, am I?" snorted old Pascal; and he glared so savagely at Lou Materoun
that the big man, too abashed to venture upon
an answer, made himself as small as he could on
the bench and with eyes downcast flicked the
ashes off his pipe on the floor between his knees.

"It is so true," said Pascal, pacified by Lou
Materoun's meekness, "that I could show it to
you printed in a book. I have heard many of
these laws and ordinances, and I cannot remember them all; but some of them I do remember—and they were the laws, mark you,
of my own time. It was forbidden to go out
after the curfew had rung; and whosoever
broke this law, and also carried with him a
dark-lantern, was liable to have all his joints
pulled apart in the strappado three times running—or he might even be outlawed from the
Comtat, at the Vice Legate's will. It was forbidden to compose, to write, to sing or to

cause to be sung, any songs that had anything whatever to do with politics; and whoever broke this law might be sent for ten years to the galleys and might have confiscated the half of his estates."

"Whew!" exclaimed the cobbler. "That wasn't anybody's twenty sous fine—as it is now-a-days."

Pascal continued: "And what will you all say when I tell you that did the Vice Legate still reign we all could be taken out and strung up in a row for the crime of assembling here together? Such was the law—to which always was added: 'If it be the good pleasure of the Legate'!"

"Lord alive!" put in Lou Materoun, this time flicking off his ashes properly into the coal-tub, "I'm glad I waited a while before I was born! And do you mean to say that just for sitting together this way in company the Pope's soldiers could have come in and jugged us? Then in those days men were not men?"

"They were men, as thou and I are men," answered Pascal. "But enough of that—those times are gone!"

Well, when Vauclair had finished reading out the Vice Legate's Laws, the crowd went hoarse with its shouting of "Vive la Nation! Vive la Révolution!" The women—hucksters, washwomen, silkweavers—all with catalan caps and tricolour cockades, were more wildly excited and made more noise than the men. They yelled, they screamed—and many of them flung themselves on the neck of the big Federal who carried The Rights of Man and fairly suffocated him with kisses.

In the thick of this confusion a big coarse woman, a tripe-seller called La Jacarasse, came rushing forward—her hair streaming loose over her shoulders, her cap awry and its untied strings flying behind her—carrying in one hand a long knife and in the other a big bag of coarsely woven straw. She climbed to the top of the altar like a wild-cat, making a great display of stockingless legs, and when she had scrambled to her feet she flourished her knife and bag screaming: " You see this here knife ? For fifty years it has ripped up pigs—last year it ripped up that cursed jade of an Aristocrat who jabbed her scissors into Patriot Lescuyer's face when the Papalists were killing him in the church of the Cordeliers. You see this here bag ? In it I carried her liver and lights and hung 'em on the latch of the Vice Legate's palace—same as the old devil did himself with

the innards of Patriots he'd ordered killed."
And then, turning to the Federal who was
holding the banner of The Rights of Man, she
plumped two big kisses on his cheeks. The
crowd applauded loudly; and "Vive la Nation!" shouted the Federal—but holding his
nose, for the tripe-woman smelt vilely of her
trade.

The drums rolled again and Vauclair stood
up straight in the very place where the taber-
nacle had been, and cried out as he flourished
his hat on the tip of his sabre: "To defend
The Rights of Man and to drag down the tyrant, I enroll myself as a volunteer in the Marseilles Battalion!"

In a moment we all were crazy with en-
thusiasm, the drums rattled their approval as
if they would burst, every arm was waving in
the air, the Marseilles men shrieked "Long
live the Avignon Patriots!" and in turn we
shrieked "Long live the Marseilles Federals!"
That was too much for me! For a moment
everything went spinning around and around;
and then, without at all knowing how I did it,
I suddenly found myself standing on top of the
altar, my red cap hoisted on top of my gun,
screaming at the top of my voice: "Death to
the tyrant! I too volunteer into the Marseilles

Battalion!" And Zòu! the drums, and Zòu! the shrieks "Vive les Patriotes!" "Vive les Fédérés!"

Far up in a corner of the chapel I caught sight of Lazuli, her little boy up on her shoulder, both clapping hands and screaming: "Bravo, Pascalet! Bravo!" As I pitched down from the altar Commandant Moisson caught me in his arms, and with a kiss on each cheek accepted my enlistment among his Marseillais. And then, louder than ever, rattlety-bang went the drums!

The meeting was over. Some good Patriots, they were porters down by the river gates, called out: "To the Porte de la Ligne! There is cool wine there!"

"To the Porte de la Ligne! To the Porte de la Ligne!" shouted the crowd; and the Battalion, falling into line and followed by the cannon and the forge, went down to the Rhône—where there was enough bread and wine and olives and nuts and garlic for all the world! We ate, drank, sang and danced I don't know how long. The great heat of the day was over, and the *tambourins* untiringly beat the farandole. But I was so stuck up with being enrolled in the Marseilles Battalion that I felt bound to behave like a grown man.

I scorned dance and song and victuals; I went swaggering from one group to another; I talked to the Marseilles men and made acquaintance with them, drinking a glass with one and touching cups with another.

But one thing bothered me dreadfully—I was so very young! Those to whom I spoke said: "Good for you, little cock! What's your name?" and then every one of them added: "How old are you?" I answered them all bravely, trying to mince my words as they did: "My name's Pascalet, I must be more than sixteen years old"—and in order to look the age I gave myself I stood up as straight as I could on my toes. I felt and felt the corners of my mouth. But my moustache couldn't be made to sprout by feeling for it. There wasn't a single hair! However, as the moustache was impossible, I tried my best in other ways to look like the men of the Battalion. I stuck a bit of willow in the muzzle of my gun; and in order to be as grimy as possible I dragged my feet in the dust. Had I dared, I would have rolled over and over in the road!

Suddenly I realized that it was a long time since I had seen Vauclair, and I wondered where he could be. While I was hunting for him, forcing my way as well as I could through

the closely pressed throng, I heard just behind
me the lively cracking of a whip and the jingling of bells; and as I turned I saw a two-horse
carriage struggling to get through the crowd.
It already was so close upon me that I could
feel the horses' noses sniffling on the back of
my neck; and in a hurry, with the others, I
stood aside to let it pass.

But, Saints above! what did I see? It was
the carriage of Monsieur le Marquis! Big Surto,
in coachman's dress, was driving; and, still
stranger, there beside him on the box was my
father, my poor old father! His face still was
marked with the weals of the whip-strokes;
he was bunched together all of a heap, looking
sick and poor and thin, and so frightened at all
the crowd of dancing and singing soldiers that
to see him hurt my heart. But at the sight of
big Surto's hard face I trembled all over and
was dumbfoundered. The carriage rolled softly
along, and inside I saw the Marquise Adelaide,
pretty Adeline with her gentle eyes, and Monsieur Robert; and down in one corner, looking
no bigger than an onion, was Monsieur le Marquis d'Ambrun. I looked again toward the
box so as to be certain that it was my father I
had seen, and my eyes met wicked Surto's
wolf's eyes—which plunged into me like two

knives and seemed to say: "I've got you this time, sure!"

The carriage passed, and the crowd surged together behind it and went on with the farandole and dance. But I, thunderstruck, did not know of what wood to make arrows.

It was against all sense of right to let my father go that way without speaking to him. But I knew that if I went to him I was lost: big Surto's eyes had told me that only too plainly. And yet—my father! A sob came up into my throat! Not knowing what to do, I started off again in search of Vauclair. With him to back me I feared no one; with him I could go to see my old father and be sure that Surto would do me no harm. I searched and searched; but Vauclair was nowhere to be found—and as I stood on tip-toe to see if I could catch a glimpse of his red plume over the heads of the crowd a heavy hand dropped on my shoulder with a nip like a vice.

I turned—it was Surto! As soon as he had taken the carriage out of the press he had given the reins to Monsieur Robert and, bringing my simple-hearted father with him, had come after me instantly—so that I should not escape him again. I tried to wriggle out of his clutch, but his fingers were iron hooks strong enough to break my shoulder. "Come along," said he. "Come before the Commantant. Your farder is going to take you back home."

"I won't go," I cried. "I am free. I've enlisted as a volunteer!" and again I tried to break away. But Surto dragged me off by main force; while my old father limped along behind us, muttering: "Yes, yes, you good-for-nothing boy, you must come home. Monsieur le Marquis has said so—and that settles it."

Commandant Moisson was not far off; and seeing that there was a disturbance of some sort he called out, "What is the matter?" and came toward Surto.

"The matter is that this rascal has been playing truant; and his old farder here vants to make him go home, vere his old mother is crying her eyes out because he has run avay."

The Commandant frowned at me sternly. "You little scamp," said he "is this the way young fellows like you treat the old folks now-a-days? Go home, the Nation does not need you yet; go home with your father who does need you now. Later, when there is a little more hair on your chin, you shall enlist with us for good and all." So saying he turned on his heel without giving me a chance to say a word. My father bowed deeply to his disappearing back, and in another moment big Surto was dragging me brutally out of the crowd—going at such a pace that my father could hardly keep up with us.

I felt that I was lost. Vauclair, who knew all my story, could have saved me; but Vauclair had returned to the house to prepare for our march to Paris, and was beyond all call. If only I had had my gun or my sword! But both were stacked up with the arms of the Battalion against the ramparts. Alone, unarmed, my heart failed me under Surto's claws; and I let myself be dragged on, more dead than alive, while I looked around vainly for Vauclair's red plume. Soon we were far away from the scene of the festival. We pushed through the quarters of the Anti-Patriots and reached the Rue de la Violette, on which was the palace of Monsieur le Marquis d'Ambrun. The carriage was there in the middle of the court-yard; where the servants, instead of unloading the baggage, were piling things into it under the orders of Monsieur Robert and Mademoiselle Adeline. When Monsieur Robert saw me brought in, dragged along like some wild beast, he sneered and said: '' Now we've got the little villain! Zòu—down with him into the vault and let him stay there!"

My father stepped forward and as usual fell on his knees and kissed that monster's hand.

When Mademoiselle Adeline heard what her brother said she clasped her hands and turned her head aside so as not to see me; and I understood that though she was sorry for me she did not dare to speak.

The end of all now seemed very near to me. We came into the hall, in the middle of which was an open trap-door showing a dark staircase leading to the cellar; and as Surto dragged me down those stairs I heard Monsieur Robert saying to my father: "Well, you've seen your good-for-nothing scamp of a son. You thought he was with Monsieur le Chanoine Jusserand, to whom Monsieur·le Curé had sent him with a letter of recommendation; but the scorpion preferred living with murderers. You saw him dressed up in his robber's clothes!"

Down at the end of the cellar was the vault. Surto drew the bolts, opened the door, and pitched me into the dark hole—saying as he did so: "Starf in there! When you get hungry, eat one hand—and keep the other for breakfast next day!"

Although I felt that I was lost, I tried to plead with him; but the beast, twirling me around as if to get a chance to kick the bones out of me, said stuttering with anger: "You little tamn rascal! I know vat a snake's tongue you haf! You haf see too much! Suppose you toldt vat you see in the hospital, or vat you see unter that pig oak! You understandt, hey? Vell, down there you haf to keep your tongue insidt your teeth!"

As I went pitching into the darkness he slammed fast the door of the vault, and I heard him shoot the bolt outside. Then I heard him go up stairs, and I heard the trap-door fall with a bang like a cannon shot. I was left alone in the blackness, the silence and the chill of death.

There was no one to rescue me. My own father had betrayed and sold me, had consented to my death. No, that was impossible. He could not in the least have understood the harm that he was doing me. He, poor unfortunate wretch, with his face all scarred with the marks of the Count's whip, still knelt and kissed the Count's hand. Oh, to think of those scars, and not to be able to avenge them! Then I thought and thought over what Surto had said about what I had seen under the big oak at La Garde. But what had I ever seen under that

oak that should make him want to shut me up
there so as to keep my tongue behind my
teeth? Suddenly, in a flash, it all came back
to me and I understood.

One day, long, long before, I had climbed
to the top of that oak to get at a bird's nest
with some beautiful nestlings; and I was in
the midst of putting the little birds into my
cap when down under the tree I heard voices.
Spreading myself flat along the branch and
looking down, I saw big Surto with Madame
la Marquise. They were holding each other's
hands and talking most earnestly. As they
separated, one to go one way and one the
other, I heard Surto say: "No fear, we'll get
rid of thy little Marquis! I swear I'll shoot
him the first day when we are hunting together
that I get the chance;" and the Marquise answered: "Act quickly, and when the chance
comes shoot true!" These words fairly made
my flesh creep. I flattened myself still closer
against my branch and waited until they both,
as I thought, were out of the way before I came
down. Unluckily I didn't wait long enough.
Surto, though a good way off, still was in sight;
and what was more he happened to look back
in the instant that I was sliding down the trunk
to the ground. I ran like a rabbit into the

thick wood, and I thought at the time that he
did not know who it was; but I was mistaken
—and I suppose that from that moment he was
bent upon my death. And so I fairly had played
into his hands, by giving him a good open excuse for killing me, when I threw the rock on
Monsieur Robert's toes.

I was in the midst of these thoughts and
recollections when I heard rats running over
broken bottles piled up in one corner of the
vault. Broken glass! Oh, what good luck!
At least I would not have to die of hunger—I
could cut open my four veins. I groped my
way toward the corner, and at each step a
spider's web brushed across my face; they
were so thick that the spiders must have been
left alone there to spin them for years and for
years. I reached the broken bottles, and was
feeling around among them for a sharp pointed
bit that would do the work well when I heard
a sound as if the trap was being raised. I held
my breath; and then I clearly heard footsteps
outside the door of the vault. It doesn't seem
reasonable, but I who at that very moment
was trying to find something to kill myself
with, began to tremble so that my teeth chat-
tered; for I was sure it was Surto coming back
to knock me on the head. I didn't mind dying

so much; but I did mind dying by that monster's hands—and above all without struggling; without making him pay for my death. I picked up the first bottle-shard that my hand found, and with set teeth faced the door; ready to spring on the wretch and bury my teeth in his neck and the bit of glass in his side. And then the bolt squeaked and the door opened wide.

Oh how dazzled I was!

With a little lamp in her hand, a blue hood on her head, I saw gentle Adeline whose first words were: "Hush, Pascalet! where are you? I have come to save you."

"You, Adeline! Oh have mercy on me. Don't give me up to your game-keeper. He will kill me!"—and I fell at her feet.

"Never, my good little Pascalet. It is just the contrary—I have come to save you from that wicked man. Follow me and do not speak. I will get you away out of this house—and may God keep you from ever falling again into big Surto's claws. He is now in the garden, digging your grave; for he has sworn that before day dawns he'll break your neck and bury you. Come!"

I followed her quickly up the stairway, into the hall, and then out by a door—so heavy that

we both together had to pull to open it—into
the chicken-yard.   Once there, Adeline said
to me: "Get over that wall and you are in the
street."   Mademoiselle Adeline actually tried
to drag out for me the chicken-house ladder.
Her utmost efforts could not stir it from its
place—and while she was tugging away at it
with her delicate little hands I, active as a
marten, was on top of the wall.   And then—I
am ashamed to tell it—I, rough and coarse as
barley-bread, had never a word of thanks for
her, but just dropped down into the street and
tore off as fast as I could toward the Place du
Grand Paradis.

At that time of night Avignon was as silent
and as lonely as a graveyard.   The full moon
was pouring bucketsful of light on one side of
the narrow street, and casting on the other side
a black shadow so thick that hidden in it you
couldn't tell a horse from a man.   Buried in
the shadow, I ran onward—taking care to keep
clear of the Papalist quarter—and not until I
came near the end of the Rue des Encans did
I hear a sound.   Then, as I turned the corner
into the Rue Sainte Catherine, I heard coming
toward me the trampling of feet.

"Heavens!" I thought, "maybe it's the
Papalist patrol!"—and I hid myself in a deep

doorway where the shadow was as thick as a fog.

The sounds came nearer and nearer, while I stood there trembling; and at last—it seemed to me a long while—the group came abreast of me and then safely passed me by. But though they did not see me in the shadow, I saw them clearly in the bright moonlight. At the head walked a big thick woman, striding along like a man and carrying in one hand a long knife and in the other a bag. Behind her came three masked men, carrying between them another man bound and gagged—a poor wretch who from time to time kicked and struggled and tried vainly to get free; and each time that he fell to wriggling and plunging, and the little procession halted until his bearers could hold him fast again, the woman turned around and cried in a harsh voice: "That's right, kick away! Kick as much as you please! You can't get loose—and I'm going to rip your bowels out before we throw you into the Rhône!"

It was La Jacarasse, the tripe-woman, who was taunting the helpless man with these blood-curdling words; and I could hear her keeping on in the same fashion until she and the masks and their prisoner disappeared around the next turn.　They went on into the Rue de la Banasterie, toward the Porte de la Ligne—and as soon as they were out of sight I took to my heels again and in another minute I was at our own door.　Jacquemart was pounding midnight on his bell, and yet there still was a light in the window of our room.　I knocked and called as loudly as I dared: "Lazuli! Lazuli!　It is I!"

"Can it be Pascalet?　Yes, it is his voice!" I heard Lazuli cry, and then I heard her hurrying down the stairs as if on wings.

The key turned and the door flew open. As soon as Lazuli saw me she caught me close in her arms and kissed me a dozen times. "Where have you been?　What has happened to you?" she exclaimed.　"I don't know how many patrols I've sent hunting for you all through Avignon."　And as we went up the stairs together to our room she continued: "Vauclair left with the Battalion.　He told me that as soon as you got back I was to send you after him on the road to Paris.　Oh Pascalet, my pretty boy, I began to fear you were lost!" —and then she threw her arms around me and kissed me again and again.

I was greatly surprised and confused and delighted.　I hardly could tell whether I was asleep or awake. I knew nothing of caresses; and these, the first I ever had felt, seemed strangely sweet to me. Lazuli's hearty kisses as she pressed my face against her warm bosom moved me curiously. Not to be rude, as I had been to Mademoiselle Adeline, I gave back kiss for kiss and hug for hug and felt I never could weary of so giving and taking. Often had I spent hours gazing at her, thinking how pretty she was and how everything she did was well done. Sometimes as she passed near me I had ventured to touch her skirt; and the touch had sent a thrill through all my veins. Lazuli's voice was honey-sweet, and when she looked on me with her lovely kind eyes her glance seemed a caress in itself. Innocent as a new-born babe in all such love matters, I didn't understand what I felt. Probably Lazuli had some notion of it. At any rate, she soon stopped petting me, pushed me away, and returned to her usual cheerful well-balanced self as she said: "You must be hungry, Pascalet. Take some bread and wine and tell me all that has happened to you." She poured me a glass of cordial and continued: "You must be off in a hurry so as to catch up with the Battalion at La Verdette, where they camp for the night. You know where that is, about half a league from Avignon? The Battalion starts from there at daylight for Paris."

While I sopped my bread in my wine I told her step by step all my misfortunes, and also how I had met La Jacarasse and the three men carrying another man to the Rhône. When Lazuli heard this she threw her arms up over her head, and exclaimed: "It isn't possible! Where are we? Is everybody a murderer? I am not going to stay here alone with my baby. I am afraid of your Surto. I am afraid of La Jacarasse. Start now. Leave here at once. Take your gun and your sword and join the Battalion. Tell Vauclair I can not stay here alone. Tell him I shall start for Paris next week by the coach. I shall pass you on the road and will wait for you in Paris. I will get ready there a little home for you both; and I will be there with you should anything go wrong. I too am a Patriot. I want my share of all your troubles.

"Here is your bundle. See, Pascalet, what I have put in it for you. Here is a nice un-bleached linen shirt; here is your gourd, full of good brandy; here is a handsome red *taiolo* to fasten round your waist; here are two pistols, with powder and ball and fresh flints; and here is your tricolour cockade. Here too, don't forget, are the three crowns given you by Monsieur Randoulet. You may need them. It is a long road to Paris, and the times are bad. They say all the people up there are Aristocrats —perhaps you will not get even drinking-water for nothing! Well, it is time to start. Come and kiss little Clairet—but come quietly, for he is fast asleep. And then be off as quickly as you can, and tell all I have said to Vauclair."

Lazuli took me by the hand and led me in softly to kiss little Clairet. Then she put my bundle on my back, fastening it on firmly with two bands which crossed over my chest, and we went down stairs. I went first, and what with sword and gun and bundle I was laden like a bee. Lazuli came behind, lamp in hand, saying over and over: " Yes, I start next week —we will all meet very soon. Say so to Vauclair."

My heart got up into my mouth and choked me so that I couldn't answer her a word. I stopped on the threshold—and before I could turn around the door was shut behind me and bolted fast. And there I was, all alone at night on the Place du Grand Paradis, my sword by my side, my gun on my shoulder—starting on foot for Paris, the Capital of France!

"And now," said Pascal, interrupting himself, "I think it is about time that the little man there and the rest of us should go and see the blind procession go by.   Good-night."

As we went out Lou Materoun said: "But to-morrow you'll tell us what happened up there in Paris, won't you, Pascal?   You're not going to leave us this way, all high and dry?"

"Yes, yes, I'll tell you all about it to-morrow," answered Pascal—already a good way off.   Lou Materoun went toward the upper part of the village while we went toward the lower, each one taking the road to his home. Sheltered under my grandfather's cloak, my eyes shut up with sleepiness, I clutched his breeches and so let him lead me to the door of our house.   And while he held up his lantern and fumbled with the key I still heard, there under the cloak, the steady beat of Lou Materoun's hob-nailed shoes as he went upward through the darkness to the high end of the village street.

CHAPTER V.

THE MARCH OF THE MARSEILLES BATTALION.

While we were at supper the next evening my father said: "My olives are to be ground to-night and I must go to the oil-mill to see after them. The first pressing will be sent home about ten o'clock, and as I can't be in two places at once somebody must be here to put it in the jars."

"Very well," said my grandfather, "I will stay at home and attend to it."

"Won't we go to the shoemaker's then?" I cried all of a tremble.. "Why, it's to-night that Pascal tells of the march to Paris!"

My father frowned as he said: "I don't see why I should be kept from looking after my olives by a blind grandmother's story like this stuff of old Pascal's."

But my mother understood perfectly how I felt—how cruelly disappointed I was. I do believe that she used to feel in her own body all that I felt in mine. Never had a boy so good and kind a mother. "There now," said she. "Go to your story-telling. I will stay up and attend to the oil."

A minute later my grandfather had lighted his lantern and we were off together; and in less time than it takes to go from the sink to the wood-pile we found ourselves at the shoe-maker's. As it turned out it was well that we had hurried. The meeting already was in full session, and the neighbours had no more than made room on the bench for my grandfather when old Pascal opened his mouth and began.

I did not loiter on the road. I followed the tow-path along the Rhône, taking a short cut whenever I could find one. The stars were shining. The red moon, looking as big as the setting sun, just touched the Rock of Justice. The Rhône went rippling along with a little noise like that of the sun-wind in the white poplars. The nightingales were trilling to each other across the river. On the meadows were tiny points of light where the glow-worms were lying in the grass. Suddenly the sound of girls' voices and of young mens' laughter startled me; and I knew that hidden by the bushes close by was a threshing-floor, and that the young people of the farmhouse to which it belonged were seated on the straw-heaps and were merry-making out of doors in the sweet freshness of the night.

But nothing could stay me. On I ran, keeping my eyes steadily fixed on the evergreen-oaks of La Verdette which I could make out faintly in the distance. And as I ran I kept saying to myself: "Hurry! Hurry! The Battalion may start without you!" I felt that no joy could be so sweet as that of being once more with the men of Marseilles, of seeing again Vauclair, of feeling myself again one of the patriot Reds of the Midi on the march to Paris to drive out our traitor King.

At last I came to the edge of the wood, and as I was looking for a place to jump the ditch that ran beside the road a voice cried sharply out of the darkness: "Halt! Who goes there?"

"Friend of Liberty," I answered, giving the countersign.

"But who are you?"

"I am Pascalet. A volunteer from Avignon."

"Why, it's our kid! Vive la Nation! Tip us your five sardines, Pascalet. We thought you were done for." And the sentry shook hands so hard that I thought my five sardines, as he called them, were done for any way.

The sentry's challenge, and his shout of joy when he found that I had got back safe again, started the rest of the men from their resting places beneath the trees. The Commandant Moisson, Captain Garnier, my good Vauclair— half the command came crowding around me. As for Vauclair, he was so delighted that he picked me right off my feet and hugged me like a bear; and we couldn't speak, either of us—we were fairly crying!

"If you hadn't turned up, Pascalet," said the Commandant, "I believe I would have marched the Battalion back to look for you. I felt something here in my heart that told me it was all wrong to let that dirty German carry you off."

"Well, it's all right now," said Vauclair as he loosened his bear-hug and set me on my feet again. "We won't talk about it. Tell me, how did you find your way here? Did you see Lazuli?"

"Did I see her? I should say I did! It was she who gave me my things and started me after you. I told her everything that had happened, and she was all worked up about it."

Here the Commandant ordered the drums to beat the assembly. "Hurry, lads," he called. "We must be off. It will be daybreak soon."

Vauclair kept muttering: "I don't wonder she was worked up. It doesn't seem possible such things could be! It doesn't seem possible!" And as we fell in he asked: "And what did she say to you?"

"She said she wouldn't stay where there were such goings on. That she and little Clairet would take the Paris coach next week and pass us on the road. She says she wants to have a hand in the row up there herself."

"I'm glad she's coming," Vauclair answered. "What you tell me takes a load off my mind. I should have wearied for her up there alone. But aren't you tired, Pascalet? You haven't had a wink of sleep—and you know we are to make one stretch of it from here to Orange, at least six leagues."

"Sleepy? Tired? Not a bit of it! And what do we want to stop in Orange for?" Booby that I was, I thought that Paris was just on the other side of the mountains and that we could get there in a single march!

While we talked, the Battalion was forming in line on the road. "Forward, march!"

cried the Commandant. The drums beat the quick-step; all the men together burst out with "Allons enfants de la Patrie!"—and we were off. I stepped out with my longest stride—trying to walk with the step of a big man—and I sung away at the top of my voice. I felt as if I were borne away on wings. My voice rang out so loud that I heard nothing else. It seemed to me that my singing could be heard in Avignon, in Marseilles, away even in my own home among the mountains at Malemort; and as if the whole round earth must hear the rattle of our drums, the thunder-like rumbling of our cannon, and our tremendous cry: "Aux armes, citoyens! Aux armes!"

I had taken my place at the head of the Battalion, close behind the drums, alongside of the tall Federal who had carried the banner of The Rights of Man through the streets of Avignon. He was a good-natured, jolly fellow; a Marseillais named Samat. Every now and then he would turn to me and say: "Good for you, kid! Good for you!" To which I would answer—wanting to please him by speaking with the Marseilles accent: "Vivo la Nacien!" and then I would go on roaring "Allons enfants de la Patrie!"

Day was just dawning as we marched through the village of Sorgues. The men in their shirts, the women in their shifts with hair loose over their shoulders, crowded to the windows to see us pass. The young men and the girls applauded us; the girls even blowing kisses to us, while the men shouted: "Death to the tyrant! Vive les Marseillais!" But the stiff-necked ones, the old women, the people behind the age, crossed themselves, spit at us, and banged-to their shutters. The village was so small that we were soon through it and out in the open country again.

The sun was rising behind Mont Ventour, and the birds were flying out from the trees and bushes. Already men were at work at the threshing-floors unbinding the sheaves and spreading them out and hammering them with the hard-hitting flails. Close beside the threshers the great winnowing-sieves, hung between their three poles, swayed backwards and forwards winnowing the grain from the chaff. The yellow grain rained straight down, forming even, pointed heaps; while the floating chaff, looking like gold-dust, was carried away by the light wind and sprinkled in little gold dots over the grass. From the grain that leaped from the husks with each flail-stroke, and from the beaten straw, there blew over on the soft wind clear to the road where we were marching with our cannon behind us a delicious smell that fairly made our mouths water—it was so like the smell of good golden-crusted bread fresh out of the oven. Farther away, off in the stubble-fields, we could see men gathering the heaps of sheaves into wagons—so piled up that they looked like little thatched houses. Sticking out beyond the shelvings the big ends of the sheaves almost touched the ground; and the load, held fast by the double rope, curved out so far over the back of the shaft-horse that he looked like a horse half buried in a stack of straw.

As the sun got higher and the day got hotter the cigales began to sing; and all around us new ones were coming out of the ground and getting off their chrysalis overcoats and then— when the good sun had given them fresh life— flying off with their harsh buzzing cry into the hot air. The little creatures came and perched on our bayonets and gun-barrels; and as we roared out the "Marseillaise" to our steady drum-rattle, they scraped out their buzzing song. So to buzz of cigale and buzz of drum we marched under the blazing sun, kicking up the dust of twenty flocks of sheep and making our throats as dry as lime-kilns.

In spite of heat and dust, in spite of thirst and weariness, no one complained as we tramped steadily on: one body and one soul with one will and one aim—and that to make the traitor King, and those Parisians who were traitors with him, cry mercy.

At midday we reached Orange, where the whole town headed by the Consul came to meet us. I can tell you I was a proud boy as I entered that town! From my shoes to my eyebrows I was white with dust. My red cap was cocked over one ear. I kept my eyes glaringly wide open, so as to look fierce and dangerous. I howled the "Marseillaise" at the top of my voice as I marched in the van of the Battalion—and I was sure that no one saw or heard anybody but me!

Samat, at the head of the column, flourished his banner of The Rights of Man; and when he saw any one who looked sulky, or who did not applaud, that unpatriotic person had to kiss The Rights of Man in a hurry!

At the Hôtel de Ville the Consul welcomed us formally in a speech in French which we couldn't make anything out of. He talked and he talked and he talked, without once stopping. And at last—as it seemed as if he never would finish—Margan, a long thin pockmarked fellow, called out: "Hold up there, Monsieur le Consul. Hearing your gab gives me the pip. Vivo la Nacien—with a jug of wine!"

Every one laughed and applauded; and the Consul, quite understanding the matter, ended his speech by saying: "Friends, I see what you need is to be well filled up. You are to camp on the Place de l'Arc de Triomphe; and there you'll find all the good wine and good barley bread that you can hold. Vive la Nation!"

We found it all as the Consul had promised, and after we had gulped our claret and munched our good barley bread seasoned with a clove of garlic rubbed on it, we went to take an afternoon nap in a near-by shady field. Some lay down on their sides, some on their backs, but the greatest number lay face down so as not to be bothered by the flies. Unbuttoning my coat and unlacing my shoes, I lay down beside Vauclair, gun in hand—for I had sworn, since my capture of the day before, that never would I let that gun go again —and with my bundle for a pillow I soon floated off in dreams. I saw myself once more at the Porte de la Ligne in the midst of the festivities, again I heard the jingle of bells and the cracking of a whip, again I felt the breath of the horses on my neck. And then—oh horror!—again a hand caught my shoulder in a grip like a vice! Frightened, panting, I awoke screaming: "Vauclair! Help! Help!" And as I jumped to my feet—this is the wonderful part of it—I really saw on the highway, close by me, the Marquis of Ambrun's carriage dashing along at full gallop with its three horses harnessed *en arbalête*—two horses abreast and the third in front—and there was Surto up on the box outside.

"What's the row? What's the matter with you?" cried Vauclair, jumping to his feet beside me.

"Look! Look!" I cried. "It is the Marquis d'Ambrun and Surto! There, up the road, in that carriage!"

"Oh," said Vauclair, regretfully, "if only we had seen them coming!"

My scream had waked up most of the men. The Commandant came up, and Vauclair told him all about my kidnapping of the day before and pointed out to him the little black speck far up the road wrapped in a cloud of dust; and then added that in that carriage were the very Aristos who had tried to kill me.

"It's a good thing for them and a bad thing for us that we didn't see them sooner," said the Commandant. "We'd have settled the score for the boy, here—and three fine horses are just what we need to drag our cannon to Paris."

But there was nothing more to be done about it. A little later Captain Garnier ordered the drums to beat the assembly, and we all fell in; and then—with the people of Orange crowding around us cheering, and with all the Battalion roaring out "Tremblez, tyrans!" and the rest of it—away we went up the Paris road.

The sun was setting behind the white poplars bordering the lagoons of the Rhône as we passed through Mornas. To our wonder the town was dead deserted. The rattle of our drums, our singing of the "Marseillaise," the rumble of our cannon, shook the whole town —but the doors and windows staid fast barred and the only living things we saw were some fluttering and squawking hens.

"Here's a pretty state of things!" said Samat; who felt quite shame-faced at having unfurled his banner of The Rights of Man in a place where there was no one who could be kicked into kissing it on his knees.

"What in the name of all thunders is everybody doing in this town of nobody?" shouted

Margan, at the same time banging with his gunstock against windows and doors. But his banging did no good. We went clear through the village without seeing the face of man.

At the end of the town we came upon more squawking chickens; and Samat said, with a good deal of meaning in his tone: "Well, at any rate there are plenty of chickens in this country!" He left the ranks and went back, and so did twenty or thirty more of our men; and when they joined us again every one of them had a cock or a pullet spitted on his bayonet—where they kept on gurgling and sighing for two or three hours, as we went marching onward through the black night.

Oh how long was that night and how weary that road! The darkness grew blacker and blacker. We were too tired to talk. Even Margan, who was a born chatterbox, held his tongue. The only sounds we heard were the rattling of the forge-irons and the rumbling of the cannon on the road, and the chirping of crickets and croaking of frogs off in the darkness near us in the fields. Drowsily we plodded on.

Suddenly, far ahead of us we saw a light

that seemed to be in the road and that tossed about and went from side to side.

"What's that?" called out one of our drummers, who led the way. No one could tell, and every one made his guess as to what it was. One thought it the mail-coach, another a carriage, another a Jack-o'-lantern. But what it actually turned out to be was a man with a lantern running toward us, with open arms as if he would bar our way, while he shouted: "Mercy! Mercy! We are all good Patriots. Have pity on us. Do not hurt us. We are poor, but we will give you all we have. I can offer no more!"

"But, my good man, who are you; and what makes you think we want to hurt you?" asked Samat, sticking the man's own lantern under his nose so as to see what he looked like.

"I am the Consul of Pierrelatte. Don't hurt me, and I will turn over everything to you. Before they ran away my Pierrelatte people said to me: 'Let them eat and drink all there is to eat and drink. Let them eat and drink it all!' Now what more would you have? I implore you not to burn or pull down or ruin the property of these my poor people!"

"You great old owl, you!" cried Margan, bursting into a laugh at seeing the Consul trembling on his little cock's legs that shook like castanets. "What do you take us for— for murderers, for highway robbers? Come, come, you must tell your Pierrelatte people that we are good Patriots, and that all we want is enough wine to keep us going from here to Montélimar."

"Well, that don't seem much to ask," said the Consul. And then he went on: "Ah, my dear sir, no sooner had the carriage driven away than all my Pierrelatte people fled into the islands of the Rhône—leaving me, their Consul, all alone to try to make you hear reason."

"What carriage?" asked Vauclair.

"A carriage that passed here at nightfall. It stopped but a moment in the Place de la Commune, and the coachman without getting down from his seat called out: 'Good people, hide yourselves! The Marseilles robbers are coming! To-morrow you all will be dead and your houses all pillaged and burned!' And then he whipped up his horses and galloped off as if he had the devil at his heels."

"We know who that man was! Eh, Commandant?" said Vauclair turning to Commandant Moisson. "We'll catch up with him at Paris—with him and his Marquis too!"

Margan, who was getting impatient, broke in with: "All right, all right, citizen Consul. As you have a lantern, go ahead and show us the door of the best cellar in the village. That is all we ask."

"Come along, you good people," said the old Consul, now quite easy about us. "Follow me." And away he went, stumping along in front of the Battalion while he rambled on to us: "Oh, if only they had known this, my people would not have hidden themselves, every one of them, in the Rhône islands. They took their goats, their mules, their asses; they even carried their rabbits with them. They took away everything they possibly could take. If you could have seen them running away—the women shrieking and screaming, the children crying, the men swearing! And so away they all went to the islands.

"Had they known that a couple of barrels of wine was all you wanted! Well, well, well—all gone except me, the Consul. I said to myself: 'Either you are the Consul or you are not. If your head is cut off, it will be cut off—but you will not do your duty as a Consul unless you stay!'"

"What are you chattering about, old fellow?" said Margan. "Are we near that cellar-door yet?"

"Not two steps farther," said the Consul. "Here we are," and, so saying, he stopped in the main street of the village before a locked and barred door. "Here is the best stocked cellar in Pierrelatte," he went on, holding up his lantern so as to see the lock. "But they certainly have carried off the key."

"All right, all right," said Margan, stepping forward. "Don't work up your bile, citizen Consul, we have keys here to open all locks," and he called: "Hallo, there, oh Peloux! Bring up the forge-truck and show what good locksmiths we are. Show how long it will take us to open the doors of the King's Castle up there in Paris!"

Peloux, who was the armorer of the Battalion, came forward with his men, dragging the forge-truck. In the glint of an eye they turned the tail of the truck toward the big door; six men took hold and drew it to the other side of the street so as to have a good start: "Oh, isso! Now then, all together!" they cried—and the ready-made battering ram whacked against the door, and burst it open with a bang! Like a swarm of eager wine-flies we rushed through the opening, and in no time had the bung out of the biggest barrel and its vent started.   Out spouted the wine in a red curve, glinting in the light of the lantern like a rainbow of rubies and filling the whole place with its rich smell.   As the big jugs were filled each man clutched one, and either glued his lips to it and sucked away or held it high up and let the wine pour directly down into his thirsty throat.   Some even stooped and drank directly from the barrel.   Round went the jugs—once, twice, thrice.   Oh how we gulped and guzzled!   Each man as he had his fill went off and lay down upon the straw on the threshing-floors at the entrance of the village; and I, when the hens began to have two heads, did as the rest and went to lie down, too.   The dawn had just begun to whiten the sky so that the white moon looked like a cymbal nailed up there.   But some of the men stayed on buzzing around the cask, kissing the vent until the wine no longer spirted out in a clear rainbow but dribbled out thick and heavy off the lees.

But in spite of our night's march, and our guzzling on top of it, we made an early start. No sooner did the red sunlight touch the top of Mont Ventour, so that it was like a lovely rose on the highest branch of a rose bush, than the Commandant—who, with our officers, had stood watch while the drinking was going on —ordered the drums to beat the assembly and we fell into line.

The Commandant, with drawn sword, took his position in front of the Battalion and said to us: "I know that you are good Patriots. I know that you will do your duty unto the end, unto death. Friends, the Country is in danger. France may perish. The King has betrayed us and has made a pact with strange peoples to destroy the Nation. It is our duty to save what he seeks to destroy. With our hearts full of rage against the tyrant, and our souls full of love for the Country, we will stride on together to Paris and show what the Reds of the Midi can do!" And to this speech we all, in one formidable shout, answered: "Vivo la Nacien!"

Then the Commandant turned toward the Consul of Pierrelatte, who had stuck to him all night long, and said: "Citizen Consul, tell your Pierrelatte people that we of the Marseilles Battalion are, as they are, children of the plough and of the workshop; that we have faith in liberty and in justice, and that we go to Paris to overthrow the tyrant. And tell them, too, that we are neither murderers nor robbers, and that we pay our debts." So saying, he drew out an *assignat* from his pocket and gave it to the Consul, adding: "Here is an order on the Treasury to pay for the wine we have drunk and the damage we have done."

The poor Consul could not believe his eyes. Greatly moved, he took off his cocked-hat; and his emotion going to his thin cock's legs they more than ever shook like castanets. So we left him. The drums struck up the march, and singing the "Marseillaise" we again started on the road to Paris.

This time, leaving big Samat and chattering Margan, I stationed myself in the rear, with the cannon, and the forge, beside Sergeant Peloux—from whom I had a favour to ask. A tremendous longing to help pull the guns had taken hold of me: for I thought that if only I could be harnessed up with the others in that hard work I would not seem so young. I fancied to myself how I would look as we passed through the towns and villages—bending over and tugging at the straps, red as fire and dripping with sweat, my eyes very wide open and rolling ferociously, sparks flying from the stones beneath my hob-nailed shoes, and all the while shouting in a voice as deep and

as hoarse as I could make it: "Vivo la Nacien!" I fancied how the women and girls
and children would stare at me; and how I
would look to them just as the men of the Battalion had looked to me when they came in
to Avignon.

But at the very first word that I ventured
to say about this to Sergeant Peloux he set me
down hard. "Your turn will come in good
time, little man," said the Sergeant. "We
haven't got to Paris yet; and before we get
there you'll have your gaiter's full of toting
your bundle and your gun and that sword that
is a good deal longer than you are!"

I didn't dare to make any answer when I
got this set-back, and I felt myself turning red
with shame. Luckily for the hiding of my
confusion, a frightened hen just then fluttered
into the ranks and every one tried to spit her
on sword or bayonet. Flying and running and
squawking as if her head was being cut off,
the hen came down the line, and as she passed
me I spitted her at the first lunge.

Proud as a prince, I stepped out so as to
gain the head of the column and show off my
hen; and as I passed up the line I heard the
Federals saying: "Look there, the kid has
her!" But Vauclair turned around frowning;

and as I came up to him he said: "Whose
hen is that?"

"It's mine."

"Have you paid for it?"

"No, indeed!"

"Then you have stolen it. Go to your
place. Don't let this ever happen again."

I never had seen Vauclair so hard; and as
he spoke I felt a sudden pang in my heart—it
was the first time that I ever had given him
pain. But I felt that he was right to blame
me. I *had* stolen that hen, and perhaps from
some poor man. I wanted to unspit her and
fling her behind the hedge, but I did not dare
to. Yet I longed to get rid of her. She was a
weight on me and made me bitterly ashamed.
I had kept on walking very fast and so had
reached the head of the Battalion. In order to
make tall Samat and chattering Margan turn
around, and also in order to hide my confusion, I began to sing "Allons enfants de la
Patrie!"

"Hullo! is that you?" said Samat.
"Look, Margan, look there—what a splendid
big hen! Where did you pick her up, kid?
What geese we were not to have caught her
ourselves!"

"Do take her, if you like her," said I; and

without any more words I took down my hen
and stuck her on his bayonet.

"He's no goose, anyway, that kid; he
wants to make me carry her! No matter,
youngster, you shall have a bit of her." And
on he marched, roaring out: "Allons enfants
de la Patrie!"

When I had got rid of my hen it seemed as
if a tremendous load had fallen from my back.
Vauclair couldn't reproach me any longer, and
all things pleased me again; the road was gay,
the sun delighted me. While the men heavily
tramped along—dripping with sweat, suffocated by the white dust, and deafened by the
shrill voice of the cigales—I, light as air, went
and came the whole length of the Battalion as
the sheep dog does with his flock. I jumped
up on the banks by the road side and gathered
big blackberries with which I stuffed myself
and my pockets.

Suddenly the drums beat the quick-step.
Samat unfurled his banner, and we steadied
our lines. We were entering the town of
Montélimar. The streets and open places were
crowded with people, and more people filled
the windows and doorways. We marched on
until we came in front of the Patriot's Club,
over which the red flag was floating; and then,

after a short halt, we went to encamp outside of
the town beside a river that they told us was
the Jabron. Here we made ourselves comfortable—roasting the Mornas chickens and
eating them with good fresh bread; and then,
having loosened the knee-buckles of our
breeches and taken off our shoes, we spread
ourselves out on the grass. Even for those of
us who kept awake it was a delicious rest to
go down on one's elbows and stretch out at
full length on the soft grass in the shade of the
poplars and willows which grew beside the
stream.

I lay that way—half awake, half dreaming,
turning over in my mind for a while the cruel
and bitter life I had passed at La Garde; and
then forgetting it all as I sleepily watched a
white cloud up in the sky that got bigger and
bigger and then slowly got little again, and at
last went quite away. Then I let my head fall
between my hands and watched with great in-
terest an ant who was carrying through the grass
a crumb of bread bigger than himself. The little
creature would get caught in a thick tangle of
grass-blades, or would slip down from a tall
stem; but off he would start again, sometimes
pushing and sometimes pulling at his load. In
pity for him, I now and then would take a

twig and help him on his way; putting the twig under him very gently, so as not to hurt him, and so lifting him over a hard pass that would have cost him an hour of climbing to get over alone. And so the afternoon wore away.

At sunset the brave Patriots of Montélimar brought each of us to eat with our bread a plaited rope of garlic, for that is the food to give strength and courage to warriors; and then the drums beat, and once more we started on the road to Paris.

We marched all night; a warm clear summer night with now and then a flash of heat lightning low down in the sky. As dawn came on we were wrapped in a cool mist that rose from the Rhône and spread out over the osiers and the fields and the flowering hedges by the road side; but the sun soon rose and drank it up. It seemed strange to us to find men reaping. In Avignon half the grain already was in the granaries; at Pierrelatte they were putting it into sheaves; and here they were only harvesting! But we were coming to the frontiers of the North. Now that we had passed Montélimar there were no more olive-trees; and the *marinade*, the soft sea-wind off the Mediterranean, was far away. Here, where the olive could

not flourish, were no more cigales—the ground
was too cold to bring them forth. When I saw
cherry-trees which were only just losing their
blossoms I could not help saying: "How far
off we are!"

Margan laughed when he heard me, and
broke out in his chattering way: "Yes, we've
come a good way, but we're not nearly there
yet. Go ahead all, and the devil take the
hindermost! Go ahead! It's not in fifteen
days, nor yet in twenty days, that we'll be
beating the moths out of the King's council-
lors. And, I say, boys, won't that make a gay
stir-about? To-morrow we'll be in Valence.
But we won't stop there. Didn't the Commandant say that the country's in danger? We
won't stop till we haven't any breath left!
And now, once more: 'Aux armes, citoyens!'" And as we crossed the bridge of the
Drôme, all singing at the tops of our voices,
we fairly made the buttresses shake!

With bunches of box and laurel stuck in
our guns and in our hats, covered with a thick
coat of dust, and all singing "Tremblez, tyrans
et vous perfides!" we crossed the city of
Valence at midday in the full blaze of the sun.
The whole population was out to look at us.
Men, women and children, all pale and un-

easy, gazed at us as we passed—not knowing whether to be frightened or to be comforted; wondering who we were and whence we came and where we were going. As we marched on I heard an old woman say: "It is Jourdain's army of cut-throats!"—and she crossed herself. as if a thunder-clap had just burst forth.

But the Commandant called out: "No stopping! The country is in danger!" And on we went, the drums beating the quick-step, and Valence soon was left behind. We sang the "Marseillaise"; and drum-beat and song echoed back to us from the limestone rocks on the other bank of the Rhône; so that it seemed as if off there, too, another army of the Reds of the Midi were marching to the assault of Paris.

Rub your crusts of bread with garlic, good Federals, good Patriots! March bravely on and on! Up there in Paris must come the hardest task of all. March on and on with bleeding feet. The way is dull and hard, the road is long—but at the end stands Liberty!

We crossed the bridge of the Isère, made our camp about sundown in the forest of Carnage; and started again toward morning so as to reach by evening the city of Vienne. As we marched along the peasants dropped their work and ran across the fields to stare at us. We frightened and astonished them; and when we joked them—calling out: "Oh, hé, ox-herd, is it fine to-day?" or "Look out, reaper, your whet-stone case is leaking!"—they answered in a patois which was neither one thing nor the other and like people who did not understand. It was easy to see they were Northern lumpkins. Why, they had a twist in their talk that the very devil must have puffed into their faces; and already they spoke like the Paris folks, with a twang in the nose.

The day went on, and toward sunset we were come close to Vienne. The city stood before us, high up on the banks of the Rhône; and above the city rose still higher the cathedral of Saint Maurice—towering above walls that seemed as big and high as those of the Roman theatre at Orange.

At the sight of this great city I was seized again by my longing to be harnessed to our cannon, and so to enter it looking like a man. I fell out from the ranks under pretence of fastening my shoes and let the Battalion pass until the rear-guard came up to me with the cannon and forge.

"See here, partner," said I to a Federal whose feet were cut and bleeding but who

was tugging away at his harness strap, puff-
ing and blowing like an angry lizard. "It
seems to me that that cannon isn't walking
alone!"

"Not a bit of it, youngster. If you'd like
to try a pull, we'll see what meat you are
made of."

"It is just what I want to do," I answered;
and without more words I laid my gun and
sword and bundle on the truck, the Federal
slipped out of his strap and slipped me into it
without stopping the march—and there I was,
pulling with might and main.

Sergeant Peloux, when he saw the first tug
I gave at the collar, called out: "Go slow, kid,
you'll be blown in no time at that rate—to say
nothing of smashing the harness."

This snubbing, though it was only in fun,
quieted me for a minute or two; but then off I
went again, tugging harder than ever. As we
started up the slope to the city all the bells
were ringing and cannon were thundering out
from the walls; and as we got higher the
townsfolk came out to meet us in swarms. It
was the Fourteenth of July, the festival of the
Federation. We had barely room to pass, the
streets were so crowded; and the people had
to look out for their toes as our wheels rumbled

and bumped over the stones. In order to be the more looked at, I bent over almost on all fours, like a beast. When I passed a group of girls I raised my head a little and, red as a flaming devil and with flashing eyes, I made my voice deep and shouted: "Vivo la Nacien!" And how enchanted I was when now and then some girl pointed me out and said: "Just look at that young fellow. Goodness, how he frightens me!" But what I did not like to hear was when they said: "Oh, poor little one! He is hardly more than a child—he hasn't a hair on his chin!" Then I would drag harder than ever at my harness, and shout louder than ever: "Vivo la Nacien!" I even thundered out big words and big oaths one on top of the other. I was very young, then!

The Patriots of Vienne entertained us well that evening; and the next morning, before leaving the city, the Battalion went to present arms before the altar of the Federation that had been raised in the open space in front of the church. Here we all bent the knee and sang the verse: "Amour sacré de la Patrie!" Hardly had we ended it when a group of school children, led by their teacher, a young Abbé, presented themselves before the altar and, kneeling as we had done, sang to the air

of the " Marseillaise " a verse that we never before had heard, beginning:

In the path our elders showed us
We will follow when they're gone.

This beautiful verse set our patriotic fires to
blazing and upset us completely. Tears were
in all eyes, and each one of us took up a child
in his arms and kissed it over and over again.
Older people embraced each other, and every
one shouted "Vive les Fédérés! Vive la Nation! Down with the tyrant King!"

Commandant Moisson hugged the little
Abbé, who had made all out of his own head
the new verse, and said: "Thanks, Patriot,
thanks! We will sing your children's verse
on the ruins of the King's Castle." And the
little Abbé, his eyes wet with tears, answered:
"Your patriotic song went right to my heart,
and sent a thrill into the very marrow of my
bones. Never before have I heard the voice of
God ring out so clear: may His blessing go
with you and His arm give you strength!"
Then the drums rattled and off we marched
to " Allons enfants de la Patrie!"

All Vienne followed us, shouting. I had
harnessed myself again to the truck. A little
monkey six or seven years old took upon him

13

to carry my gun, another one carried my sword, and a third my bundle. A swarm of children buzzed around and followed us like so many flies. From time to time the smallest had to run in order to keep up with us. I felt that no one could understand as I did the delight of these little fellows. It made me as proud as a pig on stilts to see how they admired me and how set up they were by carrying my gun or my sword, or even by my letting them finger the fine gilt buttons on my coat.

But as we went on farther and farther, and the town came to be a long way behind us, we had to tell the children that it was time for them to go home. Handing back the arms and the other things we had allowed them to carry, the good little fellows obeyed us and stopped short: and there they stood watching us, longingly, until we were hidden from them by a turn in the road. Just as they lost sight of us they all together began to sing in their high pitched clear voices the verse which the little Abbé had added to the "Marseillaise":

> In the path our elders showed us
> We will follow when they're gone.

Without any order being given, the whole Battalion halted; and we stood silent and deeply moved listening to that thrilling song. It seemed to go deep down into our hearts, and we were comforted and strengthened by it. Turning about and facing us, Commandant Moisson said: "Listen, friends, listen well—for this is the last time that you will hear the sound of Patriot voices; the voices of the Reds of the Midi. Our feet are now on Northern soil. Henceforward we shall be among the Anti-Patriots—the men who have tried to stop the Revolution by opening to strangers and enemies the frontiers of France. Let us show the Aristocrats who we are and what we want. Let them know that nothing can turn us back; that for us it is Death or Liberty!" Then the drums beat and again we went on.

We marched almost steadily for three days and nights—drinking the water of brooks and ditches, eating only bread and garlic, and taking only snatches of sleep as the chance came. Up there in the land of fogs we could not count on the soft straw of the threshing-floors for our rest by night, nor on the cool dry grass of shady fields for our rest by day. Not a bit of it! The wheat was just getting into ear in that country of nothing—which God certainly had gone through by night—and the fields were soaking with dew or mist until three or four in the afternoon: it took the sun so long to drink up the moisture.

Well, as I said, we marched for three days and three nights, and so came to the bridge of Saint-Jean d'Ardières—farther north than Lyons (which city we had passed at early dawn without stopping); farther north, even, than Villefranche. There, on the shady banks of the Ardières, we halted for some hours during the hottest part of the day. In the twinkling of an eye the Battalion was at rest beside the river. Some stretched themselves out in the shade of the willows; one dabbled in the clear water, another ate a bit of bread, another mended a tear in his clothes, and another put a stitch in his shoe. But I remained on the bridge with the cannon; for Vauclair had told me that the Paris coach might pass us there, and not for an empire would I have gone to sleep and so missed the chance of seeing Lazuli and little Clairet.

In order to amuse myself while the others slept, I seated myself on the parapet of the bridge and spread open my bundle that Lazuli had so well put up for me and had so carefully knotted and arranged. I examined my two pistols—taking out and sharpening the flints and rubbing off here and there a spot of rust—and it seemed

to me that in possessing them I possessed all
that a man could desire to own on this earth.
Then I uncorked my gourd full of brandy and
sniffed at it, and without tasting it enjoyed the
good smell.   I felt the three silver crowns that
Monsieur Randoulet, good Monsieur Randoulet,
had given me.   I tried on my sash, my fine
red *taiolo;* I looked at my black shining powder and counted my store of pistol balls; and
then, before packing all up again, I turned to
my pistols once more.   Oh, my pistols!   I
could not bear to let them out of my hands.   I
could not tire of looking at them.   And to
think that they were my own!

While I was going on with all this child's
play a noise made me jump—the sound of bells.
I thought that it must be the coach; and I
turned around and stared off into the distance
as far as I could see the road.   There was
nothing in sight—not the smallest black spot,
not a puff of dust—and yet nearer and clearer
came the sound of jingling bells.   And then,
while I listened with pricked up ears and stared
down the empty highway, there came out from
a sunken road behind a flowering hedge close
by me a little flock of ten or twelve sheep, followed by an old shepherd who, in spite of the
heat, was closely muffled in his big shepherd's

cloak. As soon as the old man saw me he bent down his head, pulled his hat over his eyes, and turned as if to retrace his steps. But it was too late. The sheep already had jumped up on the road and he had to follow them. He seemed to be less fearful when he found that I was all alone, for he came toward me and asked me the way to the ferry across the Rhône.

"I'm the wrong one to come to with that question, good man," said I, "for I don't belong in these parts."

"Who are you, then, and where are you going," he asked kindly. "You look very young to be wearing the uniform of the National Guard."

"I am a Federal Patriot, and I am going to Paris with the Marseilles Battalion to make the King hear reason and to bring him to terms."

"What do you mean by that? Bring to terms our King, our good King, the father of us all! What are you thinking about, my child?. But where is this Marseilles Battalion?"

"There is our artillery," I answered, pointing to the cannon. "Our men are down there by the river, resting in the shade."

"Oh Saints of God have mercy!" exclaimed the old shepherd, raising his eyes on high and putting his hands together in the way a priest does when he says mass. "Is it possible, my child, that you have been misled to believe that the King must be 'made to hear reason' as you call it so glibly? Listen well to me, for you are in an evil way: you are going straight into the jaws of hell. I also am a good patriot; and I tell you that you will better serve your country if you will stay here as a shepherd, as I am doing, than if you go up with your Battalion into the North. Come now, I will make you a good offer. You shall help me to take care of my flock, and I will pay you well and you will have little work to do. And when we have led the flock up into the high pastures in the Alps I will give you a third of it for your own. You will be a little capitalist."

"Desert the Battalion!" I cried. "Never! You might give me all the sheep in all the mountains and on all the plains, and you might stuff my pockets full of gold crowns—but I never would stir from the Battalion so much as a single step! Vive la Nation! Liberty or Death!"

"Poor child, poor child, your head is turned! So young, and talking of death. Unhappy boy! Don't you know that our Lord Jesus Christ when he died on the cross forgave those who put him to death? Are there no curés in your country, have you never heard good Christian words?"

"Yes indeed, there is a good curé in our village; he is as good as he can be, and his name is Monsieur Randoulet. He saved my life; he drew me out of the claws of the Marquis and his game-keeper who wanted to kill me."

"Well then, my child, in the name of that holy man who saved your life, listen to me. Promise me that until your last gasp you always will carry about you this medal on which is the image of Notre-Dame-de-Bon-Secours. She will keep you from wrong do-ing."

As he spoke, the old shepherd pulled a plug out of the top of his staff; and from the hollow place inside, as he turned the staff up-side down, there fell out shining medals and louis-d'ors. He took a medal, pressed it to his lips, and gave it to me. Then he took one of the gold pieces and also gave it to me, saying: "The medal is a coin that will save your soul from sin, and the louis-d'or is a coin that will keep your body from poverty and harm. If ever you chance to fall into the hands of those whom you believe are such wicked people, those whom you call Anti-Patriots, show them your medal and it will save your life. But speak not to any one of what you have just seen and heard. Now I must leave you. I am in haste. May God take you in his holy keeping."

As he talked to me the old shepherd gently stroked my cheeks as Monsieur Randoulet was used to do when he met me on the road to the Château de la Garde, and I felt him making with his thumb the sign of the cross on my forehead. Then, followed by his sheep, he went quickly down the other side of the road; and as he passed away from me I still heard him repeating: "Poor child! Poor child!"

I was so surprised that I just stared after him and never said thank you. I watched him until he was hidden from me by a dip in the land, and then I came back to my bundle, all open and spread out on the bridge. Somehow this encounter had upset me and changed my thoughts. Neither pistols nor red scarf amused me any more. I began to put together my bundle again; and while doing this I heard the sound of horses galloping beyond the very flowering hedge from behind which the shepherd had come forth with his flock.

I turned around quickly; and to my amazement I saw four mounted gendarmes, cockade in hat, with drawn swords and pistols stuck in their belts, riding straight toward me at full gallop as if they meant to cut me down. But they drew up short on the bridge, and their leader asked me sharply: "Citizen Patriot, have you seen pass here a shepherd with a dull brown cloak around him driving a little flock of sheep?"

My blood ran cold at this question, for it showed me that trouble was in store for the poor old man. Instantly, without stopping to think about it, I answered: "No!"

"That's a pity," said the roughest looking of the lot. "We should have stuck to his tracks. Then the country would be safer, for we would have delivered the Revolution from its worst enemy."

What the fellow said startled me. Could it be possible that the old shepherd was an enemy to the good cause? I was sorry I had said no so quickly, and I corrected myself by adding: "I did not see him, but if I do not mistake I heard the sheep-bells down there along the river path."

" That must be he," said the leader of the gendarmes; and in a moment they had turned their horses and had gone galloping along the path the old shepherd had followed when he left me.

At first I scarcely realized what had passed, and then I began to be frightened.   Ought I to hold my tongue about it all, or ought I to tell Vauclair, I wondered; while the blood mounted up into my cheeks and my heart beat fast.   I hoped that the old man had taken a cross-road and would not be caught, for I felt that I had set his pursuers on his track.   And then, as I did not know what I ought to do, I went back to my bundle and began to put it together again.   The sun was going down and I knew that it soon would be time for the Battalion to start.   Some of our men came up on the bridge —while I still was fussing over my bundle and staring along the path that the old shepherd had taken—and presently I thought that I could hear, above their talking, the sound of more distant voices and the jingling of bells.

I was right.   A minute or so later I saw red plumes showing through the willows, and then out came the four gendarmes cruelly dragging after them the poor old shepherd tied fast to a horse's tail as if he had been a robber.

He was in danger of being crushed by the feet of the prancing and kicking horses, who knocked him about and covered him with their sweat and foam. As the gendarmes rode up to us on the bridge they raised their swords and shouted "Vive la Nation!" and our men, of course, crowded around them asking questions.

"What has he done?" demanded Captain Garnier.

"It seems to me," said Samat, "that you are pretty hard on him. No doubt he is an Anti-Patriot; but let him go now and I will give him The Rights of Man to munch on "— and he began to unfurl his banner.

"He is a traitor, a miserable wretch that death is too good for. Vive la Nation!" answered the leader of the gendarmes.

At this answer each man had his own thread to spin. "Let him be tried at once and give him Marseilles plums to taste!" cried one. "No, powder's too good to waste on traitors. A rope necklace is good enough for him!" cried another. "Into the river with him!" cried a third. Every one had his say; and in the midst of it all the poor old man's heart died out of him and, pale as death, he dropped down on the road.

It was pitiful to see him drop that way.

With the help of two or three Federals who were as sorry for him as I was, I lifted him up and seated him on the parapet of the bridge beside my still open bundle; and while the gendarmes were talking together, settling how they would carry him on one of their horses if he couldn't or wouldn't walk, I quickly uncorked my brandy-flask and put it to his lips. The strength of the liquor brought back some life into him and he opened his eyes. Taking my hand in his, he whispered so that no one but I heard him: "Thank you, my child. May God repay you."

Seeing him so sickly, so weak, so old, our men changed their key and fell to pitying him, muttering that unless he were a very great traitor he might as well be let go. I was longing to get rid of the weight on my heart that came from having given him into the hands of his enemies, and these mutterings gave me courage to step up to the gendarmes who were preparing to hoist him on one of the horses and to say: "This man is half dead, he can not do any harm. What difference can it make to us whether he is a Patriot or an Anti-Patriot? Let him go and take care of his flock —which is most likely all he owns on earth, he and his poor wife and children."

"Our little man is quite right," called out several of our men together.

"He's right, is he? I'll show you if he's right!" answered one of the gendarmes angrily; and, tumbling off his horse, he flung himself like a wolf on the old shepherd and dragged from his shoulders his big cloak. And there— Saints of God! there was our old man in a handsome violet robe with a band of fine lace and a golden cross that shone on his breast! "Here's the poor man you were sorry for!" cried the gendarme. "He is neither more nor less than the Bishop of Mende, the ci-devant Monseigneur de Castillane; and, just as you see him here, he is the commander of twenty thousand Royalists who are holding the camp of Jalès. And do you want to know where he was going? He was going, the traitor, to join the émigrés and foreigners who are plotting together to ruin the Revolution. I'll prove it to you—look here!" As he spoke, he snatched the shepherd's staff from him and pulled out the plug and turned it upside down. Out poured medals and louis-d'ors; and then, as he shook it, out came a roll of parchment. The gendarme spread open the roll before us; and Commandant Moisson, reading it, cried out: "You are right.

This man is a traitor. Here is the Royalist plot!"

Our men needed no more. "To the river with him!" "Kill him!" "Death to the traitor!" they shouted; and there was a rush toward him and hands were raised and swords were drawn. But the gendarmes guarded him while they tied him fast to the tail of a horse again; and the leader said grimly: "No, friends, this piece of work we will attend to ourselves!" And so they rode away.

In a couple of minutes we lost sight of them, and then our drums beat and we started again on our march.

As we went onward our men sang and joked and talked about the lucky capture of the Bishop. But I kept silence. The louis-d'or and the medal burnt my pocket. I could not bear to think about them. Traitor or not, I felt very sorry for the old man. My heart almost failed me when, as we came out on the other side of the bridge, I saw his deserted sheep wandering about aimlessly. The poor beasts would crop a while, and then suddenly would stop eating; and with their mouths full of grass they would look around in every direction, bleating piteously for their lost shepherd. After we had marched a good way we still could hear them forlornly bleating.

Our long tramp began to tell on us, and as we marched the men became more and more silent. The kits and accoutrements, so easy to carry at first, grew to be an intolerable burden on our backs. Many of the men fell footsore and some of the lamest took off their shoes, finding it more comfortable to jog along barefoot in the soft dust of the road. I was harnessed again to my cannon, and I tugged away patiently.

We had reached an evil land, a place of Aristocrats. The country through which we were passing was dreary and dismal, and was overhung by a dreary dull sky made still more dull by the long flocks of crows flying across it. In every direction, as far as we could see, great fields of beans and beets and vetches stretched on and on with never a tree in them. The houses and huts were roofed with slates of a dismal black, and the stern and silent people living there were like the land. Everybody we met on the road or in the villages gave us sidewise suspicious glances, such as a dog gives when he is carrying off a bone. The people all looked alike—with their big, pale, pasty-white, close-shaven, dirty, hang-dog, stupid animal faces all jowl. They never gave us a smile, much less a bottle of wine; they gave us nothing, indeed, but the cold shoulder, and so slouched away. When at a safe distance, they turned and shook their fists at us. Even the sun hid himself behind a dull thick mist, like a dead man under a shroud; and yet his heat was overpoweringly oppressive.

On we tramped dully and doggedly, hungry, weary and footsore. We had no heart for laugh or song. Commandant Moisson and Captain Garnier began to be uneasy, fearing that we would lose heart. They mingled in the ranks, doing all they could to cheer us. They told us of the wretched condition of the people of France and how the wretchedness would be relieved as soon as we reached Paris and seized the King's Castle. Only nine days more of marching, they said, and the country would be saved, the Revolution triumphant. Then all men would be free and all hunger satisfied. The harvests of the land would belong to those who had sown the seed thereof; the fruits of the land would be gathered by those who had grafted the trees and delved about their roots; to the shepherd would belong the sheep.

As for me, I needed no cheering words.

Stones were bread for me, I could have eaten thistles and thorns, I could have walked on broken glass, nothing could have discouraged me.   I pulled away like a galley-slave in my harness—only wishing that I could drag both the cannon and the forge all by myself.   It hurt me to hear the older men, who had left wife and child in Marseilles or Aubagne or Arles, muttering among themselves, as if afraid of being overheard: "Who knows how all this is going to end?"   "We didn't know Paris was so far away!"   "The National Guard is all for the King and may go against us." "It seems we are to be forced to camp outside of Paris."   "Then all our long tramp will have been for nothing!"   And so they grumbled on.   It just broke my heart to hear them talk in this way.   To cheer myself and to get some go into me, I would burst out into the " Marseillaise "—and that for a moment would hearten up the whole Battalion.

But the endless road was always the same long weary way, lengthened out like a breadless day.   The villages and hamlets were always as dismal as their dull distrustful stupid inhabitants, not one of whom would have freely given us so much as a drop of water. Had their eyes been knives, they would have stabbed us through and through.   How could we, then, be light of heart?   God's fire was fast dying out of our cold breasts and we needed some great stirring to kindle it anew.

Macon, Tournus and Chalons were left behind.   We had just marched through Autun—a hateful Aristocratical hole—without any one giving us a good word.   It was about five o'clock and the sun was low.   I was pulling away in my harness and Vauclair was walking beside me.   He seemed thoughtful and sad as he said to me: "I don't see why the Avignon coach has not caught up with us. Can anything have happened to it? I feel anxious.   I long so to see Lazuli and my dear little Clairet.   Lazuli certainly told you that she would take the very first coach that left Avignon?"

"Yes, certainly; and she said she would pass us on the way."

"The coach pays tribute to the robbers of the Bos de la Damo, and so is safe from them," Vauclair went on.   "But there are the King's carabineers, who are not less, perhaps are even more, to be dreaded than the robbers. But at the very latest, if nothing has happened, the coach ought certainly to catch up with us by to-morrow at Saulieu, where we shall camp to-night. Saulieu is a town full of good Patriots——"

Vauclair did not finish what he was saying. All of a sudden we heard the shrieks of women and children coming, as it seemed, from a hut about a sling-shot away from the road—a poor little place, so low that its thatched roof looked to be almost a part of the ground.

"Help! Help!" came the cry in a woman's voice. In a moment a dozen of our men had jumped the ditch and were running across the beet-fields to find out what was the matter. As they entered the hut the cries and screams ceased; and presently they came back to us, bringing prisoner a red-faced Capuchin monk, so fat that he seemed as if he would burst his tight skin, and three bailiffs as thin as rails and yellow as saffron. After them followed a peasant and his wife, and then came a troop of ragged dirty faced children that looked just as I used to look up there in the hut of La Garde.

"What's all this row?" asked Commandant Moisson, looking sternly at the Capuchin and the three bailiffs shivering and cringing in the clutches of our men.

"The matter is," said Margan, who was always ready to put in his word, "that this Capuchin father, who already is bursting out of his skin from over-eating, brought the three bailiffs with him to carry off this poor peasant and give him the strappado because he hasn't paid his tithe of chickens."

"What! Tithes now-a-days!" cried long Samat. "Why, all that sort of thing has been abolished by The Rights of Man!" And then turning toward the Capuchin, he added: "And so we are no longer in France—you dirty bundle of lard!"

"But that isn't all," Margan went on. "The old glutton had got loose the peasant's cow and was for taking her away too—so that he should be paid for his trouble, he said."

Our men were all on fire in a moment over this outrage, and some of them began to cast loose the straps from the cannon in order to make the Capuchin and the bailiffs for once in their lives taste leather. But the Commandant raised his hand for silence and said: "It *is* strange that a thing of this sort should go on in France´ now-a-days. We must make an example of those four Anti-Patriots. They shall be stripped as bare as worms, and without a thread on them they shall haul the forge to Paris! Margan, you be driver; and if they need food to make them go, do you feed them well with dry blows!"

When the Capuchin heard this he clasped his hands and then crossed himself. Margan dragged off his habit, while some of the other Federals took the rags off the three bailiffs. Then the monk, with a bailiff on each side of him, was clapped into the harness; the third bailiff was hitched in front of them for a leader; the drums struck up the quick-step, and off we marched to

> Que veut cette horde d'esclaves,
> De traîtres, de rois conjurés ?

As for the peasant and his wife, they stood staring after us not knowing whether to laugh or to cry.

Twilight was falling as, hungry and weary and footstore, we neared the longed-for little town of Saulieu. Since we had left Vienne, six days before, we had not seen a single woman with a smiling face; nor had we heard a friendly word nor received a friendly glance. We had slept as we could—on the bare ground, on the short grass growing on the sloping road side, even in dry ditches. Our only drink had been water, sometimes from wells and brooks, sometimes from ditches; and our food had been bread and garlic. Many of us had gone bare-foot—either to ease our blistered feet or to save our precious shoes. And all of us were worn with marching. For five and twenty days, marching steadily, the Battalion had been on the road.

But at last we were to be welcomed and made much of in a friendly Patriotic town. Yet even this pleasant promise had in it for me a touch of bitterness. As I looked around me and saw all our men with their bushy dusty beards, while my round boyish face was as smooth as an egg—though I was as dusty and sunburnt as any one—I was in despair. The people in Saulieu certainly would think that I was only a little boy. To have had a nice thick dusty uncombed black beard I would gladly have been as long and thin and pock-marked as old Margan. Suddenly I had an idea. I had gathered a capful of ripe black-berries while they were harnessing up the monk and the bailiffs, and the thought came to me that I might stain my face to look like a beard. I put my fine plan straight into prac-tice. Taking the blackest and ripest berries, I crushed them under my nose, on my chin, on both cheeks, and smeared my face till I made an absurd fright of myself. Even Vauclair, who was the first to catch sight of me, did not recognise me at once; and soon all the men were laughing at my childish foolishness.

All the people of Saulieu turned out to meet us with torches and drums and trumpets, hailing us with shouts of "Vive la Nation!" "Down with the tyrant!" "Vive les Marseillais!"—while up in the church towers the bells were ringing the tocsin of the Revolution. The men of the Patriots' Club had lighted a big bonfire which was blazing away in front of the church of Saint-Saturnin, and we almost had to come to fisticuffs to keep them from feeding the fire with the fat monk and the bailiffs.

The Saulieu people were good Patriots. From father to son they had handed down the memory of the old times when their Pastourells were persecuted and tormented as our Albigenses had been. The men of Saulieu never forgot all that had been forced down their throats in the name of the King and for the sake of religion. Bitter bread had they eaten in the days of their Pastourells, and they knew that the hour of vengeance at last had struck for the downtrodden and the persecuted!

How good they were to us in Saulieu! They gave us all the wine we could swallow and all the good things we could eat. We had enough beef *à la daube* to go over our ears! The only drawback was that these good people talked in a sort of half French and half patois that the devil himself must have given them.

And what a joy it was to see them fall on their knees when we burst forth into "Aux armes, citoyens!" The roar of the voices mingled with the crackling of the flames of the big bonfire. The bright light flashed in our faces and sent great shadows flying up the church front as the men feeding the fire stooped and rose, or as caps and hats were waved in the air or brandished on pikes and guns. The huge blaze which made the sky seem darker and deeper and blacker looked like the mouth of hell belching forth whirlwinds of smoke and flame, while flying sparks circled round and round.

In the midst of the rejoicing Vauclair seized my hand and said as he drew me out of the crowd: "Come with me to the post-house. The coach may have arrived already. Lazuli and Clairet may be there now."

Off we went, finding our way as well as we could through the dark and narrow streets of Saulieu. It is but a little town, and we soon reached the Paris highway; and far off in the black night we saw a lantern dangling over the door of what we knew must be the post-house. Presently, when we had reached the lantern-lit doorway, we crossed the big yards and went by the great sheds where the carters were coming and going, lantern in hand, load-·ing or unloading their wagons or setting them in order for the march of the next day. We passed in front of the dark warm quiet stables, hearing the sound of the horses and mules munching their sweet-smelling hay or crunch-ing away at their comforting oats.

"See, look there!" cried Vauclair, much excited and quickening his pace. "There is the Avignon coach—certainly that is it! I should know it anywhere by its high leathern cover and green and yellow body and red cur-tains—let alone by the sound of that little dog's bark, the *loubet* up there on top."

We hurried on into the inn kitchen, all lighted up by a blaze of furze before which turkeys and legs of mutton were turning around on the spit. The servants were going and coming with plates and bottles and jugs. No one took any notice of us, and we went on into the big room where all the travellers were at table. And then, before we had seen her,

Lazuli flung herself on Vauclair's neck, hugging and kissing him and crying: "My own man! My Vauclair!"—and presently adding: "At last we've got here. There is little Clairet asleep on the bench in the corner. Wake him up yourself—for three days he has been calling for his father!"

Vauclair was so upset that he couldn't say a word. He followed Lazuli as she made her way among the crowded tables; and I followed too—unable to understand why Lazuli had not even spoken to me, let alone given me a kiss.

Little Clairet was fast asleep, wrapped up in his mother's fringed shawl. Lazuli picked him up, stood him on his feet, and as she shook him gently said to him: "Clairet, Clairet my darling, wake up—here is your father!" But the little fellow was so dead with sleep he could not open his eyes nor hold up his head. Vauclair took him in his arms, and as he kissed him, rubbing his cheeks with his rough beard, the child began to waken. The bright light bothered him, and at first he put his elbow up over his eyes; but his father's voice at last roused him completely and as he recognised him he hugged him round the neck.

All this time I was waiting for my turn to come; and Vauclair, seeing me, said to the little fellow: "Haven't you a kiss for Pascalet, who gave you his grapes? Come, give him a good hug." But as Clairet caught sight of me he threw himself back as if I had been the devil with all his horns!

At this Lazuli gave a little jump, and as she clapped her hands and burst out laughing, she exclaimed: "Heavens and earth! Is that Pascalet? What has he been doing to himself? What's that black all over his cheeks? Oh, what a scarecrow of a black snout!"

And then I remembered that I still was all stained with the blackberries, and feeling as flat as a quoit I ran to the kitchen to clean myself. I plunged my face into a bucket of water and rubbed hard enough to take the skin off, and then ran back. This time Clairet knew me and kissed me, and Lazuli kissed me too.

The Avignon coachman, having fed his horses, had come to the next table and gave us a friendly look as he began to eat on both sides of his mouth at once. Lazuli soaked a biscuit in wine, and while she fed Clairet with it told all that had happened in Avignon after we left and during her journey.

"You will never guess," said she, "who is in the coach with us, going to Paris! She's a nasty neighbour, I can tell you, and I haven't opened my mouth to her the whole way."

"Who is it?" asked Vauclair.

"Of all people in the world, it's La Jacarasse! She has brought along her bag and her big knife; and on top of the foulness that comes of her pig-cleaning she has a breath that fairly reeks of wine. But her nastiness is no great matter. What touches my heart is the young girl she has with her, I'm sure against her will—a child not more than fifteen who is as pretty and sweet and charming as she can be. I can see the poor little soul tremble and shiver with fear whenever La Jacarasse looks at her or makes any sign to her. Poor lamb, what will that woman do with her! There is something all wrong about it."

" There certainly *is* something wrong about it," said the coachman, turning toward us and lowering his voice. "Things are happening now-a-days that make one shudder. Did you hear that a few days ago in Avignon some fishermen from the Porte de la Ligne found in the Rhône, caught against the first pier of the bridge of Saint-Bénézet, the body of the young Marquis de Roberty, bound and disembowelled? Well, folks say that La Jacarasse and two or three other wretches cut him open and threw him into the river. And I happen to know that this very Marquis de Roberty was betrothed to the very young lady who is with La Jacarasse now. Her name has clean gone out of my head, though I knew it when we left Avignon. Now don't a two and two like that make four? I am sure that the old she devil has another crime in hand, and that she will work it against this innocent child. It is easy to see that the poor girl is half dead with fear of what may be going to happen to her."

But here the coachman suddenly remembered that time was passing and stopped short in his talk.

"We must be off in less than half an hour," he said, and fell to finishing his supper—taking a bit of bread and sopping up every drop of gravy on his plate and polishing it till it looked as clean as if it had just come out of the dish-tub. Then he got up clumsily, balancing his heavy shoulders as is the way with carters, and went lumbering off to make ready for the starting of the coach.

"Less than half an hour more," said Vau-clair. "Now listen, Lazuli, and don't forget what I tell you: As soon as you get to Paris go to my old master Planchot, the joiner.   He lives at the end of the Impasse Guémenée, opening from the Rue Saint-Antoine, a little way off the Place de la Bastille.   It is on the Place de la Bastille that you leave the coach. When you get to the house you must say to Master Planchot: 'I am the wife of Vauclair, who worked a year of his time with you. He is coming up with the Marseilles Battalion to help settle the affairs of the Revolution, and he sent me on before to hire the lodging that he used to have here in your house.'   You will see how pleased the master will be, and how gladly he will rent you my old lodging—with its little kitchen and all.   There you will be safe and quiet; and if any bad luck comes to me or to Pascalet, we will be much better off there than on a bed in a barracks or in a hospital.   But the first thing of all is that you don't forget the name of the street where Planchot lives—Impasse Guémenée.   Say it over after me, Impasse Guémenée."

"Guémenée, Impasse Guémenée.   All right, I won't forget it," Lazuli answered; and laughed as she added: "How one has to bring one's lips to a point to talk like those Paris donkeys!"

"And now another thing," said Vauclair.

"Did you get some silver money before leaving Avignon?"

"Don't worry—I sold my little trinkets and my carved ivory crucifix to Nathan the Jew, and that made me all right." As she spoke, Lazuli took Vauclair's hand and put it under her shawl, at the same time adding in a low voice: "There, feel how I have sewed my yellow and white money in the lining of my waist. The coachman swore to us that he had paid toll to all the bands that haunt the road to Paris—still, one never knows what may happen and it's well to be on the safe side."

"You're a treasure of a woman!" cried Vauclair, as he bent forward and kissed her. Almost in the same moment he turned round suddenly saying: "What's that I hear? There are our drums beating the recall; and the alarm-bells ringing, too. Something has happened. Quick, Pascalet, take your gun. Good-bye, Lazuli—a safe trip to you. Clairet, my dear little Clairet, good-bye." Vauclair took up the child in his arms and kissed him, while his eyes filled with tears. And I, clumsily loaded down with my sword and gun and bundle, also kissed Clairet and Lazuli and said good-bye.

By this time the drums were beating furiously and the bells were ringing louder and louder. One more kiss and a last word. "Lazuli, remember, when you get to Paris go straight to old Planchot's. Impasse Guémenée, you hear?" As we pushed forward to the door we heard behind us, back in the depths of the inn, the harsh rough voice of La Jacarasse calling out to the serving-woman: "Here, bring me another jug of wine!" And then the serving-woman passed us, muttering: "Dirty pig, I wish it might choke you!"

In a moment more we were in the street, running through the dark night to join the Battalion and to find out what had caused the alarm. We ran through streets and open spaces without meeting a living soul; hearing now and then a shutter pulled in and barred, or a key turned in the lock, or a bolt pushed fast by timid folk who were shutting themselves up in their houses.

The smoke from the dying bonfire and the shouting and singing of the crowd guided us on our way through the crooked streets; and, somehow or other, we came out all right on the big open space in front of the church. There we found our men all in line, with guns shouldered and bayonets mounted ready to start. In front of the Battalion was a man on horseback, at whom I stared with all my might to try and make out who he was— with his cocked hat and with his gilt buttons which sparkled in the faint rays coming from the few embers left of the great brush fire. Just then the drummers who had been drumming the recall through all the streets came back, making a most tremendous racket. The Battalion burst forth into the " Marseillaise." The crowd clapped hands, shouted, screamed, sang and howled, while the bells kept on madly pealing the tocsin. Never can I forget the roar that in that sombre night rose from the throats of thousands of men. Overtopping the roaring crowd, like a black statue sharply defined against the starry sky, was the silent motionless man on horseback.

Suddenly the horse stamped, striking out sparks from the paving stones. The horseman, raising his arm, motioned to the crowd to keep silence. As if by enchantment, the cries, the songs stopped, the drums ceased beating, the bells rang no more, and there was utter and solemn silence. Then the man on horseback spoke to us: "My brave men of Marseilles, I have ridden full speed from Paris to tell you what is being said and planned there. The Anti-

Patriots, the Counter-Revolutionists, the Aristocrats, all slaves of the King, have reported everywhere that you are brigands, that you have escaped from the galleys at Toulon, that you are the scrapings of the port of Marseilles, that you are Corsican bandits! They say that you have pillaged, burned, pulled down, murdered, and torn open all on your way hither. They even say that you crucified an old Canon at the door of the club in Avignon, and that you killed and quartered the Bishop of Mende. at the bridge of Saint-Jean d'Ardières—and who knows how much more they've said of this same sort! King Capet—the tyrant who has made a covenant with foreigners to invade France and massacre all French Patriots—wants to keep you from coming to Paris: so that he can the more easily bring his Germans and Austrians into France. The King plotted this black treason with the generals of the Emperor. If we had not caught and stopped him at Varennes the unnatural traitor would now be at the head of more than a hundred thousand foreigners: thirty thousand Austrians from the North, fifteen thousand Germans to come by way of Alsace, fifteen thousand Italians to come through Dauphiny, twenty-five thousand Spaniards to come across the Pyrénées, and as many

Swiss to invade us through Burgundy. This swarm of stranger enemies was to be spread like a pest over all our France of the Revolution; and, led by the tyrant himself and by the émigré nobility, it was to have given back full power to the King. And then—woe to the Poor! Good-bye to Liberty! Farewell to the Rights of Man!

"This same King Capet says that you shall not go to Paris; that he will bar the way. King Capet says you shall go to Soissons. King Capet in his foolhardiness does not understand that we men of the South fear nor powder nor fire nor steel! He does not know that, backed by the wrath of all Southern France, you come to abolish the throne, to smite into pieces the crown, to take vengeance for the past! King Capet says you shall go to Soissons. Has King Capet forgotten that there in Soissons is the famous axe with which his ancestor Clovis cowardly murdered his poor soldier? You, who are the strong arm of God, will lift up that same axe and with it you will cleave Capet's head from his shoulders! Up, men of Marseilles! Up, Patriots! Rise up for Death or Liberty!"

So saying, the man swung his horse around and cried out to us as he galloped off into the darkness: "I go before to tell to the men of the Revolution and to the Patriot Barbaroux that the Marseilles Battalion is advancing at a forced march on Paris. Vive la Nation!"

"Vive Rebecqui! Vive Barbaroux! Vive la Nation! Down with the tyrant!" answered we in one formidable shout as the horseman vanished into the night on his way to Paris.

Commandant Moisson flashed his sabre and cried to us: "Boys, the Marseilles Battalion starts now and rests no more. There is nor stop nor pause for us until we camp on the threshold of King Capet's Castle!"

The Battalion answered him by bursting out into "Allons enfants de la Patrie!" The drums beat the quick-step; and off we marched, with the strength of God's thunder in our bones. We were as vigorous and as strong as the day we had started on the Paris road.

Out of the way, you weak blooded monk! Scat! you sick silkworms of bailiffs! We want no more of your help. And again we harnessed ourselves to our cannon and, sweating and singing, went joyously on our way.

I kept wondering who was this man Rebecqui, this man on horseback who had spoken so well. Rebecqui, Rebecqui, who was he?

Everybody said that he was from Paris, but if so then the. Paris people spoke as they did in Avignon. He must be such another, I decided, as that Barbaroux who was waiting for us up in Paris; Barbaroux whom every one idolized, Barbaroux who was to save the Revolution. And so, thinking no more about him, I took up our chorus: "Aux armes, citoyens!"

The good red wine we had drunk, the tocsin that we still could hear off in the distance, and above all the fiery words of that Rebecqui, had put new life into us. Never had we marched more steadily, never had we felt less weariness or more go. When we were not singing the "Marseillaise" we were shouting "Down with the tyrant! We'll get into Paris. We'll get into his Castle. He doesn't want us there, but he'll have to have us!" And then we would close up our ranks and burst out again with: "Amour sacré de la Patrie!"

At daybreak, still singing, we marched through a big town—I don't remember its name—where we had been told that King Capet with his army and the people around were to bar our way. But not a soul was stirring—no one was in the streets. We made the houses shake as we marched through.

Samat unfurled the banner of The Rights of Man, but he couldn't find any one to kiss it—until he caught sight of an early beadle who was opening the doors of a church. He dashed upon the bewildered beadle, and when he had made him kiss the banner he burst into the church like a whirlwind and marched· around it holding up his banner to be kissed by all the saints of wood and stone; and when this matter had been settled to his satisfaction he came running up to us, all out of breath to take again his place in the ranks.

When the sun had sucked up the mists so that his sharp rays stung our necks like needles, we halted on the banks of a stream and ate our pittance of dry bread and garlic. But our halt was short. We were charged with God's thunder—and the thought of our high duty urged us on. Some of the men began to drag behind, limping on bleeding feet; but they struggled along bravely and would not give in. To drown the murmurs of pain, which even the best of them could not wholly stifle, we sang the "Marseillaise."

This terrible forced march lasted altogether for seven days and seven nights. As we marched we ate our everlasting garlic and bread, the bread often mouldy, and all we had to drink was water from ponds or way-side ditches. Footsore, hungry, weary—still we toiled on.

Yet we had a laugh now and then—as when we passed through a town absurdly named Melun, and made our joke about it by baptizing it Water-melon. It was a little town, packed full of Aristocrats. When its Mayor refused to let us have any bread we grinned on him with our famished white teeth—and then he changed his mind in a jiffy and promised us two loaves apiece! While we waited for it we camped outside the city gates for three hours, and when it came we danced around the baskets in a big circle to the tune of "La Carmagnole." After the bread was divided Commandant Moisson said to us: "Boys, this is the last time you will have to chew on country bread—may it set light on your stomachs. In two days or less you will taste the bread of Paris—and you will take the taste for bread out of the tyrant's mouth!"

What the Commandant promised came to pass. The next day we marched through such a forest of oaks and ash and beech that it seemed to me I was back again on Mont Ventour. The wood was so shady, the turf so thick and soft, that we made a halt; and as we were resting, some of us seated on fallen branches, some leaning back against the trees, some stretched out at full length on the soft grass, we were puzzled by hearing a queer noise—a dull humming roar, or buzzing murmur. Each of us in turn made a guess as to what it was. "It's bees swarming," said one, and we stared up into the branches to see them. "I should say an earthquake," said another, "only earthquakes don't last so long." "The sound seems to come from underground," said a third; "and yet it almost sounds like far off talking, or the firing of cannon very far away."

"As for me," said long Samat, "I think there is a spring near here that rushes between rocks, like the fountain of Vaucluse."

"If we weren't so far from Marseilles," put in Margan, "I should say it was the noise of the sea beating against the rocks of our good mother, Notre Dame de la Garde."

"If only it isn't an army of Aristocrats who are coming to bar the way,'" said Sergeant Peloux, frowning as he spoke.

The Commandant, smiling to himself, listened to all our guesses and then said: "Well now, if I didn't know you came from Marseilles I should say you were from Martigues—

that town where the people gulp down every fool-story that is told! That noise which puzzles you so is neither swarm, nor earthquake, nor waterfall, nor breakers on the rocks, nor is it the roar of an army; good comrades, it is neither more nor less than the voice of that great Paris we come to see! It is the sound of hammers on anvils, of the rumbling of carriages in the streets, of the hum of the market place; it is the voice of the people, the sobs, the laughter, the angry cries, the joyous shouts, of the hundreds and hundreds of thousands of souls in the Capital! In it are blended the clarion notes of Liberty, the frank voice of Equality, the sweet tones of Fraternity; and also, alas! the threatening lying voices of selfishness, of despotism, of hypocrisy and of tyranny. Friends, it is said that that dull roar of Paris, that jumble of songs and cries and sobs and laughter, can be heard five leagues away from that great city!"

Hardly were the words out of the Commandant's mouth than we were on our feet, our guns shouldered and our kits fast on our backs. We sang, we shouted! Could it be that we were so near to Paris! Vive la Révolution! Vive Marseilles! Vive Toulon! Vive Avignon!—and we tore branches from the oaks

and the beeches with which we dressed our
guns and our red caps and the gun carriages,
and we danced a round to the tune of the
"Carmagnole." The drums, instead of beating the everlasting quick-step, set up a buzzing like the *tambourins* on the Saints' days in
our villages; and off we capered in a farandole
—leaping, jumping, swaying, cutting pigeon-
wings, hugging, crying, and all the while shouting Paris! Paris! Paris—at last!

We went on in this crazy fashion for a good
half hour before we quieted down and got into
rank once more; and then we marched gaily
out of the shady forest with never a thought of
our past hunger and thirst and weariness and
pain. As we came from under the trees the
Commandant, pointing with his sword,
showed us far away on the edge of the green
plain a grey line that took up the whole horizon and was broken by towers and spires and
had floating over it a little bluish cloud.

"There is Paris!" said he.

The whole Battalion, as if the order to halt
had been given, stopped short. We stood
silent, staring at the horizon. Something
gripped fast at our throats and would not let
us sing the "Marseillaise." Our eyes were
blinded with a rush of tears. The Comman-

dant made a sign to the drums and off they
rattled the quick-step; and as if their rattle
had given us back our voices we burst out all
together with

> Allons enfants de la Patrie,
> Le jour de gloire est arrivé!

Wild, stern, fierce, we ran rather than
marched. The carriage of an Aristocrat was
driving toward us, but when the coachman
caught sight of us he was so frightened that
he turned tail and whipped back to Paris at
full speed.

By sundown we were come fairly within
one of the outlying suburbs, on the borders of
a stream of which I forget the name; and there,
suddenly, we saw a lot of people coming to
meet us shouting and waving their arms.

"Vive les Marseillais!" they cried.

"Vive les Patriotes!" we answered—and
in a moment we had broken ranks and flung
ourselves into the arms of the crowd. I can
tell you there was hugging and kissing! And
as fast as the hugging was over, it all began
again. Kissing and crying like women, these
friends who had come to welcome us told their
names—Barbaroux, Rebecqui, Danton, Santerre.

Barbaroux, the famous Barbaroux, the Deputy from Marseilles, who with his sweet voice could fairly beguile the soul out of you, hugged our officers all round and said: "To-morrow at daybreak you shall enter Paris and go right to the tyrant to bring him to reason. Here is Santerre, the Commandant of the Garde Nationale, who has promised to meet us with forty thousand men, all ready to cry with us: 'Liberty or Death!'"

At this, every one shouted "Vive Barbaroux," and a few in the crowd shouted also "Vive Santerre!" But a good many of us didn't like the looks of this Santerre the brewer. He spoke in French fashion through his nose, for such is the pretty way of the people up there in the North. Then he did not let out his feelings as Barbaroux and Rebecqui and Danton had done; nor did he even shake any one's hand. He seemed a sort of imitation fine gentleman, who put on gentle airs and who sneered at our huggings and dancings and singing of "La Carmagnole."

All this time we of the rank and file were making friends with the good people of the suburb, Patriots all. They mingled with the Battalion and the women and children kissed our hands. They wanted us to sup and bed at their homes—fairly fighting to have us, and not being contented unless they had two or three of us apiece.   I went off with Margan the chatterer to sup and sleep at the house of a fine fellow of a gardener.   And what a feast he gave us!   Because we came from the South, he gathered from his hotbeds the very first of his tomatoes and young egg-plants—that he might have sold for almost their weight in gold in the Paris markets—and with them made for us a paradise of a fricassee!   I can tell you our jaws wagged over it after our weeks and weeks of munching only dry bread and garlic and drinking ditchwater!   And then we slept in a real bed with our shoes off and our legs bare.

Name of a name, what a short night it was! At two o'clock in the morning, long before the first ray of dawn, the drums beat, the shutters flew open, the doors were unbarred, and the Federals poured out from everywhere, their kits on their backs and their guns on their shoulders ready to march.   As for me, down in my pocket I found two well dried blackberries with which I yet managed to make myself a famous pair of moustachios—that I might go into Paris looking like a man.

Something, I don't know what, kept us

from starting; and for all our early rising we did not get off until the sun was tipping the poplars with fire and the little birds were beginning to twitter as they waked up in the trees. But this time we started for Paris itself! Barbaroux, Danton, Rebecqui, with some other deputies to the National Assembly, headed the column; then came the drums beating the quick-step; then the two cannon and the forge, to which last I was harnessed; then the Battalion, with well sharpened swords and with guns loaded and primed ready to fire off! Big Samat displayed his banner of The Rights of Man, and the whole Battalion struck up: " Allons enfants de la Patrie!" Oh, Holy Liberty! had we but met the tyrant in his carriage with all his guards we would have made but a mouthful of them and him that day!

Soon we began to see the first houses of the Capital—and what enormous houses they were! The very lowest was higher than the spire of our church, so that to look at the eaves you had to put your neck out of joint. As we drew closer to the city its people came out to meet us—headed by a skirmish line of children who capered around us and shouted and danced and sang. There were workmen, shopkeepers, soldiers, and women of the people with woollen cockades in their caps showing the national colours of blue and white and red. And they all were clapping their hands and shouting "Vive les Marseillais!" Presently they got into line along the road side so as to let us pass, and waved their arms to us in sign of welcome. It was easy to see that they were good Patriots. But as we went farther into the town, between the big stone houses with their balconies and their beautiful doors, the look of the crowd began to change. We met carriages coming and going, with their silk-stockinged valets perched up before and behind. In them we caught glimpses of stiff Aristocratical mugs, all frizzed and perfumed. As soon as he saw these long Samat ran up to them and, willy-nilly, made them kiss his banner. In the crowd, that was crushed up against the wall in order to give us passage way, we saw, too, many sedan-chairs all gilded like an altar and lined with silk. Two very serious-looking men, in cocked-hats and embroidered coats, carried each of them—one man before and one behind. Sometimes a beautiful powdered lady all lace and ribbons would be in the chair, sometimes a marquis—dry as a stock-fish or as fat as an urn—in a coat of velvet with buttons of gold. But woe betide if footman or lady or marquis did not wear the tricolour woollen cockade. In a flash a Federal would go up to them and snatch away the cockade of silk ribbon and stick in its place the woollen tricolour that some woman or man of the people would give from off their own clothes. All this was done instantly, in passing, in the push and rush and stir of the march.

A great crowd followed us; drawn on partly by the steady roll of the drums ás they beat our marching-step, but more strongly by the terrible chant of the '' Marseillaise ''—which all the five hundred men of the Battalion sang in one tremendous voice loud enough to jar the plaster off the walls. Soon the crowd caught the words of the chorus and sang with us— and then it no longer was five hundred, but a thousand, ten thousand, twenty thousand, singers singing with one voice! That awful roar of '' Our soil's athirst for traitor blood!'' brought hot tears to every Patriot's eyes and sent a glowing thrill through every Patriot's breast. And all those arms flourishing in the air together, all those starting eyes sending forth the same gleam, all those thousands of open jaws uttering the same cry, were enough to drive one wild!

Bending forward, stooping almost on all fours, I dragged at my cannon and sang as if I would tear my throat open. From time to time I would raise myself and look back to see the overwhelming, howling, terrible flood of people pouring on close behind us. It seemed as if the houses, the trees, the very street with its paving-stones, were following us. It seemed as if a great mountain were galloping after us and was near upon us with its peaks and valleys and forests shaken and riven by the avalanche, the tempest, the earthquake of God!

The torrent burst into the Place de la Bastille, already crammed with a crowd into which the Battalion slowly bored its way. On each side of us and in front of us was a tremendous crush as men and women were pressed together like grain on the threshing-floor; and as they closed in behind us there was a surging eddy in our wake. The ruins of the Bastille were covered with people screaming, shouting, clapping, waving their arms. The broken walls, the heaps of stone and plaster, the riven beams, the roofless turrets, the windows wide open to the four winds of Liberty—all bore their loads of sightseers so close packed that their heads came together like a bunch of grapes.

I dragged away at my harness and, be-wildered, glanced aside at the mountains of people roaring and flourishing their greetings to us; until, by a lucky turn of my eyes, I caught sight of Lazuli up on a wall with Clairet on her shoulder, laughing and crying with de-light and shouting: " Vive les Marseillais!"

But it was not the sight of Lazuli that all in a moment made my voice grow husky, my blood stop running, my legs that had carried me so far give way under me, and my eyelids tremble with blinding tears: it was that I saw beside Lazuli, holding her hand and clinging to her as though for shelter, a pale young girl lovely as the Virgin—and knew her to be Ade-line, Mademoiselle Adeline of the Château de la Garde, the angel who had saved my life!

Old Pascal's voice broke, and for a moment he could not go on.   And in that very instant bang! bang! bang! came three blows on the shutter, and we heard outside the voice of Lange, Pascal's brother, calling: " Come, come. Are you going to spend the night here?   You have made me get up at two o'clock in the morning to look for you.   Come right away home!"

Two o'clock in the morning! Who would

have believed it? We all were on our legs in a moment; and the next moment we all were out in the darkness and scurrying off on our various ways through the blackness of the night.

CHAPTER VI.

It was very clear that after my sitting up till two o'clock in the morning I would be a desperate sleepy-head all the next day. My dear grandfather, I am sure, puzzled his brains through a good part of his own short night to find some way by which I could be kept awake during the next evening, and so not miss old Pascal's story—which he himself enjoyed as much as I did and would not have missed for the world. And the good old man did find a way that worked very well indeed.

Usually he was off at daybreak, with his hoe and his wallet, to his vine-yard or saffron-field. But that morning he pottered about the house until after ten o'clock. And then, as if he were asking a favour, he said to my mother: "I'd like to take our boy out with me this morning. A piece of my wall fell down in the last rains and must be set up again. I want somebody to hand me the stones. Then I can get along faster and finish it to-day."

"Well," said my mother, "he went to sleep again after I called him and so has missed his school, and I suppose he might as well go along with you and work like a man."

And so off I went for the day with my grandfather. But I did not hand him any stones—oh, no! Before he set hand to the broken wall he hunted out a sheltered corner where the sun shone warmly, and there he made me a soft bed of dry leaves on which he laid me; and on which I slept like a saint the whole day long.

When evening came I was as bright as a button, and so hungry that I ate supper enough for two. But hardly had my grandfather made an end to his own eating, by pushing away his plate and snapping his knife together, than I was up and had lighted the lantern and was tugging at him to hurry him away. Off we went, a pair of children together; and we had no more than taken our seats in the shoemaker's shop than Pascal began.

As I was saying, up there on the ruins of the Bastille, I caught sight of Lazuli with little Clairet on her shoulder, and Mademoiselle

Adeline close beside her holding fast to her arm as though in dread that some one might try to snatch her away. I tried to stop to make sure that my eyes were not playing a trick on me. But there was no stopping then. I could no more stand against the forward push of the crowd than if I had been a fly. The cannon seemed to be alive—to be galloping on of themselves. When I half halted, to turn around, the wheels of the truck came on me with a bounce and I had to start ahead in a hurry. And so on I went with the crowd, and the Bastille quickly was left behind. I felt my heart sinking. Something seemed to grip it and wring it until I hardly could bear the pain. To give myself strength and courage again I burst out with the rest into "Aux armes, citoyens!" and fell to dragging at my harness like a wild bull.

Presently something seemed to be going wrong ahead of us, in the Rue de Saint-Antoine, and we were pulled up short. And then we found that the Garde Nationale of Paris was there, barring our way. Santerre, the famous Santerre, had met us with a poor two hundred men—in place of the forty thousand that he had promised—and, instead of joining us, he was trying to prove to our Commandant that it would be folly to attack the

King's Castle; that the time had not yet come.

He was full of all sorts of excuses, this Santerre, for putting off the attack. Nothing was ready for it; the cannon we were to carry off from in front of the Hôtel de Ville were too strongly guarded to be taken; Mayor Pétion had said that we must wait until the Assembly could come to a vote. Mayor Pétion didn't think that this was the right time to force the King—and so on, with this, that and the other, until it was enough to drive one wild.

But in the end these peace-lovers carried the day against us, and it was settled that we should go along the Boulevard quietly to our barracks: and behold, then, Monsieur Santerre with his two hundred Parisians at the head of the procession—while we Marséillais marched along behind him meek as lambs! As for the crowd—the howling, roaring crowd that had followed us with fists and teeth ready for fighting—when those in it saw that there wasn't to be any attack on the Castle they dropped away from us by tens and twenties: and so left us to go through the Aristocratic quarter alone. Then we knew that Santerre had tricked us.

As we marched on we met only gilded carriages and silk-curtained sedan-chairs in which were fine court ladies in laces and furbelows, and powdered and pomatumed dandies in velvet coats and breeches, with silver-buckled shoes and with knots of ribbon at wrist and knee and wherever a knot of ribbon could be stuck on. These, we could see, were laughing and sneering at us; but Samat and Margan, who were not the sort to be laughed at by any such riff-raff of Aristocrats, stopped the coaches in a hurry and made the frightened porters put down the sedan-chairs—and then all those musk-scented dandies and mincing dames had to beg our pardon by kissing The Rights of Man! The poor things fairly shook in their shoes as they saw our glittering teeth, white as the fangs of the wolves on the Luberon, and our flashing eyes under dust-white brows. We made short work of them—pulling off their hats and their silk cockades and ordering them in our strong Provençal tongue, deep and mellow as the roll of drums, to cry with us Vive la Nation! It was good to see their shaking and trembling and their pinched disdainful faces as they joined in that Patriot shout.

The people in this quarter of the town, far from welcoming us from doors and windows and balconies, hurried away from us into the depths of their houses and all the welcome we got was the banging-to of shutters and the grating of bolts and bars. But welcome or no welcome, our drums rattled on and the chant of the "Marseillaise" rang out on the air.

At last, glowing with excitement, hoarse with shouting, and dripping with sweat, we came to our barracks; that stood in a puzzle of streets in the very middle of Paris. We found ourselves far off from the National Assembly, far off from the King's Castle, far off from everywhere. It was all the doings of that Santerre! Don't talk to me about people who keep their feelings inside of them and who neither laugh nor cry!

Santerre started to make us a speech; but he jabbered away in French, and we could not understand more than five words in ten. I think he was trying to tell us why we hadn't gone straight to the Castle; and then he tried to smooth us down by saying that we were to have a feast offered to us that evening at the Champs Elysées.

But here Margan caught him up short. "Mister Parisian," said our big pockmarked Sergeant, "you must excuse me if I cut into your speech. I should like, if possible, to get into your head that we didn't come all the way to Paris in order to string beads, nor did we swallow two hundred leagues of blazing dust in order to end off with a spree. Down in Marseilles each one of us has his own little *cabanon*, his own quiet nook by the sea-side or on the hills, to which he can go for his summer pleasure—taking along his garlic and oil to make *aïòli*, and the fish and saffron for his pot of *bouillabaisse*. We can do our junketting at home. I tell you squarely that all we came here for was to upset the King and save the country. We came for nothing else; and if you think you can take the taste of that out of our mouths by stuffing us with pastry, why——"

But here Barbaroux broke in with: "Hush, hush, friend Margan! You are quite right—but listen to what Patriot Danton has to say, and you will see that we all are of one mind."

In a moment Danton had mounted on a table and had started off with a speech that went like a bugle-call! He could talk for half an hour at a stretch and always say just the right thing. It was a great pity that he had to speak in French; but even in French we could understand that he was speaking well. *There* was a man for you! *He* was not like Santerre! When he finished, while we were cheering him, Barbaroux flung himself into his arms

and they hugged and kissed before us all; and
then they both promised us that within three
days they would take us to the King's Castle.

While all this was going on, we had served
out to us rations of wine and bread and ham,
and we were mighty glad to get them. By
that time it was two o'clock in the afternoon,
and as we had not tasted a mouthful since before sunrise we were as hungry as wolves.

But what Vauclair and I most wanted was
to hunt up Lazuli, and we made short work of
our rations and hurried off. Our guns we left
at the barracks, along with our bundles; but
into our red *taiolo*, drawn tight about our
waists, we stuck our pistols, and we carried
also our swords. And then off we started for
the house of Planchot the joiner in the blind
alley close by the Bastille.

The streets were still all topsy-turvy after
our passage. But doors and windows were
open again, and groups of people were standing on the thresholds and at the crossways
whispering among themselves. As we passed
them they stopped their talk to turn around
and stare hard at us; but we took no notice of
them—beyond sticking our hands into our red
sashes and holding fast our pistols all ready,
should there be need for it, to draw and fire.

All this while I had not said anything to Vauclair about my having seen Mademoiselle Adeline with Lazuli. That sight had utterly bewildered me. I wondered if I really had seen her? If, after all, she had not been a sort of vision that had come to me—begotten of my hunger and weariness and my excitement in the midst of the tremendous rushing and roaring of the crowd?

On we went, turning corner after corner and crossing little and big open spaces, and coming at last to the Impasse Guémenée without having had any adventures at all. As we stood outside the door we could hear the smooth "hush, hush" of a big plane as it threw off the long shavings; but the planing stopped short at our loud knock, and then the door flew open and there was Planchot himself. It was plain that he knew Vauclair on the instant; but instead of shaking hands and welcoming him he turned his back on us and rushed off like a crazy man shouting: "Vauclair! Vauclair! The good companion Vauclair!"

A moment later we heard Lazuli, upstairs, screaming: "It is he! Clairet! Clairet! Come quick!"—and Clairet's little voice crying: "Papa, Papa!"

We met them on the staircase, and how

we all hugged and kissed! How sweet Lazuli's hearty kisses were, and how entrancing the feel around·my neck of her dear arms! The blood rushed through my veins and my heart beat hard. I was no longer a child, but I was not yet enough of a man to understand why a kiss should so upset me.

After a moment Lazuli exclaimed: "You haven't seen us all yet. The family has grown. Poor little Mademoiselle Adeline is with us— you remember her, Pascalet? She saved you from wicked Surto's claws. And now I believe I have saved her from death. She is very sad, poor child, but she has a good spirit of her own. I must tell you all about it. I was so sorry for her on the trip from Avignon to Paris. It was she La Jacarasse was so rough to in the coach." As she spoke, Lazuli opened the door, adding: "I know, Vauclair, you will say as I do—when there is enough for three, there is enough for four."

It was lucky we had not far to go just then, for this news upset me more than all our long march in sun and rain and dust and wind. I, who had dragged at my cannon like a beast of burden and had thought nothing of it, felt my strong legs give way on hearing the name of this young girl. There she stood, white as wax, her beautiful large soft eyes dim and sunken; and in an instant I had flung myself at her feet and was kissing her hand. She brought the past back to me. My village, our hut of La Garde, my mother, my father! It seemed as if in her flowing robe, in her soft laces, she bore the scent of the wild clematis and of the broom-flowers that bloomed far away in our lanes. The hand I was kissing was the same that had given me the bit of white bread; the same that drew the bolts of the dungeon door at Avignon! And—was it possible?—she too was deeply moved. She took me in her arms and kissed me as Lazuli had done! Oh how utterly delicious it was! Suddenly I felt her delicate slender body yield and sway; and as I held her fast I saw that she had fainted.

Lazuli caught her from me; and, as if she had been a little child, gathered her up in her arms, saying: "Don't be worried, it is nothing but a fainting fit; and no wonder, poor child! That journey was such an awful thing for her. She suffered and wept the whole length of it." Still holding in her arms the sweet girl, who as she lay there, limp and helpless, looked like an armful of flowers, Lazuli disappeared into a little dark room—leaving us all upset and flustered out in the kitchen to stand staring at each other.

Just then we heard the clatter of old Planchot's wooden shoes on the stair. He had come to greet Vauclair according to the rite and ceremonial of their craft. To make this greeting what it should be he had put on his Sunday hat and his best wig; and before he said a word he laid a square and a compass down between himself and Vauclair on the floor. At once Vauclair made the proper motions of hand and foot, to which Planchot replied properly; and then, under their raised hands, they embraced over the *quilibret;* that is, the compass and square.

"And how goes it with you, my Avignonnais?" Planchot said. "And how goes it with you, La Liberté?" Vauclair answered. And then they went on with greeting after greeting, and never would have stopped at all had not Lazuli, her finger on her lip, come back to us.

"It will be nothing serious," she said; and as she turned to Planchot she added: "Our little girl has had a fainting fit. The crowd, the heat, the excitement of seeing her father, was too much for her. But she is better now. She soon will be all right."

"What a pity," said Planchot. "She is a delicate child. She is as pale as pine shavings." And then, tapping Clairet's cheeks, he went on: "Here's a fine little man! You are not like your sister; you don't get frightened when you see our Patriots, our Reds from the beautiful South, march by!" He turned to Lazuli, who was making signs to us to be quiet, and asked: "Wouldn't you like a little orange-flower water for the child? Speak right out if you would. We are all good Reds together, and everything in the house is yours. I wouldn't talk that way if you were Aristos—those wretches who are only waiting for the Austrians and Germans to come to help them ruin the country and kill the Revolution. There is nothing for Aristos here—except powder and ball and the sharp edge of my axe! But I'll leave you now. You need rest, and I've got more than enough work to do."

Planchot stopped his chattering and turned to leave the room—but took Vauclair with him to the threshold and whispered: "I have an order for seven guillotines. I must have them ready for the Jacobins within the fortnight." Then he left us, and we heard his sabots go clacking down the stairs.

Lazuli pushed-to and fastened the door and

17

brought out a bottle of muscatel and some bis-
cuits; and then, seating herself at the the table
as close as she .could get to us, she began to
tell in a low voice how she had saved Adeline
and had passed her off to Planchot as her own
child.

"You remember," she said, "how at Saulieu I told you about the poor young girl who
was travelling with La Jacarasse? Well, just
after you were called away by the drums, they
came to take their places in the coach. La
Jacarasse was very drunk. She staggered
every which way, and in getting into the
coach she stumbled and fell sprawling—dropping her big bag, out of which fell her pig-
killing knife. But she managed to climb in
and take her seat; and after her came the poor
young lady, blushing and ashamed and scarcely
daring to call her soul her own. She was crying, but trying to hold in her sobs like a child
who is afraid of a whipping. In the coach we
all looked at each other, shaking our heads;
for, though no one spoke out about it, the
sight went to our very hearts. And then I
made up my mind that I was going to find out
who that poor child was, and that I would
do my best to rescue her.. So I sat down
beside her, in front of La Jacarasse—who fell

asleep and snored away to the jolting of the coach.

"Then in the dark I whispered in the girl's ear: 'My dear, what is the matter? You are crying. Tell me what hurts you, perhaps I can help you.'

"'Thank you so much,' she answered in a trembling whisper. 'How kind you are! But there is nothing to be done for me. That woman will see the end of me. There is some plot against me that I can not understand. How could my mother have given me into such a creature's hands? It would have been better had she sent me to Paris alone.'

"'Who are you, dear child? Who is your mother?'

"'I am the daughter of the Marquis d'Ambrun. My narne is Adeline. My father and my mother, with my brother Robert, started for Paris some time ago. They were in a great hurry to be off to help the King of France, who is in some sort of danger. I had had a dreadful fright and was too weak to go with them, and so they left me behind for this horrible woman to bring me to Paris in the first coach from Avignon. Oh, Great Saints! Oh, Holy Maries of the Sea! Shall I ever reach home alive! And even should I reach home——'

"'Should you reach home? Why, then you will be safe, of course. Your mother must love you so; must be so good to you.'

"'It is not of my mother that I am most afraid, but of a wicked man, a German, who is our game-keeper. He and La Jacarasse have agreed between them to get rid of me, I am sure. They all are blind to that German's wickedness; and the blindest is my mother. It is not long since she—who used to be so kind to me—threatened me with a blow because I blamed him. I fear him even more than I do La Jacarasse. I am certain that the two have sworn my death. What can I do? I pray God to take me soon to himself!' As she said this she began to sob and cry so pitifully that I got to crying with her. It almost broke my heart.

"Of course I knew the whole story as soon as she told me her name; and I made up my mind that I would risk anything to get this dear little girl, who had saved our Pascalet's life, safe away from that wicked Surto and out of the claws of La Jacarasse. Over on the seat in front of us the good-for-nothing beast of a Jacarasse still was snoring; and so, drawing closer to the dear child, I whispered: 'I am nothing but a poor woman of the people, with all my riches in my twenty nails. Yet I took little Pascalet into my home—the Pascalet from La Garde whom you saved alive out of the vault—and I will take you into my home too.'

"When I said this, the poor girl flung herself on my neck and as she kissed me again and again she sobbed out: 'Oh, save me! Save me! I will follow you anywhere to get away from that awful woman and her great knife that she threatens my life with when she is drunk.'

"'Be careful, she is stirring. Now get it clear in your mind, my dear, that when we come to Paris and I get out of the coach you are to follow right behind, as if you were my daughter.'

"'I will do just what you tell me. I trust you because you were good to little Pascalet.'

"'Hush! We must not talk any more now. Day is almost here and La Jacarasse is waking. Remember what I have told you. When we leave the coach do you follow me, that is all.'

"Just then La Jacarasse gave a tremendous yawn, and then began to stare around her with her half open piggish eyes as though she didn't know where she was.

"Mademoiselle Adeline no longer sobbed.

Every now and then she glanced at me as much as to say: 'I know you will save me from that woman!'—and I, under our shawls, would give her hand a little squeeze.

"The coach with its three horses abreast and a fourth ahead went at a good rate, stopping before the inns of the towns and villages we went through only long enough to leave the letters and to let La Jacarasse swallow a glass of wine or brandy. The nearer we drew to Paris the drunker she became, until at last she could hardly see the coach door when she got in.

"'So much the better for us,' I whispered to the dear little girl. 'Let her drink like a sieve. The drunker she is the easier it will be to give her the slip.'

"At one of our stops I got a chance to tell the coachman what I meant to do, and he was as kind. as he could be about it—you saw at Saulieu what a nice a sort of man he was. 'I like to see a good woman like you,' he said. 'Of course I'll help you all I can. Now listen. We stop in Paris before the inn of the Soleil d'Or. I will get La Jacarasse out of the coach first by taking her off to have a drink with me —and then do you and the young girl get away as fast as you can. Don't bother about your baggage. I'll look after it, and you can get it whenever you please.'

"Two days after the coachman and I had this talk we got to Paris. It was about night-fall when we came in, and almost dark when we stopped in front of the Soleil d'Or. The coachman gave me a wink as he opened the door and called out: 'Who is going to stand treat to a glass of brandy?'

"'I am! I am!' cried La Jacarasse, in her rough voice—and went stumbling across our feet and legs, dragging her nasty smelly bag after her, and lurched out through the coach door. The coachman kept her from falling by catching her under the arms and dumping her down on the pavement, and off they went for their drink.

"That was our chance. I made a sign to the darling as I caught up Clairet in my arms, and to the wonder of everybody we got out and hurried off—leaving all our things behind us—and in ten steps we were lost and hidden in the crowd of people coming and going on all sides.

"Of course we didn't know the way; but I had a tongue in my head and asked a man selling red, white and blue cockades how to find the Impasse Guémenée. 'It's only two

steps off,' said he. 'Turn the corner of the
Place du Faubourg de Gloire into the Rue Saint-
Antoine and follow your nose for no more than
half a minute—and there you are. Vive la
Nation! Won't you buy a cockade?'

"Cockades indeed! That was no time for
buying cockades! We started off as fast as
we could go—giving a look back now and
then to see if La Jacarasse was after us, though
we did not feel much afraid of her; and in a
very few minutes we found ourselves all hot
and panting in the Impasse Guémenée and in
front of Planchot's door. It was Planchot himself who opened the door to us; and when I
told him who I was and showed him Adeline
and Clairet and said, 'Here are Vauclair's children,' he and his good wife Janetoun hugged
and kissed us as if we were their very own.
Nobody could have been kinder than they
were. They got beds ready for us, they
lighted the fire to get our supper, and in every
way they treated us as if they had known us
all their lives. We talked away to them of
our South Country, and they asked a thousand
questions about you and about the Marseilles
Battalion; and so in a moment we were
friends. But if I had told who Mademoiselle
Adeline really was I am sure there would have

been trouble; and I am sure that unless we keep our secret, and go on calling her our daughter, there will be trouble still."

"You have done exactly right," said Vauclair. "I know Planchot all the way through, and better dough never went to the making of a man. He is kindness itself. He carries his heart in his hand. But if he knew that Mademoiselle Adeline was the daughter of a marquis, of a noble, who had come to fight for the King, he would be quite capable of turning her neck and crop out of doors. Not a word must be said about it—be sure, Pascalet, that you keep your tongue inside your teeth. If that girl went back to her family she would simply be going into the jaws of the wolf. It is clear that Surto and La Jacarasse and the Marquise understand each other like three pickpockets at a fair. Mark my words, the three of them have sworn the death of the Marquis d'Ambrun and of Count Robert and of Mademoiselle Adeline. As to the Marquis and his son Robert, I don't care a button what happens to them. Let them be hanged or have their throats cut— it is no more than they deserve. But we'll save Adeline, or I'll know the reason why!"

"No, no, I won't have it! I won't have it!" cried Adeline, as she suddenly joined us.

"Do you think I will let my father and my brother die without going to their rescue? I heard what you said about them, and I know that Surto and La Jacarasse surely will try to strangle or stab them. I must go home to protect my people! Take me home—our house is near here in the Rue des Douze Portes." And then, turning from Vauclair, Adeline flung her arms so tightly around me that I scarcely could breathe and said imploringly: "Thou, Pascalet, thou canst not refuse me. Promise to take me home. Death is nothing to me if I can save my father and my brother!"

"Hush, hush, my dear little girl," said Vauclair. "Remember, no one here must know who you are. We'll save your father and we'll save your brother, too; but you must be silent or we shall all be lost. Hark! I hear some one coming up the stairs!"

As for me, the touch of Adeline's arms had so upset me that I scarcely knew what I was about. I cried in company with her, and kept saying: "Oh yes, yes, we'll save them, and I'll take you home!"

How strange that was! Who would ever have thought, when I left my village, that a day would come when I would consent to save from death the Marquis d'Ambrun and, still more wonderful, his son Robert! Count Robert who had nearly killed my father, beating him like a dog and leaving him for dead; Count Robert who had shut me up to die of hunger in the vault!

There was a knock at the door, and when Lazuli opened it there was Janetoun, Planchot's wife, come up to greet us. Then came no end of hand shakings and how-de-does and how d'ye do again, and compliments too! "Oh, what fine handsome fellows!" cried Janetoun. "That's the kind of men we have in the South—*they* are not afraid of a long march! *They* are not like these dried up Parisians who are neither fish, flesh nor fowl and can out-talk the wind. Like the dogs, they find a safe place and then bark from it. *You* won't do like that! When *you* get hold of Capet, as they did last month, you'll squeeze his neck for him—and serve him right too!

"And now I've a bit of news for you. It is arranged, you know, that you and your comrades of the Battalion are to be given a banquet to-night in the Champs Elysées. Well, the Aristocrats will be there and they will try to start a fight with you. They are arming for it now. But don't you fight with

them.   Tell your friends in the Battalion what
is coming, and tell them to let the Aristocrats
alone.   Now I've warned you—and forewarned
is forearmed!"

"Janetoun is right in telling us," said Vauclair, "and we must be off.   If things are as
she says they are, we must be with the Battalion.   Right about face, Pascalet! March!
And as to any Aristocrats stopping us, I'd like
to see them do it while two good watch dogs
are by me, and I have this sharp walking-stick
at my side!"—and he touched as he spoke his
pistols and his sword.   "But tell me, Janetoun," he added, "will that Santerre be there?
Do you know him?"

"You must not think I want to get rid of
you," said Janetoun, lowering her voice; "but
really I do think that to-night you ought all to
be together.   As for Santerre—well, you had
better talk to Planchot about him; he knows
him, and knows how much he can be trusted."
And then, with her finger on her mouth, she
whispered: "I can tell you this, though—only
last evening he was seen stealing out of the
King's Castle just at the edge of dark!"

Janetoun stopped for a moment, and then
speaking in her natural voice, she went on:
"But don't let what I've told you worry you.

As I said, forewarned is forearmed. We know here all that is going on. Planchot goes every evening to the Jacobin Club; and they are wide awake, those Jacobins! It is they who have ordered the seven guillotines! You understand ? Well—a word to the wise, you know." She suddenly turned, and as she ran down the stairs in a jiffy, she called back to us: "I must melt the glue. The guillotines must be ready in a fortnight. There isn't much time to spare!"

"What is a guillotine, Vauclair, anyway ?" I asked.

"I'm sure I don't know," Vauclair answered. "The Jacobins have ordered them—like enough they are seats or tables, for the club house."

"They're a puzzle to me," said Lazuli. "I can't make out what they are; but they certainly are neither chairs nor tables. Come and see—we have one here in the little room. Planchot lent it to us to use as a bed for Adeline."

We were as full of curiosity as so many children and we all went in together laughing to see the queer piece of furniture. What we saw, lying flat on the floor, was a sort of case or box, somewhere about three feet long and half as wide, from which started arms at least six feet long into each of which was cut a deep groove running its whole length. At the top the arms were held together by a solid cross-piece, in the middle of which was a little pulley.

"I think," said Lazuli, "that it is meant to stand up, with the two arms in the air. When we came here, Father Planchot had only one bed for the three of us; so he said that he would fetch one of his guillotines up stairs, and that we could make it into a bed for Adeline. You see, by laying it down this way and filling it well with shavings, it makes a very fair bed indeed. There is room enough for a child, or indeed for a grown person, in here between the arms."

While Lazuli was talking we were looking at the queer affair. Vauclair raised it and turned it over and looked at it carefully. But he ended by making a little puzzled sound, as much as to say: "Deuce take me if I can guess what the thing is for at all!"

And then I ventured to say that perhaps it was to be used in making triumphal arches or something of that sort, for some grand festival —such as the Fête-Dieu in Avignon.

"You've hit it, I do believe," said Vauclair. "No doubt they are for some great festival of rejoicing. What geese we were not to see it right off." And then we went back into the kitchen and began to get ready to leave.

While we were tightening our red sashes Adeline once more threw her arms round my neck crying: "My Pascalet, you will surely come back to me, and surely will take me to my father's house?"

Vauclair saw how upset I was and answered for me. "Yes, dear little girl," he said, "just as soon as we have taken the King's Castle we will take you to your people, that I promise you. Then the Marseilles men will be the masters and will make laws for Paris. Surto and the wicked Jacarasse, when we find them, shall be shut up tight in prison so that no one will ever see them again. You must be a very good girl and let us leave you quietly now, and we will come back to-morrow. If you don't keep very quiet· La Jacarasse will find where you are hidden and will carry you off; and she, certainly, will *not* take you home."

As he spoke, Vauclair gently loosened her tightly clasped arms from about my neck; and I, encouraged by Vauclair's words, added: "Yes, yes, we'll take you home; and we will

protect you, too, from that horrible Jacarasse."

As she tried to thank me I closed her·
mouth with a kiss; and then Vauclair caught
me by the hand and led me out of the room.
As we went down stairs I heard Lazuli laughing and saying: "Come, come, you will be a
most unreasonable girl if you keep on crying
after a kiss like that."

Oh, that kiss! How I felt it thrilling through
me! Though we were out in the big street I
neither saw people nor carriages coming and
going. My cheeks felt as red as fire, my ears
sang, my legs could hardly support me. Oh,
how I longed to go back to the house to kiss
Adeline once more and tell her all that I wanted
to tell! But little by little my senses came
back to me and my cheeks cooled down. After
all, I wasn't much more than a boy, and I was
full of a boy's curiosity. I stared at the people, the carriages, the sedan-chairs; I gaped at
the painted and gilded signs, which were made
in all sorts of fantastic shapes and swayed in
the wind over the shop-keepers' doors. By the
time that we reached the Place de la Bastille—
or, as they called it then the Faubourg de la
Gloire—I was quite myself again. In the
morning we had seen the ruins of the strong-

hold crowded with people; but without the people it took even more of a hold on me. It seemed as if it had been tumbled down by an earthquake. When we had walked all round it, looking at it from every side, we went into the Soleil d'Or—where the Avignon coach had stopped, and where the coachman had given Adeline and Lazuli their chance to run away from La Jacarasse.

In this inn I saw a queer thing that bothered me a great deal. There hung from the ceiling two big figures stuffed with straw, just like the "Carmentrans" we parade around on Shrove Tuesday. They were dressed up in paper—one as a general of the army, the other as a crowned lady.

"Don't you know what those are?" Vauclair asked. "Well, I'll tell you. The general is Lafayette, and the fine lady is the Queen. Every evening the Patriots of the quarter, who hold their meetings here, carry those two figures up to the highest window in the house. And then—kerflop! and down they go on the pavement to the shouts of the people, who join hands and dance around them to the tune of 'Ça ira.' All of which means that some day in the King's Castle we will do the same thing!"

When we came out of the Soleil d'Or, we turned down and went along the banks of the Seine, a river that flows through Paris. It is not near as wide as the Rhône, and is very dirty. The water is so foul that it looks like the last skimming of olive-oil or the drainings of a stable-yard; and, compared with our Rhône, it flows along so slowly that it is hard to tell which way it goes.   .

The sun was almost down as we passed in front of the Hôtel de Ville; and had set by the time we reached the Champs Elysées—where we found all the men of the Battalion with the Paris folks who were giving us our feast. The table was spread in a cabaret called the Grand Salon; and it truly was a grand salon, I can tell you, for there was room in it for five hundred men.

The gardens of the Champs Elysées were crowded with people, some shouting "Vive la Nation!" others, the Anti-Patriots: "Vive le Roi!" and "Vive la Reine!" Next door to the Grand Salon was a cabaret in which another festival was going on; and this other festival had been started by some of the sprigs of the nobility—who, as well as their serving-men, were dressed up as National Guards. Nice National Guardsmen they were! They were the King's dogs; and they had come on purpose to make a disturbance and so to pick a quarrel with us. Well, they got what they came for—and also something they didn't come for, as you will see!

We were no more than seated at our table, with Santerre to preside over us, than this Royalist rabble, right under our windows, began to sing songs in honour of the tyrant and of his Austrian Queen. We let them go on, but soon the good Patriots of those parts took the matter up and began calling out: "Down with the foreigners!" "Down with Coblentz!" "Down with the Austrian!"—and at this the cowards drew their swords and shamefully fell upon the women and children. That was the kind of fighting that suited them, but it did not suit us! "Help, Patriots, help!" the women shrieked. And then: "Help, Marseillais!"

We would have had snails' blood in our veins had not our hearts sprung up in answer to that cry. In spite of Santerre—who tried to quiet us by calling out: "It is nothing, nothing at all. Stay in your places"—we all were on our feet in a moment. Some of us ran out at the door, some jumped out of the windows; all of us with drawn swords and pistols, and all as eager as wolves! But when the Aristos caught sight of us, instead of staying to fight, off they ran like rabbits—some of the hindmost being spurred on by the toes of our boots as well as by the points of our swords. They all made for the drawbridge of the King's Castle, while we burst out laughing at seeing them run away before they were hurt.

One big fat fellow fell head foremost into a mud-puddle. I was sorry for him and helped him up; and when he was on his feet I found that he was so tall that my head was not much above the level of his fat stomach. All the same, I put the point of my sword to his big paunch and cried: "Shout 'Vive la Nation!' —or in it goes!"

All covered with mud as he was, he made an awful face at me and answered: "I am Count Moreau de Saint-Merri!"

"The deuce I care who you are," I answered. "Shout 'Vive la Nation' or the point of my sword will make a new button-hole in your breeches!"

"Vive la Nation! Vive la Nation!" shouted he—and then I let him run off to the Castle.

As we were on our way back to the table in the Grand Salon we saw marching up from the other end of the Champs Elysées a company of Anti-Patriot National Guards, who were coming to support the lot we had just driven off. One of these, an officer with silver epaulettes, aimed at a Federal and fired; but his pistol flashed in the pan. Instantly the Federal turned around and blew out his brains. The Aristocrats, seeing their officer killed, broke in disorder and fled. This time we did not pretend to stab; we stabbed in earnest. The slowest and the timidest cried for quarter, and at the end we found ourselves with about a dozen prisoners in hand. Santerre joined us, and for once was earnest enough. He begged and implored us to let our prisoners go. He said he would answer for them himself; that they really were on our side; that they were our brothers, but had been tricked into acting against us. He talked and talked so in his French jargon that he finished by making us do what he wanted.

Our feast was all spoiled. But we carried off the food to our barracks in the Rue Mirabeau le Patriote, and there we spent what was left of our evening quietly—eating, drinking and singing as if we had been at home down in the South. Barbaroux and Danton joined us there, and comforted us by promising that in not less than three days we certainly should attack the Castle.

"If the Assembly and the National Guard won't act," they said to us, "we will take matters into our own hands. We will put down the tyrant and save the country all by ourselves." Santerre, who had come with them, could not say no to this; and he promised that in three days his men would march with us to the attack.

Then we stretched ourselves out on the stone floor and slept there for the rest of the night like logs; and the next day we were up at cock crow and off to see the town.

Nobody stayed in the barracks but the men on guard. Some of us went to take a good look at the King's Castle, and at the bridges and streets and alleys leading to it. Others went to the National Assembly to hear what they were chattering about in that place; others were satisfied to stare openmouthed at the dancing bears and into the shop windows, until you might have thought they had just landed from Martigues! Vauclair and I, of course, made straight for the Impasse Guémenée to see our dear people.

As we entered the workshop, Planchot drew Vauclair aside, and with a very mysterious air whispered in his ear: "The Jacobins have just ordered another seven guillotines. That makes fourteen. I am counting on your help. Fourteen guillotines to be ready in a fortnight! I never can get through a piece of work like that alone."

"Surely, surely, brother Planchot," Vauclair answered. "Of course I'll help you. That's what I'm here for. And isn't it for the good of the Revolution, too? Just wait while I run up stairs to say good-day to my wife and children, and then I'll put on my apron and take hold of my plane."

Lazuli and the others had heard Vauclair's voice and they all came running down stairs. Lazuli kissed Vauclair, and Adeline put her arms round my neck and kissed me. And then there was a fire of questions.

"Has all gone well?" "Is the King's Castle taken?" "Is any one dead?"

"No," we answered. "We haven't taken the Castle; we haven't even seen the King. It will be for to-morrow, or the day after to-morrow."

Old Planchot, his hands folded under his apron, kept grinning at our hugging and kissing and finally said: "Look here, Vauclair, it seems to me these young people are on mighty good terms with each other!"

"When the affairs of the nation are all settled, brother Planchot," said Lazuli, laughing, "we'll have a wedding. We'll marry them in front of the Liberty Tree."

As Adeline heard these words she remembered her training as a well brought up young lady and blushed furiously, while her eyes filled with tears. Unclasping her arms from about my neck, she covered her face with her hands.

To make things easier for her, I acted as if nothing had happened. Taking off my sword and pistols and my fine National Guard coat, I rolled my shirt sleeves up to my elbows and said to Planchot: "You want help. Here I am all ready to help. What shall I do?"

"Now that's the sort of boy I like," said Planchot, slapping me on the shoulder. "Well, take this plane, and square the arms for the guillotines. Do it carefully. See, you are to plane down to the black mark. There is enough here to keep you going for a week.

"As for you, Vauclair," Planchot went on, "you are a master-workman and I'll give you some of the finer work to do. You will make the mortises in the lower blocks and chisel out the long grooves the whole length of the arms.

Those grooves must be as straight and true as the lines on music paper."

"And can't we help too?" asked Lazuli and Adeline and Clairet all together.

"Yes, yes," Planchot answered. "There's work for us all. You can sweep away the shavings and hand us our tools, and you can melt the glue—and among us we'll have such guillotines as never were seen!"

I started in and planed away like a good one. Soon the floor beside me was covered with shavings—some long, some short, some delicate and shining like silk ribbon—all twisting and curling together like Adeline's pretty hair. The pine wood with its sharp sweet fresh smell made me feel almost as if I were once more in the pine forests up in my own mountains at Malemort. Close by my bench Clairet and Adeline played in the shavings; and whenever I asked for the straight-edge or the square Adeline hurried to get it for me.

"Master Planchot," said Adeline, "we all will go to the Feast of the Guillotines, won't we? Where is it to be?"

Planchot opened wide his eyes, and for a moment shut his jaws together so that his nose almost touched his chin, as he answered: "Yes, I'll take you all there, and you shall see how we'll use them. That will be a gay festival. Nothing like it has ever been seen."

That was enough for us; we all were sure then that those things were to be used as triumphal arches for the festival that was to take place after we had captured the King's Castle.

"Father Planchot, will there be farandoles at the Guillotine Feast?" asked Clairet one day.

"Oh yes, yes, fine farandoles," said Planchot, winking at Vauclair and me.

"And will there be wreaths of box and lovely flowers twined all around the side-pieces of the guillotines?" asked Adeline.

"Oh yes, yes, plenty of flowers—and all of them red," Planchot answered.

Vauclair and I asked no questions. We did not want Planchot to see that we did not really understand how the guillotines were to be used.

"Master Planchot," Adeline went on, "please lend me your pencil. I want to put my name on the guillotine that I am using as a bed. Perhaps I will know it again on the day of the feast."

Our little lady was the only one of us who knew how to write, and when she had finished her fine performance we all went to look at it. On the upper cross-piece, beside the little pulley, she had written in big letters:

ADELINE

Oh that name! It is more than sixty years ago that she wrote it there—yet to-day I see it as plainly as I saw it then!

We sawed and planed and worked together steadily for eight days. Every evening Vauclair and I went back to the barracks to sleep, and every morning early we came again to Father Planchot's; when the first questions would be as we crossed the threshold: "Have you taken the King's Castle? How many were killed?"

But our answer had to be always the same: "No, we haven't taken it yet."

We were beginning to think that we never would take it. Sometimes it was Santerre who stopped us by declaring that he was ill and we must wait for him to get well again; sometimes it was Pétion, the Mayor of Paris, who stopped us by pulling a long face and saying mysteriously: "We must wait or all will be lost. It is not the right moment"; sometimes it was the National Assembly that chimed in with: "Yes, you must wait, or something will go wrong!"

At last one day our pockmarked Margan stood up in the gallery of the Assembly and shook his fist in the face of all the deputies as he cried out: "You are all afraid. You sit there shaking like reeds. You always are fearful that something will or won't happen. And while you talk, we wait—we the Patriots, the Reds of the Midi who have tramped through the heat of the sun and the chill of the night our two hundred leagues; we to whom you have not allowed even enough mouldy bread to keep our bellies from crying hunger! Shall I tell you what we think of you? We think you are cowards! All we fear is your fear! Our only dread is that if we wait for you to start the Revolution there never will be any Revolution at all!"

But Margan's speech did no good; and we of the Battalion were wearied and over wearied by our waiting for the signal to start. And as we lost heart the Aristocrats gained heart. They saw that nothing happened, and they began to pluck up their courage once more. The time-serving shop-keepers, the money-makers, painted fleurs-de-lys on their signs, and stuck up for mottoes over their doors "A fig for the Nation!" or "Vive la Reine!" or "Vive le Roi!" And all this while swords and guns and pistols, with plenty of balls and powder, were carried into the King's Castle by the Royalist dogs who freely went and came—while we were stuck fast like so many posts planted in the ground!

That sort of thing could not be allowed to go on. We raised our voices so loud that at last we made ourselves heard. We swore that if the others held back, and if leaders were denied to us, we would march without leaders on the King's Castle and would take it alone. Then Barbaroux and Danton came to our help. They talked with the Federals from Brest, and with the true Patriots, the true Revolutionists, of the National Guard; and among them they arranged that our quarters should be shifted across the river to the building that had been the convent of the Cordeliers—where the Patriot Club used to meet—because from there we could march on the Castle easily. Danton himself came to lead us to our new barracks, and as he served out cartridges to us he shouted: "Liberty, Equality, Fraternity—or Death!"

At the Cordeliers we found Barbaroux waiting for us, and he made us a speech that set all our hearts to beating with joy. "To-morrow," he cried, "the fight that you have been

longing for shall be fought. In spite of all
Paris; in spite of the National Assembly; in
spite of Pétion (of that Pétion who boasted
that he would march you out of the city in no
time if the Assembly would but make him a
grant of seven thousand crowns); in spite of
them all, I say, and in spite of all the gods in
heaven and all the devils in hell, the tocsin
shall ring to-morrow night—and by the morning we all will be dead or the King's Castle
will be ours!"

That time there was no trickery. The next
day all Paris was in a ferment—while we worked
on at the guillotines. We knew that we should
not be wanted before evening, and the last of
the fourteen was almost done. Early in the
afternoon we finished it and threw down our
planes.

"All they need now," said Planchot, rubbing his hands, "is the razor of Equality. But
that is another man's affair. 'Tis no part of a
carpenter's business to shave!"

That last day's work was the hardest of
all. Everybody knew that there was thunder
in the air. From early morning the streets
had been crowded: heavy covered wagons
trundled along mysteriously; the King's
mounted gendarmes clattered hither and thither

at a gallop; in all the quarters the drummers were beating the assembly on a hundred drums.

Lazuli and Adeline understood that at last the fight was coming in earnest. They spoke little. Without asking for orders they loaded our pistols, and then they turned to Father Planchot's grind-stone and fell to sharpening our swords. But when the time came for leaving them they fairly broke down. Oh, how they cried, and how they begged us to take care of ourselves and of each other!

"You needn't either of you be in the very first rank."

"If you should get the smallest hurt, come right back home."

"Vauclair, listen. Take good care of Pascalet; and you, Pascalet, don't leave Vauclair's side."

And then more kisses and more tears. At the last Adeline said to me: "If you see my brother or my father, promise me that you will not hurt them." And I, carried away by her kisses, answered: "I will not. I give you my word!"

While we were in the thick of our good-byes Planchot had left us and had gone up stairs to his bed-room. Suddenly he appeared among us again, dressed in his uniform of the Paris National Guard—and a great-looking object he was! He was a little bit of a man, with a hooked nose like an owl's beak, a pointed chin, and not a tooth in his head. Like all old carpenters, his right shoulder was higher than his left. What with his cocked hat too big for him, his coat too long for him, and his spindle legs, he was a regular Punch!

Janetoun came clattering down the stairs after him and burst into the room at his heels crying: "Thou shalt not go! I say thou shalt not go! They can get along without thee— thou art too old to fight. Leave fighting to the young folks. Thou wilt be killed by everybody! The very horses will trample thee down! Tell him, Vauclair, to stay at home. He only will be in your way. Why, his sword is longer than he is—he can't draw it out of the scabbard! Listen to reason, my own Planchot; listen to reason, and stay here with me!"

But Planchot wouldn't listen to reason; and he answered her in French, speaking with his strong Southern accent: "La révoluchion, il nous appelle, nous vaincrons ou nous mourrissons!" ("The Revolution calls us. We conquer or die!")

"That is all very well," said Janetoun; "but what am I to do if you have an arm cut off or a leg shot to pieces?"

"La libarté ou la mort! Passe-moi mon ache que z'ai aguisée pour tranca lou cou du tyran!" ("Liberty or Death! Give me my axe. I have sharpened it so as to cut off the tyrant's head!")

Janetoun had lived a good while in the world and she knew there was more than one way of catching martins. When she found that talking to her man did no good she tried another tack—all of a sudden giving an awful scream and striking her hands together and going down on a heap of shavings in a bunch.

Planchot stopped talking bad French and shouted in honest Provençal: "Heavens and earth, my wife has fainted! Quick, get the vinegar!"

Lazuli and Adeline rushed up stairs for the vinegar and orange-flower water, and the moment they were gone Vauclair and I nodded to each other—and off we went without more ado.

Once in the street we had no chance to think of those we had left behind us. In an instant we were in the thick of a pushing, crushing crowd. We got ahead as we could, often being forced back two steps for one step that we had gained—as a squadron of gendarmes crushed their way through the press, or a band of Aristocrats came along roaring: "Death to the brigands!" or a company of Patriots crying: "Vive la Nation!" Some carried red flags, some black; we even saw a bullock's heart, all bleeding, carried high on the point of a pike. Women with their hair hanging loose over their shoulders were pushing this way and that, while above their heads they waved their bare arms. Barefooted men were strutting along brandishing rusty pikes and nicked swords and crazy old guns. Even the children were flourishing everything they could lay hands on that looked like a weapon. And from all the Patriot throats would come storming forth from time to time the Patriot song:

Dansons la Carmagnole,	Dance we the Carmagnole!
Vive le son, vive le son,	Hurrah for the roar! Hurrah for the roar!
Dansons la Carmagnole,	Dance we the Carmagnole!
Vive le son du canon!	Hurrah for the roar the cannon roar!

As we worked our way along toward the King's Castle there went by a company of Royalist regulars—all pomaded and be-powdered and be-curled, wearing silk stockings with buckled garters, and with swords and pistols all bright and shining in the sun.   They carried a banner of blue and white, the King's colours, on which was written: "Hurrah for the Austrian and Prussian armies who will enter Paris victorious!"; and as they marched on toward the Castle they sang the Anti-Patriot version of our "Ça ira":

Ah! ça ira! ça ira!	Oh, all goes well! Oh, all goes well!
De mal en bien tout change en France!	From bad to good all France doth turn!
Ah! ça ira! ça ira!	Oh, all goes well! Oh, all goes well!
Car c'est Louis qui règnera.	For Louis will reign over us
Antoinette l'on chérira,	And Antoinette will cherished be
Et les Jacobins l'on pendra!	While the Jacobins shall hang!

As the singing soldiers passed on toward the Castle the sun was setting—down the line of the Seine—in a burning blood-red glow. From close to us down far away to where clouds and earth came together, everything touched by the sunrays—spires, domes, the tall houses and the walls of the Castle—was blood-red.   The river seemed running with flaming blood—that looked still redder and brighter because of the piers and arches of the bridges which made black splotches against its crimson glow.

We stopped for a moment to look at this strange sight; and as we went on again Vauclair said, very seriously: "That means that there will be a great killing of men!"

It was almost dark when we got back to our barracks in the Cordeliers; and there we found Barbaroux and Danton and Rebecqui talking away—while they strode backwards and forwards in the courtyard—to a group of Federals who evidently had been saying that they dreaded more of Santerre's tricks and delays.

"I tell you," cried Barbaroux, "that this time Santerre surely will come—or his days of coming and going on this earth surely will end. Look here!" (as he spoke he unbuttoned his coat and threw it open) "Look here! You always have seen two pistols stuck in my sash. Now there are none. And this is what has gone with them. I gave one of them to a Patriot whom I can trust as I trust myself, and I said to him: 'You know Mandat, the Commandant-Général of the National Guard of Paris? Well, follow him by day and by night—and if he dares to turn his men against the troops of

the Revolution take this pistol and blow out his
brains. So will you serve the cause of our
country and of Liberty!' And that good Patriot, answering me, said: 'I swear that you
shall cut off my head if I fail to obey you!'

"And the other pistol I gave to another
good Patriot, and I said to him: 'You know
Commandant Santerre! Well, follow him by
day and by night—and when the drums beat
the assembly and the tocsin rings if you do not
find him at the head of his men coming to join
the troops of the Revolution take this pistol
and blow out his brains. So will you serve
well the cause of our country and of Liberty!' And that good Patriot, answering me,
said: 'I swear that you shall cut off my head
if I fail to obey you!'

"And so, you see," Barbaroux went on,
"those two are provided for. One other man is
left who may play us false, and that is Pétion,
the Mayor of Paris. But he also is provided
for. At this moment fifty tried and faithful
Jacobins have Pétion shut up in the Hôtel de
Ville; and they will neither let him go out nor
let him speak to any one until the Castle is
taken and the King and Queen are our prisoners."

Before Barbaroux had finished, Margan,

gun in hand, jumped up on the table beside him and shouted: "What do we care whether or not the Parisians will march? When did they ever do anything for the cause of Liberty? For near a fortnight we've been waiting here like a pack of gaping idiots. These Parisians, every one of them, have chicken-hearts. They called for help; they called to us to come up and help them—and now they are afraid of us! And they are right to be afraid of us, for we will crush them if they stand in our way. We are come from Marseilles, from Toulon, from Avignon, from all over the hot South, to save the Country and proclaim the Revolution. We'll do it! God's own thunder won't stop us! We'll march in spite of Paris! If we must, we'll march against Paris!—and we'll rush to the assault shouting 'Death or Liberty!'"

"Well said, Margan! Well said!" cried Samat, as he sprang up on a table and waved his banner of The Rights of Man—while all of us, shouting together, filled the courtyard with an angry roar.

Another Marseillais made himself heard: "In the National Assembly," he cried, "they are all cowards! Pétion, this Mayor of Paris, is a traitor. It was he who said, 'Give me seven thousand crowns, and I'll get rid of the Marseillais.' Tell him to come here with his seven thousand crowns! Are we a herd of pigs and is he our herdsman, that he dare to say we are for sale? We must give this traitor Parisian the lie. Here is my pistol—and I swear that if the Marseilles Battalion doesn't march to the assault before day comes I, I who am speaking to you, will blow my brains out that I may not die of shame!"

"He's right, the Patriot's right!" called out one of our men who stood in a far corner and who hammered with his sword upon a table until he made himself heard. "He's right. With us it must be Death or Liberty! Not one of us ever will go back into the South again until we have thrown down the tyrant and brought Paris to reason. What are these Parisians, any way? When we are off in our far provinces they look down on us; they cry out at us for dregs and starvelings; they sneer at us because we don't talk through our noses with their own duck-quacking 'couin! couin! couin!' But now that we are here, and they see us, they tremble! We must show them who we are and what we can do. So far, they have only barked from a long way off. If they come nearer, showing their teeth; if

they try to stop us in our good work—then
will we quiet their nose-talking once and for
all!"

We all believed that there was good reason
for these bitter words against the Parisians,
and at each one of them we cheered and
cheered. For the whisper had gone around
that the National Assembly was trying to find
some excuse for sending our Battalion packing
out of the Capital; and we also had been told
that the National Guard of Paris, instead of
joining us, would fight against us in defence of
the King. But Danton, the good Jacobin,
knew better; and presently he was up again
on a table and making a speech to us in which
the whole matter was set right and clear. Ah,
he was a man! He spoke French, and we
couldn't understand all his words; but we
understood all his thought.

He began by telling us, shortly, that whoever said all the Parisians would be against us
lied; and then he told us very clearly and carefully how the attack on the King's Castle was
to be made. The battalions of the Faubourg
de Gloire, he said, were to march to the Place
du Carrousel (as they called the open space in
front of the Castle) by way of the Place de la
Grève and the Arcade Saint-Jean; the bat-

talions of the Faubourg Saint-Marceau were to come up to the Horse Market, and from there were to follow the river and cross it by the Pont-Neuf; and we, the Marseillais, with the Federals from Brest and the students from the schools, were to cross the river by the Pont-Saint-Michel and enter the Place du Carrousel through the galleries of the Louvre. It was a plan, he said, that had been carefully thought out and that promised well; and all the forces pledged to take part in it could be trusted to the death. For the signal of attack, he said finally, an alarm-cannon would be fired on the Pont-Neuf and the tocsin would ring from all the church towers—and then the good fight would begin!

Our eyes filled with tears as we listened to him, and while those who were nearest to him embraced his knees we all cried together: "God grant that your good words be true!"

The night had run onward while all this talk went on. It was late—within an hour of midnight. We remembered that we were hungry, and fell to eating our rations of garlic and dry bread. Suddenly a shot was fired in the street almost at the door of our barracks. In an instant we had seized our arms and were filing out in line. Our Commandant and Barbaroux and Danton tried to hold us back. The drums had not yet beaten the assembly, the time to march had not yet come, they shouted —but our own drummers already were beating the quick-step, and in spite of all they could say we were off. Feeling our cartridges, to make sure that they were in order, away we went through the dark streets as silently as a flock of sheep; keeping time with our footsteps to the quick rattle of our drums.

My mouth was dry. I chewed and chewed away at a bit of bread, but could no more swallow it than if my throat had been held close by an iron band. I was all of a tremble, just as if I had a fever; and I was shaking with an excitement I could not understand. It was about midnight when we came out of the tangle of narrow streets through which we had been marching upon the wide way beside the river. The weather was soft and warm; the stars shone brightly in a clear sky; on the bridges and along both banks of the river rows of lanterns were swinging in the wind.

But there beside the quiet river we struck upon such a tremendous crowd and such a whirl of confusion that it seemed as though we had got to the very end of the world. All the bridges were held by Anti-Patriot soldiery.

Mounted gendarmes were galloping backwards and forwards, making the crowd cry out and reel and surge in angry waves. In one moment we would hear a bugle-call, in the next the roll of drums. From the other side of the river came the clatter of troops of horse and the rumbling of gun-carriages. Everywhere there was a dull roar made up of the shoutings of thousands and thousands of voices, with now and then a clear cry rising sharply of "Vive la Nation!" or "Vive le Roi!" And all the while that we were pushing our way slowly through the crowd we could see looming high before us—rising up like the crags of the Luberon—the black mass of the King's Castle outlined against the sky.

Our orders were to cross by the Pont-Saint-Michel; but our leading files halted as they came to the bridge and our drums stopped beating. We all pushed and crowded to the front to see what was the matter; and we found that Commandant Moisson had gone forward alone and was talking with the commander of the detachment of Anti-Patriots by whom the bridge was held. Presently he came back to us, saying that the guard on the bridge had orders to let no one pass—a piece of news that set us to stamping with anger, until the good thought occurred to us to bring up our cannon and clear a passage with a dose of grape.

"Steady, men!" called out our Commandant. "Steady! We mustn't spoil things by going too fast. We have our orders, and we must obey them. Not a shot must be fired until the alarm-cannon gives the signal that the work is to begin."

"And where is this alarm-cannon?" asked Margan; who hardly could speak plainly, he was in such a towering rage.

"It's on the Pont-Neuf," answered our Commandant; "and the bad luck is that it is in the hands of the Anti-Patriots."

"If that's all," said Margan, "I'll start the attack in no time. Anti-Patriots or no Anti-Patriots, I'll fire that gun!"

"Silence!" cried the Commandant. "Trust yourselves to me, men. I promise you that we'll cross at the hour settled on, and that you shall be in the tyrant's house ahead of them all."

But no silence followed the Commandant's order. Everybody fell to chattering about what ought to be done or not done. The whole Battalion was talking at once.

It was in the thick of all this palaver that

Margan and Sergeant Peloux and I broke from the ranks and went out upon the bridge to where the first line of the National Guards barred the way.

Here Pascal stood up, slapped Lou Materoun on the shoulder, and said: "See here, it won't do to have last night's nonsense over again. My brother Lange says he won't come for me again. He says that if I won't come home in good time of my own accord he'll bolt me out. And I know the stuff Lange is made of—he'll do what he says!"

After that there was nothing to wait for and we all got up too. I rose more slowly than the rest, for the cat was asleep on my lap and I did not want to wake her. I laid her down on my little bench so gently that she only half opened her eyes and gave a drowsy gurgling purr, and instantly went off to sleep again. By way of good night, I ran my hand softly over her soft fur; and then, holding fast to my grandfather's breeches, I too went off to bed.

CHAPTER VII.

THE STORMING OF THE KING'S CASTLE.

ALL night long I dreamed of that famous alarm-cannon which Margan had declared he would fire off. The next day I saw old Pascal sitting on the block in front of his mule's stable. I was playing at marbles with oak-galls, all by myself, and I rolled them nearer and nearer to him while I tried to bring up my courage to the point of asking him just one question: "Did they fire it off?" But my courage would not rise so high. I even sent an oak-gall in between his feet; in the hope that he would speak to me as I was getting it, and so would give me a chance to ask that question that was burning the tip of my tongue. I don't think that he even saw me. He certainly took no notice of me. Perhaps his spirit was wandering over the sands of Egypt, or dreaming under a pomegranate tree in Spain.

Night came at last, supper was over, the

lantern was lighted, and I already had my hand on the door-latch. But my grandfather, instead of following me, went down into the cellar by the other door. Presently he came up again carrying a big bottle, holding nearly a gallon, of rich-coloured malmsey. "This is Saint Martin's Eve," said he. "The neighbours will enjoy a good cordial with their Saint Martin's chestnut feast."

A blind man would have known that it was Saint Martin's Eve. From every house came the appetizing savour of roasting chestnuts and the sharp sweet smell of the blazing faggots of thyme; and above the hum of the spinning-wheels we heard the rattling of the chestnuts in the roasting-pans and the laughing shrieks of the girls as the corks popped and burst forth from the bottles of new wine—just brought up from the cellars to be drunk in honour of the good Saint Martin: the patron saint of all honest lovers of a bottle and a glass.

As we entered the shoemaker's shop La Mie called from the depths of the kitchen: "Oh, Pascal, do wait a minute. The chestnuts are almost done," and as she spoke we heard the last of them going off with sharp pops in the pan.

"Don't get excited, La Mie—it's bad for

the blood. I'll wait for you," Pascal answered.

In five minutes she came in with a huge platter of roasted chestnuts—covered snugly with a sack folded four-double so that they would be well steamed—and when she had set it on the stove, and had placed glasses beside my grandfather's bottle on the dresser, all was ready for Saint Martin's feast.

But we still had to wait a little for the story. Just as La Mie had seated herself Lou Materoun said to her: "I don't want to order you about, La Mie, but I wish you'd get me a straw from your broom to clean out my pipe-stem."

"Confound you!" exclaimed La Mie, crossly, as she jumped up to go and get the straw. "Haven't you any broom in your own house ?"

" It's not every house," Lou Materoun answered, " that's as well furnished as this one —where there's not only a broom but also a mop !" *

"You beast of a chatterbox!" cried La Mie, plumping back into her seat. "Find a

---

* *Panoucho* means a cleaning-rag fastened in a handle, and it also means a slut, a dirty woman.

straw for yourself—you shall have none of mine!"

"No matter—my pipe has cleaned itself."

"Mops indeed!" she repeated. "Every one knows that you mop up your floor by dragging your wife around by her hair!"

"I do the best I can, La Mie. I'm not a shoemaker—I haven't a leather strap."

"Oh, hold your tongue, Lou Materoun!" said my grandfather. "We're not here to listen to your clapper clawing. We are here for Pascal's story."

"Yes, Lou Materoun," said old Pascal, "you seem to be working up a little sour—like wine that is going wrong. You'd better keep still for a while and let yourself settle."

And so, order having been restored, old Pascal settled himself on the bench and went on.

Well, as I told you yesterday, Margan and Peloux and I broke from our ranks and went out on the bridge to where the National Guards barred the way. Margan knew French, and by drawing his nose together and speaking through it he could talk just like a Parisian; we being close behind him, he fell to talking away with three men who stood a little in advance of the enemy's line.

But he found in no time that they were not enemies at all. They were good friends of the Nation, and they wanted as much as anybody to make the Revolution a success. Then Margan saw his way to what he wanted (though that was more than we did) and said to them: "Since you are good Patriots, show it by doing what I ask. Lend us your cocked-hats and do you take in place of them our red caps. It will be only for five minutes—while we go up to the Pont-Neuf and come back again. But in that five minutes the Nation will be saved!"

They were good fellows, those Parisians. Without stopping to ask questions they did what Margan wanted, and in the darkness—that they might not be questioned by their companions — they drew away toward our ranks.

Margan did not keep us waiting long to find out what he was driving at. In a low voice, but dead in earnest, he said to us: "If you are good Federals, good Reds of the Midi, you will put on those hats and follow me. We are going to the Pont-Neuf and we'll leave our skins there or we'll fire that gun! Do you,

Peloux, get ready a good fuse that will burn well; and do you, Pascalet, get flint and steel that you may light it when the moment comes. I will tackle the officer in command on the bridge, and while I keep him in talk you must manage between you to touch off the cannon and give the alarm.''

Then we understood, and we were ready to jump for joy! Peloux got out a good fuse —and with it, in case the cannon should need priming, a handful of powder—and turned over to me his flint and steel; and off we started through the darkness and the crowd. In five minutes we had reached the Pont-Neuf, where we were halted with a sharp ''Qui vive ?''

''Friends,'' Margan answered. '' An order from the Commandant of the Pont-Saint-Michel.''

'' Pass !''—and we were on the Pont-Neuf, walking along between two files of the Anti-Patriot guard. But we were safe enough under our blue-plumed cocked-hats. They took no notice of us—and in a moment we had come to the middle of the bridge and were close to the gun. It was trained toward the river, and standing around it were the four men of its crew.

"Attention!" cried Margan, as though he had commanded gunners all his life; and as the men stepped forward—no doubt thinking he was an officer with orders—he pulled a paper out of his pocket, opened it slowly in the dull light that came from the bridge lamp, and held it up as if he were going to read.

Peloux and I did not lose an instant. As the gunners came forward, we slipped into their places; while Margan got out his paper, Peloux made sure of the priming and I struck my flint and steel together and the flying sparks lighted the fuse; and just as Margan held up the paper, as though to read it, we got the burning fuse to the touch-hole, and—Bang!

That gun-shot—only a blank cartridge, that did not even ripple the quiet-flowing river over which it roared—shook the world: for it knocked to pieces the throne of France!

Before even its echo came back from the walls of the King's Castle, every belfry in Paris was ringing out the tocsin of the Revolution. Our own drums—joining with a hundred other drums—began to beat over on the Pont-Saint-Michel. We heard their lively sharp rattle in the same quick-step that so often had cheered and helped us in our long march northward. But what brought tears to our eyes and made

our hearts beat high was hearing our brothers
of the Battalion burst forth with the " Marseillaise " :

Allons enfants de la Patrie,	Onward, children · of our land!
Le jour de gloire est arrivé;	Now the day of glory dawns!
Contre nous de la tyrannie,	Blood-stained banners rise to · flout us
L'étendart sanglant est levé.	Held aloft by tyrant hands!

" Who dared to fire the alarm-gun ? " cried
the officer in command on the bridge, rushing
at us and speaking in a voice hoarse with
rage.

And instantly we three, Margan and Peloux
and I, as though we had settled it all before-
hand, had our pistols levelled at his head and
were shouting " Vive la Nation! "

" Vive la Nation! " shouted the gunners
after us, for they too were good Patriots.

That settled the Commandant—who went
white as a sheet when he saw in front of his
nose the three muzzles of our pistols, and then
turned around and stammered out an order to
his men. But his men, who heard the assembly beating everywhere, had so lost their heads
that they paid no attention to orders; and a
moment later up came the Patriot battalions

from the Faubourg Saint-Marceau and took possession of the Pont-Neuf without striking a blow.

We had done what we came to do, and away we went again to join our fellows on the Pont-Saint-Michel. There we waited for our supporting column, the Patriot troops from the Faubourg de Gloire, while all around us we heard the call of trumpets and the roll of drums.

While we stood there, chafing to go forward, a commotion of some sort—a tremendous pushing and crushing—began in the closely pressed crowd over on the other side of the Pont-au-Change. We heard cries and roars without knowing what they meant—until twenty or thirty Patriots burst out from the crowd and came upon our bridge, dragging along a dead body hacked to pieces and covered with blood. It was the body of the Commandant Général, Mandat. He had no more than begun to issue the orders which were to stop the Patriots than the man to whom Barbaroux had given the pistol stepped forward and blew out his brains.

"Liberty or Death!" we shouted, and all the crowd with us—and then the traitor's body was dragged to the middle of the bridge and tumbled over into the stream. For a moment it whirled around under the arches like the body of a dead dog, and then it was gone. From the Faubourg de Gloire all the way to the Castle rose shouts of "Vive la Nation!" And all the bells, as though they too wanted to shout with us, pealed louder and louder the tocsin of the Revolution.

We heard the rattle of drums advancing from the Faubourg de Gloire, and knew that our support was coming up. "Forward!" cried Commandant Moisson, and off we started to take the lead—for we were determined that the first to march to the attack, and the first to step over the threshold of the King's Castle, should be the Reds of the Midi!

The street of Saint-Honoré, into which we turned, was wild with noise and confusion. Our two drums beat steadily. We sang the "Marseillaise" with all our lungs. The wheels of our gun-carriages and of the forge clanged on the pavement. Behind us the battalions of the Faubourg de Gloire were shouting the "Ça ira" to the rattle of their fourteen drums. All together we went on through the quarter of the Aristocrats like a furious torrent, like a mighty wind.

Now and then a high up window would be opened and a shot fired down at us—but we laughed and marched on. "We can't stop for pop-gun work now," cried long Samat, hoisting still higher his banner of The Rights of Man; "We'll attend to them to-morrow," cried Margan. "Then they shall swallow the same sort of plum-stones that we'll give to the tyrant to-night!"

As we drew closer to the Castle the fire got hotter. Shots kept popping out at us from cellar-windows, from balconies, from the roofs. But nothing stopped us. On we marched, faster and faster—and roaring louder and louder the "Marseillaise."

So we came to the Place du Carrousel, and found it full of Anti-Patriots: grenadiers, pike-men, gendarmes. But they fell back as we advanced. The gendarmes broke in no time. The grenadiers and pikemen held their ground a little better; but as we pressed upon them— with our howling chorus, "Tremble, tyrants! And you, traitors!"—they too gave way. In a moment their ranks were broken and they were crowding back against the iron gates of the Castle court; and in another moment the gates were opened and the whole pack of them, gendarmes, grenadiers, pikemen, had rushed pell-mell inside. The Place du Carrousel was ours!

Our Battalion halted, and we formed our lines in front of the gate of the Cour Royale— the gate that had just banged-to on the backs of the runaway soldiers of the King. We were separated from the Castle only by its three courts—the Cour Royale in front of us, the Cour des Princes to the right, the Cour des Suisses to the left. Day was breaking, and the Castle no longer loomed up before us a mere black mass. We could see it all plainly; and we could see the mattresses piled in the windows, with loop-holes left through which the guards could fire as we came on.

Our support came up—the battalions from the Faubourg de Gloire; the battalions from the Faubourg Saint-Marceau, wearing their plumes of cock's feathers; the Federals from Brest in their red coats—and we greeted each other with shouts of "Vive la Nation!" that rang in the air.

At that instant, as our great shout of Liberty went upward, the first sunrays of that August morning struck upon the highest walls of the Castle; and we saw that the sun was rising, as he had set, blood-red—as though God himself wished to be with us and had given us a sign.

The drums no longer were counted by two

or by fourteen. Two score of them, a hundred of them, were rattling away together the *pas de charge!* No longer was it hundreds but thousands and thousands of voices which were crying together: "Death or Liberty!" Drums and voices rang out so loud and rose up with such tremendous force that the houses and the very stones in the streets were shaken, as though an earthquake had come.

Commandant Moisson went up to the great gate of the Cour Royale, and cried loudly as he struck it three times with the pommel of his sword: "Open, in the name of the People and of Liberty!"

But there was no answer and the door remained shut fast.

I was in the front rank. The Commandant turned to me. "Pascalet," said he, "suppose there were ripe cherries on the other side of that wall. Couldn't you manage to get your share of them?"

There was no need for him to give me an order. I knew what he wanted—and in a moment my gun was slung over my shoulder and I had begun to climb. In another moment, going up lightly as a cat, I was a-straddle of the top of the wall. "What next, Commandant?" I called down.

"Tell me what's going on in there."

"They're all running away like rabbits, Commandant. May I—— ?" and I drew and levelled my pistols. "I could make a splendid double shot!"

"Don't fire! Don't fire!" he cried.

"Well, it's too late now—they're all safe inside. The gendarmes, the green grenadiers, the red Swiss—the whole riff-raff has got safe away.

"No! No!" I went on. "There's still one left—and I do believe it's the King! Hello, Capet, is that you? Pull up or I'll shoot! Oh, it *must* be the King. Shall I fire, Commandant? Oh, mayn't I fire?"

"No, you may not," answered the Commandant sharply.

"He's gone," I said, lowering my pistol. "It's a pity you didn't let me shoot him, Commandant. He certainly was the King. He came out of the little house by the door, and he was splendidly dressed in an embroidered coat and velvet breeches and white silk stockings, and he had silver buckles on his shining shoes. It was the King for sure!"

"Oh you little numskull," laughed the Commandant, while all the men of the Battalion who had heard me laughed too. "Why, that was the porter!"

"Then I'll do his work for him," I cried—and down I dropped into the court, and in ten seconds I had lifted away the bar and drawn the bolts and the gate was open wide. In marched Commandant Moisson and the Battalion after him—and the Reds of the Midi were the first to enter the Castle of the King!

At that very instant—though we did not know it until later—the tyrant and his Austrian woman were running for their lives on the other side of the Castle through the gardens. Liberty came in triumphant, while Despotism slunk away like a fox smoked out of its lair.

But we thought that the King still was inside, and so made our arrangements to hold him fast. Our Battalion, with the Brest Federals, occupied the Cour Royale; the Cour des Princes and the gardens were held by the men from the Faubourg de Gloire; the force from the Faubourg Saint-Marceau took possession of the Cour des Suisses—and so we had the Castle surrounded on all sides.

The King's soldiers were standing ready for us. Along the whole front of the Castle and up the steps leading to the main doorway was a barricade of human flesh—gendarmes, grenadiers, pikemen—that we would have to break our way through; and in front of this line were the black muzzles of fourteen cannon. Inside, the red-coated Swiss filled the hall and the stairway; and on the balconies and at the windows and on the terraces of the garden were posted dukes and counts and marquises, and all the small-fry of the nobility beside. There were ten thousand of them, I suppose, and we had to get rid of them all!

But at first it looked as if there would be no need for a fight. As we entered the court some of the King's gunners shouted "Vive la Nation!," and at the same time some of the Swiss threw us their cartridges in proof that they did not mean to fire. Finding things going so well, and doubting nothing, some of us stooped to pick up the cartridges and others of us went forward to press the hands of the men who were showing themselves to be not the King's servants and our enemies but Patriots and our friends.

But we were going too fast in failing to reckon with the Aristocrats who were looking down at us from their loop-holes with their guns in their hands.

Suddenly there was a deafening crash in the air above us—and from all the windows poured down upon us a hail of balls. At that first volley Commandant Moisson fell with both legs shattered, and seven of our men dead and twenty wounded were lying on the ground.

Our line fell back—but only a few steps and only for a moment. Our Commandant, desperately wounded though he was, rallied us. Raising himself on his arms he shouted "Vive la Nation!"—and at those words our lines steadied, the muzzles of our guns went down as smooth and even as a wind-pressed fence of canes, and at the command "Fire!" we began to pour in upon the traitors in the Castle a steady rain of balls. Before our fire gendarmes and grenadiers and pikemen went down in heaps, blood spirting from their wounds like wine from a cask. Horses fell dead or reared and plunged in the terror caused by their hurts; and bits of stone and plaster came rattling down from the walls.

But we also were getting it. Balls whistled all around us and among us—coming from windows and roofs and balconies, from everywhere all at once! The spat! spat! as they struck the ground was all around me—with that queer softer sound that a bullet makes when it breaks in upon human flesh and bone. I was in mortal terror, and I said to myself: "Oh, oh, oh, poor Pascalet! If you don't die to-day you'll never die at all!"

Right beside me, Samat was struck between the eyes by a ball which blew his head open. He fell upon me, still holding his banner of The Rights of Man. In the thick choking smoke, I did not know what really had happened. I thought that I was wounded—and I felt myself all over to find where I was hurt. But I couldn't find any wound; and then I made out that the heavy weight upon my breast was what was left of poor Samat's head. Well, he was dead—and all I could do for him was to drag his body a little away on one side, close to the foot of a wall.

I set to work with my gun again—though the thick smoke so blinded me that I could not well make out what I was firing at—and fired steadily. At least two thirds of our shots were wasted against the Castle walls. The luck was against us, for the Royalists at the windows and on the balconies could see where to aim and nearly every one of their shots went true—wounding and disabling when it did not kill. And above all the rattle and roar of the firing, above the clatter of the drums, keener even than the sharp words of command, I heard the dreadful cries, the horrible screams of the wounded men. A poor Federal was stretched out in front of me, and as I stepped over him he caught me by the leg and shrieked: "Finish me! Put an end to me. I am choking with a coal of fire!"—and showed me a frightful wound where a ball had crashed through him from breast to side. But I could not kill him, and I pulled myself away from his grasp.

I was ramming down a fresh load into my piece when there came an eddy of wind that thinned the smoke so that I had a view of one of the windows on the floor above. My heart gave a great throb—for in that window I saw Count Robert, gun in hand, firing down on our men! Over his shoulder, in another moment, I saw Surto leaning forward and handing him a fresh-loaded gun.

"Now," thought I, "my time has come! Monster, murderer of my father, it is my turn now!" I levelled my gun at him and took careful aim. He was fairly at the end of my barrel, and my hand was on the trigger. But I couldn't fire. A tremor came over me, and the look that Adeline gave me as I parted from her flashed before my eyes. I had promised her that I would not hurt her brother. I lowered my gun!

But I had made no promises about Surto. He was fair game. But, try as I might, I could not get a shot at him. The coward hid himself so well behind his master that all I could see of him was his arm as he reached foward every moment or so to hand the fresh pieces with which the Count kept up a steady fire.

And while I stood watching for my chance I saw something so startling that I scarcely could believe my eyes. While the Count leaned forward, aiming, Surto's big hand came in sight holding a pistol. In another instant the muzzle of the pistol was close to the back of his master's head. There was a flash—and Count Robert, his head blown to pieces, fell forward across the window-ledge while a stream of blood ran down the wall to the ground.

I was utterly bewildered. I pinched myself to make sure I was not dreaming. But it was no dream. There was the Count's body across the window-sill, his arms flopping down outside. Of Surto I could see nothing. He had fired his traitor shot and run away.

That was no place for stopping to think. While I still was looking up at the window there was the tremendous report of a cannon loaded with grape, and I found myself nearly blinded with smoke while all around me was the sharp whistle of flying balls. Our men

were mowed down like grass. The ground
was strewn with dead and wounded. Our
line broke and we fell back toward the gate—
while the Royalists set up a great cheering of
"Vive le Roi!" and "Vive la Reine!"

Captain Garnier, who had taken command
of the Battalion when our Commandant fell,
was the only one of us who stood firm. He
was clear grit, that man, and he showed his
grit then. He did not fall back a single step.
There in the whirling smoke, among the dead
and wounded, he stood alone. We saw him
wave his sword, and we heard him cry: "To
me, men of Marseilles!"

And then came another shout, but from our
rear. Our old gunner Peloux had not yet had
a chance to make his dogs bark, and it was his
voice that we heard. "Room for the guns!"
he shouted. "You call yourselves Marseilles
Patriots and back down before Parisian Aristocrats! I'll teach you how to get rid of Anti-
Patriots. Let me get at them with these
bronze squirts of mine. Out of the way, all
of you! Room for the guns!"

The coolness of our Captain and our gunner put us to shame. Our panic was ended
and we grew steady again. Some of us made
a clear path by dragging aside the dead and

wounded, while others tailed-on to the ropes or tugged at the wheels of the guns. In no time we had them both, loaded as they were to the muzzle with grape, planted right in front of the great entrance to the Castle. Through the thinning smoke we could see clustered on the steps the grenadiers in their hairy caps; and behind them, in the vestibule, the red-coated Swiss were crowded like a swarm of bees. They fired on us steadily. The black entrance was bright with the flash of their pieces. It was like the mouth of hell.

But Peloux paid no attention at all to the balls that went whistling around him—ploughing up the earth, knocking big splinters out of the gun-carriages, making long silvery streaks on the bronze guns. Without in the least hurrying himself, he trained the muzzles of both pieces straight toward the doorway, carefully primed them, and flourished his linstock to bring it to a glow. In his easy-going, devil-may-care way, when all was ready, he mockingly took off his hat and bowed to the Castle; and as he touched off his cannon he cried mockingly, as though he had been emptying slops out of a window: "Look out below!"

Bang! went the first gun, spitting out

grape on the Swiss and grenadiers and cutting a swath like a scythe-stroke in a clover-field! It was our turn to roar then, and we yelled "Vive la Nation!" at the top of our lungs.

As the smoke cleared away a little we saw our harvest of dead and wounded. The steps were strewn with fallen men. The grenadiers had broken and were crowding back into the Castle upon the Swiss, while some of them were squeezing down into the cellar-windows or running toward the garden.

"Té!" shouted Peloux. "They don't like the way our guns spit. Wait for the other one!" He blew up his linstock, made another mocking bow, and cried: "Look out behind, gentlemen!"—and so fired the second gun through the doorway of the Castle right into the thick of the crowd. Soldiers of all colours, red, green, white and blue, fell dying in heaps.

That time it was the Aristocrats who were panic-struck. They stopped firing at us from the doorway, and we had only the peppering of shots from the windows above. Our drums, which had stopped beating when we were driven back, broke out loudly with the old quick-step; Captain Garnier, rushing ahead of us, shouted "Forward!"; and with lowered bayonets we charged up the steps into the Castle—the hornet's nest, the snake's lair!

"Oh, the devil!" cried Margan, as he plunged into the thick of it with his head down, like a bull broken loose in the city streets. "Now we're going to get pitch-forks in our hides!"

And pockmarked Margan was right, so we were! All the way up those stairs it was nothing but sword points and bayonets. The grenadiers and Swiss stood four men to a step, giving us cut and thrust as we came on—and the others higher up poured on us a steady fire. At each step four men had to be got rid of by bayonet, sword or pistol.

It was slow work. But with Captain Garnier and Margan to set the pace there was no balking. Vauclair was close up with them. We all set our bayonets and pressed forward.

Peloux, who made fun of everything, pointed to the red coats of the Swiss mixed in with the green coats of the Grenadiers and called out: "Hello, boys, we're going to pick tomatoes! Forward, all who like tomatoes!" and as he spoke, he let fly into the crowd above us two grenades which went off with a tremendous noise.

That was the turning point of our fight on the staircase. Through the blinding smoke we could hear the crash of broken glass that followed the bursting of the grenades, and then the groans of the wounded. We surged forward, yelling "Vive la Nation!," with such a rush that the steps trembled under us. The explosion, the shouts, the trembling of the stones, made the Anti-Patriots believe that the staircase was breaking down under them—and suddenly there was a rush and a crush and a scamper that can not be told!

Some of the poor Swiss, losing their heads, flung themselves down upon our bayonets or jumped over the balusters and broke their bones on the stone pavement below. They no longer kept a steady front against us, and upward we went—spitting with our bayonets and slinging behind us those of them who did stand firm, and who cried in the very moment they got their death-thrust "Vive le Roi!" Vive la Reine!" As we killed them, these men did not seem to weigh an ounce. We stuck them through and tossed them behind us as though we had been turning sheaves on a threshing-floor. Margan was right, it was pitchfork work indeed!

We got up almost to the first story; but it

seemed as if the more men we got rid of the more sprang up before us. We were covered with blood from our heads to our heels. Blood was pouring down the staircase as though hogsheads of wine had been stove-in above. My wrists were strained and sore. My bayonet was bent by all the bones it had struck against in breasts and thighs.

It was Peloux who cleared away the group at the head of the stairway with a couple more of his grenades. There was another tremendous crash as the grenades exploded; and then most of the Royalists left alive, and with legs to carry them, scattered like a suddenly discovered nest of rats and made off for the King's apartment.

A few of them, seeing that fighting was useless, surrendered; and some of these we spared. The poor Swiss, who only were doing their duty, were given their lives; and so were the wretched National Guards—the men of the people, as we knew by their rough shirts and hard hands, who were fighting us against their will. But it was another matter with the sprigs of nobility, the counts and marquises with their lace jabots and their silk-tied queues. For them there was no mercy. It was a knock on the head or a span of cold steel in their breasts—and then out of the window to Coblentz!

Our catechism was a short one. "Ah, you are one of the people. Good. Shout 'Vive la Nation!' Be a good Patriot. Go your way!" Or it would be: "Ah, you wear silk stockings and your hair is powdered. Good. Swallow this plum!" and crack would go a pistol-ball through his skull. I tell you it was a good thing on that Tenth of August to wear a coarse shirt and have rough hands!

For two hours and more the good work went on. We hunted everywhere: in passages and in parlours, in big rooms and in little rooms; in garrets and in lofts. And everywhere we found people hidden away so frightened that they didn't dare to call their souls their own. We routed them out from closets, from on top of wardrobes, from under beds; we dragged them down from chimneys; we caught them stowed away in the rafters under the tiles; we chased them over the roof.

At last, when we thought we had cleared out the whole place, we came to a landing between two stairways where an Aristo was standing guard before a bolted door. He was a brave fellow, that Aristo. "Halt," he cried.

"You can't enter here!"—and he cracked off his pistol and the ball cut through Margan's cap and just shaved his skull. Yet it was Margan who saved his life for him. The rest of us would have finished him in no time; but Margan stood by him and we let him go— although the pig-head could not be made to cry "Vive la Nation!" at any price at all!

We bounced him down stairs, and as we burst the door open there were cries and screams from within. In the room we found three grand court ladies, and a younger lady as lovely as the day, all dressed in silks and laces. The oldest of them called to us to save from death her niece, meaning the beautiful young lady, and said that if any one must die it should be herself—and as she spoke she went down on her knees before us and bared her breast to our swords.

Her devotion moved us and filled us with wonder. Captain Garnier made short work of the matter. He caught the lady's hand and pulled her to her feet, saying: "Get up, hussy! The nation has no need for your life" —and then he detailed four men to escort the women to some place where they would be safe.

Those, certainly, were the last of the traitor

Aristos left in the Castle. It was midday, and the fight was at an end. There was not a whole pane of glass left in the windows. Everywhere the doors which we had burst in were lying flat or hanging crazily on their broken hinges. The furniture was tossed and tumbled everywhere. The carpets, the walls, the hangings, were splashed with blood. Dead men were lying around everywhere on the floors. In one of the front rooms I saw the body of Count Robert still hanging across the window-ledge, just as he fell at Surto's traitor shot.

We entered the King's apartment, all hung with white and blue. "See, that's his portrait up there!" said Margan—and in a moment he had snatched it off the wall and flung it on the floor. We joined hands and danced a farandole around it, each of us as we passed spitting on the tyrant's face, and all of us roaring out

> Dansons la Carmagnole,
> Vive le son du canon!

Since our supper of the night before not one of us had had bite or sup. Yet we went on as though we were drunk, hugging and kissing the brave Federals of Brest and the Patriots from the Faubourg de Gloire and dragging them into our farandole. And so, farandoling, we all went on into the apartment of the Queen.

There all was gold and silk, and.mirrors covering the walls to the very ceiling, and pictures to take your breath away, and curtains and laces, and carpets as soft as down. And all had a sweet delightful smell. Margan caught hold of the bed and dragged it into the middle of the room; and as he tumbled and rolled on it we took up our crazy round again and danced about him singing the worst thing we could think of to sing:

> Fai, fai, fai te lou tegne blu, panturlo!
> Fai, fai, fai te lou tegne blu!

It was while I was in the midst of this dance that I suddenly fell to wondering what had become of Vauclair. Could he be wounded, I thought, or—dead! The thought made me shiver. I dropped from the round and ran searching for him through the rooms—stopping now and then to turn over a dead man, lying face downward on the floor, to make sure that it was not my friend. I looked out from the windows upon the courts, the terraces, the gardens. I saw National Guards in plenty, crowds of Patriots, some even of our own men. They were helping the wounded or they were hugging each other and crying and laughing. But I did not see Vauclair.

But from one of the windows, looking down upon a corner of the gardens cut off from the rest by a thick hedge of laurel, I did see a very strange and dreadful sight. There was old Planchot, drawn close against the wall, standing straight up and watching a cellar-window as a cat watches a rat hole. Some poor Swiss, who had taken refuge in the cellar when they saw how all had gone wrong, were trying to get out by the window and so give their legs a chance to save their skins. Poor wretches! As soon as one of them stuck out his head—crack! Planchot's axe split his skull! And then Planchot's hands dragged him out and laid him on one side. The game evidently had been going on for some time, for there was a ghastly heap of bodies; and in the midst of all this carnage Planchot was fairly chuckling with delight. It was a sight so frightful that it made my blood run cold.

While I stood watching him, rny eyes held fast by horror, I saw another sight that, while not so dreadful, was still more strange. There stepped out from behind the laurel hedge a big man, wearing the uniform of the National

Guard, who went straight up to Planchot and spoke to him. For a moment I felt dazed and everything whirled around me; for the big man—there could be no mistake about it—was Surto; and to see Surto in that dress, and talking that way to Planchot, seemed to me to see about the most impossible thing in the world!

But my wits did not stay long wool-gathering. "Oh you miserable dog! Oh you murderer!" I cried, "I've got you at last!" And I sprang back from the window and rushed down the stairway four steps at a time, pistol in hand.

Half way down I plumped into a man coming up. It was Vauclair, who was looking for me as I had been looking for him. "Hello, Pascalet!" said he, "what's the matter? Where are you bound in such a hurry? You look as wild-eyed as if you had seen a ghost!"

I did not let him stop me. "Come along! Come along!" I shouted back. "Surto's down there with Planchot. I'm going to kill him like a mad dog!"

Vauclair turned and came tearing down after me, and followed me through rooms and passages until we got out of doors. We ran round the Castle, and presently I found the place that I was looking for. There was the laurel hedge; there were the dead Swiss lying in a pile as Planchot had thrown them—but as for Planchot and Surto, they had vanished like smoke!

I was wild, crazy, my eyes were starting out of my head, in the same breath I wept and cursed with rage. Vauclair looked at me queerly, and then with a kind touch laid his hand on my arm. "Come, come, Pascalet," he said, "your eyes have played a trick on you. You are weak for want of food and your wits are not steady. The boys are waiting for us. There, don't you hear the drums beating the recall? Come!"

I let him lead me away, but I knew that my eyes had not played a trick on me and that my wits were all right. There was the laurel hedge; there was the cellar-window; up above was the window out of which I had seen Planchot and Surto as plainly as ever I saw anybody in my life. As we walked away I kept looking back over my shoulder in the hope that Surto might show again, but the place was bare.

The men of the Faubourg Saint-Marceau were assembling in the Gardens, and the men of the Faubourg de Gloire in the Place du

Carrousel. We followed the call of our own drums to the Cour Royale. There we found Captain Garnier, a bloody handkerchief wrapped round his hand, getting the Battalion into line, and Vauclair and I fell in. Our men were shaking hands over their good luck in coming through the fight alive, and telling each other what they had done in it, and sorrowing over the wounded and dead.

At the first calling of the roll only two hundred of us answered to our names; but stragglers came in every moment to fill some of the vacant places in the ranks. Many of our men had been detailed to take prisoners to the National Assembly, and others had gone there of their own accord to deposit valuables which they had found. When I met Vauclair on the stairs he had just come back from taking to the Assembly a purse full of gold louis d'ors which he had found on the floor of the King's apartment. Others had taken jewels left scattered on the carpets or lying on the smashed furniture. Tears of joy rolled down our cheeks as each new man took his place in the ranks.

When some time had passed without the return of more of our comrades, Captain Garnier again called the roll—slowly, company by company. When a name was called to which there was no answer the drums rolled mournfully—and that meant: " He died for Liberty!" Two hundred out of five hundred men were missing. As we found later, twenty of these were dead, and one hundred and eighty wounded.

While this sad roll-call went on the National Guards had brought biers and were carrying off the dead bodies scattered everywhere in the courts and gardens and inside the Castle. They lifted up poor Samat from the place against the wall to which I had dragged him in the morning, and as they brought him toward us the Battalion presented arms. Sobs choked us and tears blinded us. In a moment we had broken ranks and had surrounded our poor dead comrade, crying like children. Each one of us in turn kissed the poor cold hand hanging from the bier: that Patriot hand that for two hundred leagues had carried, as though it had been the Host, the Declaration of the Rights of Man.

As we fell back into line and stood ready to march I felt something warm, like a little stream of warm water, trickling down into my shoe; and for a moment I felt sick and faint and a flash of lightning seemed to pass before my eyes. I looked down to see what was happening to my foot and what it was that felt warm—and, behold! it was my own blood dropping down in big drops like great red currants from my little finger! How queer it was! I did not in the least remember being wounded. I couldn't help calling out: "See! See! The first joint of my little finger has been shot away!"

I was so delighted to think that I really had been wounded in the fight that I jumped up and down with joy—just as a cat does when she feels the weather is going to change. "I'm wounded, I'm wounded, too! Vive la Nation!" I cried—and I held up my bleeding stump so that everybody could see I'd been hit. Our men all burst out laughing at me, and at my joy that the tip of one of my fingers had been shot off.

But what was queerer than my having been hit without knowing it was that as soon as I did know it my finger began to throb and smart with pain. But I did with it what I had been used to do when I smashed my paws in cracking almonds—I put it into my mouth and sucked it; and so, feeling like a hero and looking like a finger-sucking baby, off I marched with the Battalion to the barracks.

Our work was over and we were free to

rest ourselves and have a good time. Away
we marched, our men singing the holy chant
of Liberty:

> Allons enfants de la Patrie,
> Le jour de gloire est arrivé!

But I couldn't sing because I had my finger in
my mouth! I could only comfort myself by seeing all along the Rue Saint-Honoré the proof of
how the Paris people had changed their tune. In
that very street, the night before, they had fired
at us from the windows and stoned us from the
roofs; and as we marched back by daylight
the same windows and roofs were crowded
with men, women and children welcoming us
with shouts of "Vive les Marseillais!"

Oh, but it was fun to see the fat shopmen
bowing and scraping to us in their doorways
and to hear them cheering us—while they sent
painters scampering up long ladders to daub
out in a hurry the fleur-de-lys, and the Royal
arms, and all the Anti-Patriot stuff they had
stuck on their signs! Out came "Vive le
Roi!" and "Vive la Reine!" and "Devil take
the Nation!"—and in their place came "Down
with the tyrant!" and "Vive la Nation!" and
"Vive les Marseillais!"

As we came to the Arcade Saint-Jean the
crowd grew so thick in front of us that we

scarcely could make our way through it; and then we found that it was dammed up against the section of the National Guard of Paris commanded by the famous Santerre. There, in that place so far away from the King's Castle, we found that Santerre's precious National Guard had spent all the night and all the morning— ready to join the winning side as soon as they knew which it was! There they waited, ready to greet us with open arms or to fall on us and kill us for rebels, just as our luck at the Castle should decide. And as luck had been with us —as they knew that the Castle was in ruins and the throne upset and the King the people's prisoner—they stuck their hats on their bayonets and came toward us shouting with the crowd: "Vive les Marseillais!"

But we weren't exactly idiots, and we said to ourselves: "These Parisians are a nice lot— we opened the door, and now they want to push in ahead of us and be greater Revolutionists than we! Prudent Monsieur Santerre, who always had a thorn in his foot when we wanted him to go ahead with us, now wants to get in front of the whole procession! To-morrow it will be Santerre who has thrown down the tyrant and saved the country all by himself!" And in our thoughts we added:

"If only he doesn't go and spoil all we have begun so well!"

Already the jackals were at work. Crowds of pilfering good-for-nothings, ragged scamps, drunken and dishevelled women, even National Guards, were robbing the houses and churches and palaces. And the tigers were at work, too. We met strings of people getting hauled along to prison tied fast like thieves—priests, nobles, honest middle-class folk, all half-dead with fear. The only charge against them was that they were Anti-Patriots; or, if not quite Anti-Patriots, that they were so far behind the times as still to have some respect left for their King and their Queen. We, the Reds of the Midi—who had been cried out at for brigands, for galley-slaves escaped from Toulon—would have thought it quite enough to have made them shout "Vive la Nation!" and then go their ways. But these Parisians who had shirked the real fighting, who had let us all by ourselves save the country and The Rights of Man, felt that they must draw blood from the Aristocrats in order to wash out their shame. By the time that we reached our barracks, that is to say by the middle of the afternoon, all of the Paris prisons were full of Aristocrats or of poor wretches who were taken for Aristocrats. We had believed that we were opening the gates for Liberty to enter in and possess the land; and, behold! we had let loose the foxes of rapine and the wolves of revenge and the scorpions of hate! I, who was then but a boy, saw it all only too well.

When we got to our barracks we had all the bread and wine that we wanted, and we just stuffed till we were packed full. And as I still had by me two heads of garlic I made the best meal of them all. Good-hearted Margan had tied up my finger, with a bit of amadou that stopped the bleeding, and I was all right after my first swallow of wine.

Vauclair and I kept looking at each other while we were eating; and I knew that he was thinking, just as I was, how glad Lazuli and Adeline and Clairet would be to see us safe and sound. Before we had fairly finished he said to me: "Well, Pascalet, you know who wants to see us. How do you feel about going home?"

How did I feel? The words were barely out of his mouth before I had given a last kiss to my bottle, wiped my lips on my sleeve, clacked my tongue, and stood up ready to start!

All the way from our barracks to the Impasse Guémenée we had to push our way through a yelling, frightful crowd. The streets were full of people half drunk or half crazy, all flourishing swords and pikes and all screaming and shouting. But our uniform made us sure of a welcome everywhere as we went along. The very people who the day before had stabbed us with looks of hate were the first to cry "Vive les Marseillais!"

At last we reached Planchot's door, and Planchot's wife and Lazuli and Adeline and Clairet were all there ready to open to our knock and call. Vauclair and Lazuli threw themselves into each other's arms; I caught Adeline to me and kissed her as though she had been my sister; and little Clairet hugged away at his father's leg.

But there was no Planchot to greet Janetoun. When she found that he was not with us she covered her face with her apron and burst forth into lamentations and sobs and groans. "They have killed my Planchot!" she cried. "I ought never to have let him go. Who will give me back my Planchot?" And down she fell on the bench and then rolled off and lay among the shavings on the floor. To tell the truth, we all were so much taken up with our own affairs that we paid no attention to her.

And it did not matter; for while we still were kissing each other the door flew open and Planchot came in. He was frightful to behold. He held his bloody axe in his hand, and was so covered with blood from head to foot that at first his wife did not know him. Not until she had taken a long look at him did she scream out: "It is indeed my Planchot!" But she did not venture to touch him. "What has happened to you? Where are you wounded? Has some one killed a pig and tumbled you into the tub of blood?"

"I am not wounded anywhere," Planchot answered; "but my wrist is a good deal strained. That axe, just as you see it there, has cracked the skulls of seventeen Aristos. Yes, I, Planchot, I all by myself made a heap of dead bodies that I believe would fill up this room! And afterward, with the help of a good Patriot who joined himself to me, I was able to catch and to deliver over to the people all the nobles and Anti-Patriots here in our Quarter. It is only a moment since I gave up the last one, a noble in the Rue des Douze Portes, the Marquis of—of—— Devil take his name, it makes no difference what it was. Oh there will be plenty of heads for our holy guillotines!"

"Oh Blessed Mary help!" cried Adeline; and as she spoke she fell back pale as death.

"Hold your tongue, Planchot!" cried Vauclair. "Don't you see you are frightening that child out of her wits?"

Planchot's wife had thrown her apron over her head again and was rocking back and forth saying: "Oh, it can't be possible! It can't be possible! It can't be my man who has done such things!"

Planchot was delighted with having so terrified his wife; but as he wiped his bloody hands with shavings he said, gently: "Yes, the poor little girl is faint. If I had known it would hurt her I wouldn't have said a word. Get some orange-flower water, wife. She'll soon come to."

Janetoun and Lazuli and I, together, carried Adeline up stairs and laid her on Lazuli's bed; for that very morning her own had gone off with the rest of the guillotines. When we had left the room, as Vauclair told me afterward, Planchot went on: "It's really too bad about her, poor child! But how could I know that what I was saying would upset her so? It's lucky I didn't tell about the horrible big woman who wanted to bleed the little Marquis with her pig-sticking knife. I stopped that game, however.   We must draw the line somewhere, and I wouldn't let her do it—the dirty jade! "

" A big woman with a pig-sticking knife," broke in Vauclair.   "What was her name, Planchot?   Was it La Jacarasse ? "

" Why yes, La Jacarasse.   That was the name, sure enough," Planchot answered.

" Then shame to you, miserable man that you are! " cried Vauclair.   " It must have been the Marquis d'Ambrun that you delivered up. And as to that famous Patriot who was helping you, he is the servant of the Marquis—a murderous dog of a German who only this morning was fighting against us at the King's Castle—no Patriot at all.   He is the lover of the Marquise, and he has betrayed his master to death so that he may steal safely his wealth as well as his wife.   Is it possible that you, Planchot, honest Planchot, Planchot la Liberté as the Companions call you—can it be that you have lent a helping hand to that Anti-Patriot hound ? "

Planchot frowned and shook his head in answer to all this abuse; but all that he said in reply to it was: " Are you sure that what you tell me is true ? "

" I am as sure that it is true," Vauclair answered, " as I am sure that I have on my hand four fingers and a thumb. Pascalet can prove it to you, for this German, this fellow Surto, twice has tried to kill him. And I must tell you another thing, Planchot—it is no time for concealments, now, and you shall know the whole truth. Adeline, the dear good girl who is with us, is not our child: she is the unhappy daughter of this very Marquis d'Ambrun. We saved her out of the clutches of La Jacarasse. Her own mother and Surto had given her to that beast of a woman to do anything with—they did not care what—that would put her out of the way. What do you think of that, Planchot?"

"What do I think?" cried Planchot, sputtering with anger as he picked up his axe. "Why, I think I have done just what I ought to have done. And I don't see why I shouldn't crack your head open with my axe now that I know how you have tricked me into having an Aristocrat's daughter in my house!"

"And I," answered Vauclair, as he stuck the muzzle of his pistol between Planchot's eyes, "would blow your brains out did I not know that you would come with me and with Pascalet to rescue the Marquis d'Ambrun, and to deliver up in his place Surto the murderer and the abominable Jacarasse."

Planchot had plumped down on the shavings when he saw the pistol levelled at him, but Vauclair kept it pointed straight at his face. Trembling with fear he answered: "Don't point that thing at me. I will do whatever you please. But it's too late now to rescue the Marquis. Paris is full of prisons—and how can we ever find the one that he's in? And there's nobody in the house any longer. The German—if he is a German—and La Jacarasse, and another woman who said she was the German's wife—it must have been the Marquise, I suppose—were clearing everything out of it while we were tying the Marquis to take him off; and when we left they left, too. How are we ever going to find them, either, I should like to know? I tell you the track's lost."

"All this is worse and worse," said Vauclair. "You say yourself that you saw them ransacking the house and carrying off the valuables. Why, surely, that must have opened your eyes? Is it possible that a Patriot like Planchot could have had a hand in such doings? What, Planchot, my old master Planchot, a robber!"

That word robber was too much for Planchot. His axe fell from his hand and his eyes filled with tears. "Forgive me, Vauclair," he said; "and don't say a word about what has happened before my wife. I am a wicked wretch. I neither thought nor reasoned. What can I do to set things right?"

"You can help Adeline to find her father again, and to get back again what you helped Surto and La Jacarasse to steal."

"So I will," Planchot answered. "You are entirely right in the whole matter, Vauclair. What could I have been thinking of? I, Planchot la Liberté; I, who never wronged any one of so much as a sou, am to-day no better than a robber. To-night, to-morrow, the day after to-morrow, as long as I have breath in my body, I will work to clean away this black spot from my name. I swear to you, Vauclair, that I will search all Paris, house by house, to find Adeline's father alive or dead— and to find those robbers, Surto and his harlot marquise and La Jacarasse."

At seeing his old master so broken down by shame and sorrow Vauclair was almost as much moved as Planchot was himself. When I came down stairs I found them hugging each other with tears in their eyes.

And then we held a sort of council of war together and settled on what we were to do and how it best might be done.

From that day on the three of us had but one hope and one aim: to find for Adeline, who lay almost dying of grief and horror, her father and at the same time to find and to punish the three robbers who had stolen her heritage.

I will not try to tell you the whole long story of how day after day we tramped over Paris on our search; often starting out before daylight and hunting until night. We divided the city among us, and each of the three hunted through his own part street by street; asking such questions as we dared to ask, listening for bits of talk that might put us on the scent, looking always for the lair of the three murderers and for the prison in which the old Marquis was shut up waiting for his death. We would get back home at night tired out, more dead than alive; and then we would have to make up a story full of big lies to comfort poor Adeline.

Fortunately, Adeline only knew that her father had been cast into prison. She did not know that Surto had murdered her brother, and she thought that her mother still lived in the house in the Rue des Douze Portes and waited in sorrow for her to be found and brought home. We let her keep on believing this, and every night we promised her that

the next morning we would take her to her
mother. When the morning came we would
find a reason for keeping her with us for yet
another day. As the time passed, and hope
seemed to have forgotten her, she grew thinner
and still more pale.

But in spite of the pain that it gave me to
see her sorrow, and in spite of my dread of the
day when she would have to know all and
might fall dead of grief and horror, I loved the
time that I spent with her in Planchot's little
house in the Impasse Guémenée. Each night
at supper she waited on me and cut up my
bread; but before supper, and that was most
delightful of all, she cared for my wounded
hand. Very gently she would unwrap the
bandage and put on fresh lint—her delicate
hands touching me with a touch as soft as if
she had on silk gloves. As she bent forward
to wrap the bandage I would see the curve of
her slender neck, and her lovely hair would come
close to my lips. Then she would take a big
handkerchief and fold it into a sling, and in
order to tie the sling properly she would have
to put her arms around my neck as though she
were going to embrace me. Her sweet mouth
would be just in front of my mouth, while her
frank gentle eyes looking straight into mine

would make my eyelids fall. Sometimes her loose curling hair would brush my cheek; and as I felt its soft play, and still more as I felt the sweet weight of her arms on my shoulders, thrills of exquisite delight would run through me—which I never tried to explain, but only enjoyed.

For days this troubled and weary life, that yet had in it for me so much happiness, went on and on. We found nothing that could put us on the track of the wretches we sought; we found no trace of the poor old Marquis; we had no news to give Adeline that would at all quiet and comfort her. We saw that soon we would have to tell her the whole truth.

At last the time for truth-telling came. It could be put off no longer—for the Marseilles Battalion was to be paid-off and discharged. The work that we had come to do was done, and well done. Pay for the time we had served in Paris had been voted to us by the National Assembly, and when that pay was in our pockets all would be over with the Battalion and we would be free to go back again into the South.

On the eve of the pay-day we held a whispered council in Planchot's shop, and there the matter was settled. It was decided that while Vauclair and I went to get our money the women should tell poor Adeline everything, and should make her understand that the best and only safe thing for her to do was to go back with us to Avignon and share our bread until better times should come.

I left the house very early in the morning that I might certainly be out of the way when Adeline's cry of pain should break forth. Only to think of it broke my heart.

I was at the barracks before Vauclair had left the Impasse Guémenée; and the sun was just gilding the eaves of the houses as I fell in with Margan and Peloux and a half dozen other gay Federals—all of whom, as soon as they saw me, held up their pouches and jingled the seven crowns they had just received.

"Hurry up, kid!" cried Margan. "Make your grab, and then come along with us. We're off for a good time. We mean to see some of the sights of this big village before we leave it for good!"

They took me to a corner of the barracks where I found a sergeant of the Battalion, and with him a paymaster who tinkled seven silver crowns into each Federal's hand. I got into the line, and presently I too was paid; and when I saw those seven silver quoits—which slid about among my fingers like eels as I tried holding them first in one hand and then in both—I did not know what to think of myself nor where to put my riches. But Margan, who was in a hurry to start off for his good time, slipped my money into my pocket for me; and then, as he caught me under the arm, he called out: "Forward, march! Now we'll set sail and cut up high!"—and off we all went together, arm in arm and taking up the whole width of the street.

At the first cabaret with a red cap over the door we went in and called for brandied grapes —which set us to cackling away like so many hens after egg-laying as we walked along. We hadn't the least notion where we were going, but that made no difference at all. The next tavern we came to, in we all went and had two or three glasses all around of some fiery stuff. Then we cocked our caps over our ears and off we went again. Everywhere the Parisians, at sight of our uniform, made way for us. Since the Tenth of August they had taken good care when they saw a Marseillais coming to make room for him by standing with their backs against the wall!

We crossed the river and went through the

Place du Carrousel, and as we passed the tyrant's Castle we roared out together:

Tremblez, tyrans, et vous perfides!

But for all that I was having such a good time, every now and then the thought of Adeline in her trouble would come back to me and give a sharp tug at my heart.

Presently we came to another tavern, over the door of which was the sign: "A la galère d'Avignon."

"This is the place we've been looking for!" shouted Margan. "We'll go right in. Here we can get wine from the Crau, and black olives, and cod-fish fried in olive-oil from Aix."

We were all sharp set by that time, and in we crowded in a bunch.

Getting in there was like getting home. The hostess was a jolly girl from Aramon who had been carried off to Paris by one of the King's salt-tax collectors. She made us welcome with a will, setting out good strong wine with white bread and a pot of olives to stay our stomachs until the fricassee should be ready, and all the while chattering away to us in Provençal. In a twinkling we had bolted the wine and bread and olives and had called for more, and while we were eating the second round there came to us from the kitchen a delightful tasty smell as the oil bubbled and snapped in the pan. At last in came our hostess, her cheeks as red as tomatoes, carrying a great dish of cod-fish as yellow as gold. The pieces were at least two inches thick, and as the knife touched them they fell apart in flakes like flints. With a dash of vinegar it was all that a man could desire!

Peloux, to be sure, said that perhaps it was a little too salt. But Margan took him up short. "Salt's all right," said he. "It's good for cuts, and it makes a body dry."

That salt cod-fish did make us dry! We poured down glass after glass of red wine from the Crau, and after that of white wine from Sainte Cécile. Then we took to strong brandy and quince cordial; and we ended off by drinking all the home-made cordials that the Aramon girl had in her house.

While we were sitting there, filling ourselves up like hogsheads, carts full of Aristocrats began to go rumbling by—on their way to Versailles, somebody said, because the prisons of Paris were jammed full. A howling crowd of men and women and children surrounded the carts, shaking their fists at the prisoners and throwing mud at them.   At sight of all this we paid our bill in a hurry; and out we went again, arm in arm, to see what was going on.

Behind the carts came another sort of procession.   At the head of it was a woman beating a drum, hitting the case much oftener than she did the drumhead; then came another woman, wearing a red cap and carrying a head stuck on a pike, and then a crowd of sans-culottes shouting the "Ça ira."

We turned to go with the crowd; but when I saw that the head on the pike was that of a fair-haired woman, young and beautiful, everything suddenly seemed to go whirling around.   I remembered my Adeline left unguarded—what if anything should happen to her!   Peloux and the rest had joined in the "Ça ira," and to hide my feelings I tried to sing too.   But I couldn't.   I burst into tears and scarcely could get along.

Margan was the first to see that there was anything wrong with me.   "Dear! Dear!" said he.   "The kid's crying.   His drink makes him dismal."   And then, by way of comforting me, I suppose, he and Peloux caught me under the arms and began to jump me up and down to the tune of the "Ça ira."

We came out on an open space on one side of which was a high tower. Here the crowd began to dance about, yelling; while the more furious shook their fists at the grated windows —for inside that tower the King and his family were prisoners. The woman carrying the head on the pike—it was the head of the Princesse de Lamballe, I heard the people around me in the crowd saying—took it close up to the tower and held it as high as she could reach toward the window, while she screamed out: "Come down, you wretched old blackguard of a Capet and kiss this jade. And tell your Austrian that her head will grin on a pike to-morrow as this one grins to-day!" And then the hag suddenly lowered her pike and smeared a handful of mud over the poor pretty dead woman's face.

But what was still worse, just then another brute of a woman went close to the window and held up before it the Princesse de Lamballe's still bleeding heart.

Even Peloux, who never was shocked at anything, couldn't stand that. But he didn't like to own up to what was the matter, and so he made an excuse. "See here, Margan," he said, "my throat's as dry as tinder. Let's go somewhere where I can wet it."

"All right," we answered in a breath, glad enough to get away; and then in we trooped to a tavern called the "Révolution" where we kissed a good many more glasses of red wine and white. As night came on, and we got hungry again, we had a grand *crespèu* for supper; and then, while we went on drinking, Margan sang us a song of his own—that he had composed in French, he said, on purpose to make the Parisians stare. And they did stare, I can tell you! Off he went with the first two verses, telling how the Aristocrats came forth from their villages in all their finery to save their King and Queen:

> Quand je partions de nos villages
>   J'étions fringants,
> J'étions vêtus de pied en cape
>   Comme galants.
>
> Je portions des chapeaux de paille
>   Large et pointus
> Avecque des coucardes noires
>   De papier blu!

How the Parisians did clap and stamp and shout! But when Margan came to his last verse, in which he told how the Marseilles men were too much for the Aristocrats, they made him sing it over and over again!

Pour aparer le roi, la reine
J'étions venus,
Mais le bataioun de Marseille
Nous a battus!

As for me, my poor head was going round and round, and the lights were dancing before me, and I didn't know in the least what I was doing or where I was. I took Peloux for Vauclair, and I babbled on in a stream of talk to him; yet all the while feeling that the words I was saying didn't mean what I wanted to say. The others were in much the same fix; and by the time that Margan had got through with about the twentieth singing of his third verse we all felt that we had had drink enough —and something to spare!

Out we went into the streets once more; but we could not walk straight, and at one moment we banged against the wall and the next we stumbled along in the midway gutter. Drink had driven all sense out of me and I can't remember in the least a single street that we passed through. My comrades must have kept a few gleams of sense about them, for they managed to get themselves and me into a great big house, all full of lights, that I found out afterward was a theatre. All that I can remember about it is that I saw a big handsome woman in a lace dress—so thin that she might have left it off without anybody's noticing much difference—who shrieked out a song in a way to make your ears tingle, and who all the time she was singing twisted about and shook herself as a dog does when he has a bone caught in his jaws. And when she got through everybody clapped and clapped as if it had been the loveliest song in the world.

When she had finished her howling, Margan shouted: "Come along, boys! Let's show the young lady an Avignon round!" and then in the midst of the astounded audience standing in the pit, we danced the craziest round to the ribald "Fai, fai, fai!"

Just as on a sunny day in summer the little whirlwinds strike the threshing-floor, gathering up for a moment a column of dust and husks and then going as suddenly as they came, did we whirl around before the amazed Parisians and then vanish through the corridor into the dark street.

But after that performance we had the grace to be ashamed of ourselves, and we agreed that it was time to go back to the barracks. The trouble was, though, that we didn't in the least know which way to go. Paris at all times is a puzzle for a Marseilles man, but it is most a puzzle at night.

"Look there," said Margan, staggering a little as he spoke. "Do you see that lantern? Well, I know that lantern—I saw an Aristocrat hung up to it only two nights ago. If we go down there past it we'll get to the river, and then we'll be all right."

Margan's reasoning was so good that we went the way he pointed out to us; and it did bring us to the river, sure enough. We knew where we were, then, and we set to singing as we crossed the bridge and turned to walk up stream. But all of a sudden there was no river in sight, and we were all tangled up again in the narrow crooked Paris streets.

"It's all right," said Peloux. "I know where we are. That light off there is the barracks lantern, for sure."

We headed for the lantern, and as we got nearer to it we heard the most infernal racket inside.

"Well, I'm glad we're back again," said Peloux. "The boys are having an oldfashioned good time."

"Why, this isn't the barracks," said Margan.

"You're right, I believe it isn't," Peloux

answered. "But no matter. Let's go in and see what's going on. The doors are open and there's nothing to pay. Come on!"

We followed him, and as we were stepping across the threshold we met a couple of sans-culottes dragging along a man whom they threw into a cart waiting on the opposite side of the street.

"Oh," said Margan, "it's a tavern; that's what it is. Didn't you see the drunken man those fellows were carrying out? Pooh! These Parisians can't hold any wine at all!"

As we talked, we went into a great vaulted entrance-hall—filled with a shouting, yelling crowd—at the far end of which went up a stairway to the floor above. Excepting a few women, with their sleeves rolled up to their elbows like hucksters, all the people about us were sans-culottes; and although they were armed in every sort of way—with swords and pikes and iron bars and even staves—they all were armed.

Every one was pushing toward the stairway; and as we stood on tip-toe and looked over the heads of the crowd we saw that at the foot of the stairs was a little red table at which sat three sans-culottes, with red caps on their heads, looking as stern and serious as judges. A flickering candle stuck in a bottle stood on the table and lighted up the picture.

While we stood watching, there was a movement up in the shadows at the head of the stairway; and then down into the light came an old priest. He was as pale as death, his hands were bound, and he was between two jailers who pushed and jostled him to make him go faster. As soon as he stood in front of the table at which sat the stern-looking judges, a sharp voice cried out: "He has refused the oath." And then the judges all together cried: "Death!"

On the instant, two or three iron bars struck him down. Pikes and swords were thrust into him. He was dead. And then two sans-culottes dragged out his body to throw it in the cart—the same whom we had met dragging out the man that we thought was drunk.

This sight so sobered me that I dropped Margan's arm and edged my way forward through the crowd toward the front rank that I might see what was going on. The farther I pushed the tighter I was squeezed; and at last I was caught fast among a lot of men and women all so much taller than I was that even on tip-toe I could not get a clear view. But by stooping I managed to see out under the elbow of a big National Guard who had a bloody iron bar in his hand.

I was just settled in my place when a young and beautiful lady was dragged down the stairs. She caught at the balusters, and when she was forced in front of the judges she fell on her knees and her screams and prayers for mercy fairly broke my heart. "Poor girl!" I thought. "Surely they won't dare to kill her?" But in a moment three brutes of women, three furies, flung themselves upon her; and while two of them scratched gashes in her face the third dragged down the waist of her dress and like a mad dog bit and tore her tender breasts. Saving her from this torture, a sans-culotte ran her through with his sword.

The work went on rapidly. One after another, quickly, prisoners were dragged down the stairs; sentence was passed on them in a breath; and in another breath they were killed and carried away to the cart.

All this while the big National Guard in front of me had not stirred. Suddenly he stepped forward, and in the same instant I heard the high-pitched feeble voice of an old man, a voice that I well knew, crying out: "Ah, there you are, my good and faithful fellow. Save me! Save me!" In answer to that cry, the big National Guard raised his iron bar and brought it down with a terrible blow on the head of the poor little old man who was begging for his life.

Then I recognised big Surto: at last he had murdered his master, the Marquis d'Ambrun! As the Marquis fell, La Jacarasse came out from the crowd, and with her pig-killing knife coolly began to cut off the gold buttons from his coat. Surto stepped forward and stamped on the face of his master with his hob-nailed shoes.

With one bound I was in front of the monster, and as I shook my fist at him I cried: "He is a murderer, an Anti-Patriot! Arrest him!" But instantly a half dozen of the men and women, of the hundreds who were shrieking and howling with delight at the bloodshed, seized me and dragged me before the judges. "Thou art the traitor!" they cried. "Thou art the Aristo! Death! Death!"

Happily for me, one of the judges rose from his place and laid his hand upon my head, and so protected me from the iron bars already raised. When the anger of the murderous gang was a little quieted he asked me to give an account of myself, and to tell why I wanted to revenge the death of a Marquis who had come from the other end of the country to help the King.

I began to answer, speaking in as good French as I could muster: "I am a Federal Patriot belonging to the Marseilles Battalion."

"Death! Death!" shrieked the women, breaking in on me; while a sans-culotte who had drawn a paper from my pocket and glanced at it cried out: "Look here! Read this bit of paper—it is his death-warrant!"

It was Monsieur Randoulet's letter recommending me to Canon Jusserand. The judge took the paper, and for a moment there was silence. Up on the stairs above us a line of prisoners was waiting until my affair should be settled to be brought downward to death.

The sans-culotte judge frowned as he read the paper, and I was sure that I was lost. Truly enough, the recommendation of one priest to another priest was a death-warrant in those days. I looked around and called to Margan and Peloux to come forward and prove the truth of what I had said; but the two, having lost sight of me, must have staggered out into the street thinking that they would find me there.

"Death! Death!" shrieked the sans-culottes, crowding around me and raising their iron bars to beat out my brains as soon as the judge took his hand off my head.

. But just then a voice from a strange quarter was raised in my defense. "Wait! I will tell you the truth in this matter. I swear to speak the truth—I who so soon shall appear before my God!"

It was one of the prisoners on the stairs who was speaking. As the judges turned toward him he went on: "That unhappy boy most certainly is a Federal Patriot, a member of the Marseilles Battalion. I know it only too well. That very boy gave the information to the gendarmes of the Nation which led to my arrest on the bridge of Saint-Jean d'Ardières. In proof of what I say, tell him to show you the medal of Notre-Dame-de-Bon-Secours that I gave him then."

Then I knew who it was that was speaking for me: it was the old shepherd, the Bishop of Mende.

I put my hand into my pocket and pulled out the medal and gave it to the judges. They looked at it for a moment, and then said together: "What the boy has said is the truth. He is a Patriot, a Marseillais."

"Then let him be off and join his Battalion," cried a red-coiffed woman; and, seizing me by the shoulder, she thrust me into the crowd toward the door.

I wanted to thank the Bishop of Mende who had saved me from death; but that could not be. As I turned around I saw him kneeling— then the iron bars fell and he dropped in a heap!

I looked for Surto and La Jacarasse, determined to revenge myself on the two monsters; but they had slipped away during the stir caused by my affair, and no doubt had gone to join the worthless Adelaide—the traitress Marquise.

There was nothing left for me but to come away too. I worked along through the crowd and got out at last to the street; and glad I was to be in the quiet of the dark streets, and alone. The sight of Adeline's father had stirred me deeply. I seemed still to hear ringing in my ears the sound of his weak, piping, old-man's voice; the very same voice that had called out to the swine-herd who had given me such a whack when I picked up the cabbage-stalk: "Well done! Well done! What is that little rascal doing there? Does he want to take the food out of the mouths of my pigs?" And now I had seen that old man murdered by his own servant in cold blood!

By that time I was no longer a staggering drunkard. I was entirely sober. A great fright had come to me. Death had been close to my shoulder—so close that I had felt her cold breath upon my neck. The fumes of wine had been driven out of my brain. And suddenly, there in the darkness and silence, all that had happened to me during that day, and most vividly what had happened during these last moments of it, flashed before my eyes. As I saw it all there came over me a fear, an anguish, a shame, no words can tell. How could I ever confess to Lazuli, to Vauclair, to Adeline, how I had passed that day? They could call me anything bad, and it would be true. I could make no denial. Very likely they would have nothing more to do with me —would turn me out of doors.

Then I thought of my money, and began to hunt in my pockets for it—every sou of it was gone! I must have spent it in my stuffing and guzzling. Yet that money did not belong to me to spend. It really belonged to Vauclair. I owed it to him. Just out of pure goodness and kindness of heart, he had sheltered me and cared for me for six long months. It was his money that had gone in my gluttony and drunkenness.

What a sin I had committed! Truly I did deserve to be looked down upon by Vauclair —drunkard that I was! Lazuli would be in tears. Poor Adeline, in all her bitter trouble, would have more trouble and of my making. She would be ashamed to touch me, to speak to me. Never could I dare to see them in such pain and sorrow because of my wickedness; never could I dare to face them again after what I had done. Better would it have been had the Bishop of Mende held his tongue; better had the sans-culottes dashed out my brains. That would have ended all!

In an unending bat-like whirl these dark thoughts flew round and round in my soul. On I tramped, recklessly, aimlessly. I turned one street corner after another without knowing where I was going. I tried to hold the tears back, but they kept rolling down my cheeks. Never had I suffered so bitterly since that night when I came back to the hut of La Garde and found myself without father or mother, alone. The same despair seized me that had seized me then, and the same dark thought came to me—the river! The river would not be frozen like the pond at La Garde —and oh, the good bed that it would make for me! Where was that good kind river?

All that I wanted was to find it and throw myself into it—and so be forgotten of all the world.

As I looked around me I saw that the gutter was running red with blood—the blood of the unhappy wretches they were killing in the big building out of which I had just come—and I knew that this red stream must flow down to the river. I only had to follow it and it would lead me to the great river for which I so longed.

I stepped out quickly, but carefully kept sight of the little red stream that rippled on leading me to my deliverance. And presently, turning a corner, I dimly saw the river before me—overlaid by the friendly morning mist that veiled from me my dismal grave. And then, as before at the pond of La Garde, I drew back for a spring.

At that very moment I heard the rattle of drums. I hesitated. I stopped. Off on the other side of the river, in front of what had been the King's Castle, drums were beating the assembly—just as they did on the morning when we made the attack. What could that drum-call mean, I wondered. Could it be for the departure of the Marseilles Battalion? Could it mean that the tyrant had come back? But, whatever it meant, it put fresh life into me.

Instead of jumping into the river I hurried across it to the drums.

When I came in front of the Castle I found a platform set up on which were three Patriots. One of them was waving the flag of the Nation, blue, white and red; another held up a placard on which was written: "The Country is in-Danger!"; the third had before him on a table a book in which he was writing down the names of volunteers for the army of the Revolution.

Men of all ages were pressing forward to be enlisted: old fellows with grizzled moustaches, youths, boys like myself. They all were of the poorer class, and as they gave their names to be written down they gave everything that they had to give—their blood and their life. Each man, as he passed in front of the altar of his Country and placed his name on the roll of his Country's army, shouted "Vive la Nation!"—and so went on to take his place under the command of a sergeant who ranged the volunteers in line. As each fresh company was formed its men were given guns and powder and ball: that was the whole of their accoutrement. Then came the order: "Forward, march!"—and then and there they started on a forced march to the frontier.

My heart thrilled. The Country in danger? What! We had pulled down the King and smashed his throne to bits and now outsiders were coming to set up King and throne again and to ravage our land! That should never be! On the instant my mind was made up. I marched to the platform and gave in my name as a volunteer, and shouted "Vivo la Nacioun!" as I turned to take my place in the ranks.

"Stop, citizen," said the Patriot who was writing down the names. "Here is your pay for a month," and he handed me three crowns. And then, looking hard at me, he went on: "Surely I know your face. Haven't you been living lately with my good neighbour Planchot?"

"Yes," I answered.

Hearing Planchot's name startled and moved me. Right away I seemed to see Adeline and Vauclair and Lazuli, and fear and shame and sorrow came back into my heart and the tears came close to my eyes. But I held myself together and forced back the sob that was mounting in my throat—for it never should be said that a Marseilles volunteer had wept before a Parisian moustache!

And so, having steadied myself, I said to

the Patriot: "As you are our neighbour, I want you to say good-bye for me to my people at home and to give them these three crowns. Please say to them: 'Pascalet sends you these three crowns in remembrance of your great kindness to him. He is now a volunteer in the Army of the Revolution. The country is in danger and he has started for the frontier.'"

As I spoke, I placed my three crowns in the Patriot's hand—and with them I seemed to lay down also my load of sorrow and of bitter shame.

The bright sunshine was gilding the eaves of the King's Castle about which pretty blue pigeons were flying blithely. Our drums rattled the quick-step. My company moved— and I was started on my march for the Frontier of the North!

Old Pascal was silent for some moments, and we all were silent with him. Even the chattering Materoun, for once in his life, was too deeply interested to wag his tongue. Then Pascal, sighing a little, went on.

With my regiment, I was back in Paris a year later to the very day—the sixteenth of

Fructidor in the year II. We had fought at Valmy, and on the borders of the Rhine even into Holland, driving the last Prussian out of the territory of the Republic. Then our regiment was ordered to the South; and we were halting in Paris to enlist more men before joining the Army of Italy.

That sixteenth of Fructidor I was stationed on guard at the guillotine that was chopping off heads on the Place de la Révolution—standing with shouldered arms on the scaffold, close to the National Knife. I was half sick with the horrible doings going on there, and with my back to the guillotine I stood looking out over the eager shouting crowd.

From where they turned a far corner, I could see the tumbrils full of condemned Aristocrats as they slowly made their way through the crowd to the scaffold steps. Some of the Aristocrats were very brave, looking as cool and quiet as if they were going to a festival; but others, poor things! seemed more dead than alive—so pale, so broken, that to see them fairly drew my heart out of my body. But it made no difference how they looked or how they behaved. Up the steps they came— and the big knife, without resting, cut off head after head. At each fall of the knife the whole scaffold shook, and a cold shiver ran through me—while I longed and longed to be quit of my horrible task.

At the end of what seemed to me a very long time I saw the last cart coming, and with only three people in it: two women and a man. It was nearly over, I thought. I would have to hear the fall of the knife and feel the jar of the scaffold only thrice more. Full of pity, I watched the on-coming cart.

As it rounded the end of the scaffold, passing right 'beneath me, I saw that the man crouching in one corner suddenly started and then leaned still more forward as though to hide his face; as if he had recognised me, and did not want me to recognise him. I looked hard at him, and as I looked my heart gave a bound—it was Surto! In another moment I saw that the two crouching women were the Marquise Adelaide and La Jacarasse!

Oh, that time the guillotine was doing good work! That time I did not turn my back as the knife fell! With burning eyes I looked at them as they were pushed out of the cart and up the scaffold steps. I stared hard. I wanted to make sure of them. But I had not made a mistake: their time had come!

Surto, coward that he was, drew back so

that the women might go first. The Marquise trembled and groaned and muttered her prayers. La Jacarasse squealed like a sow that already feels the knife stuck in her throat. The executioner was used to all that. He had no time to waste. He caught hold of Surto and pushed him down in front of the red block. I tried to speak. I wanted to curse them for all their crimes. But the words stuck in my dry throat, and all that I could do was to point to the sharp knife shining above them. The Marquise, looking upward, fell on her knees with a bitter cry; and even I started back, troubled and amazed. It was not the sight of the knife that so thrilled us; but the sight, above the knife on the cross-piece of the guillotine, of a name that cried vengeance:

ADELINE.

Three times the great knife fell. Three times the heavy stroke shook the scaffold. Three times there fell into the basket a head with eyelids that still fluttered and with jaws, still working, that bit the bloody saw-dust.

"Well done! Oh, well done!" cried La Mie, jumping up and clapping her hands. "How I wish I had been there to see them get their deserts!　To think of that awful Marquise —who had her son and her husband murdered and who turned over her daughter to La Jaca-rasse!　It seems impossible!"

"And that Surto," put in Lou Materoun. "What a Dutch devil he was!　But, to tell the truth, I don't believe that he was the only one who killed his master in those days.　We all know of others who got their hands on what belonged to the Aristos who emigrated or were guillotined—and they are the very ones who now-a-days wear green ribbons with a fleur-de-lys in their buttonholes, and are forever taking off their hats to every nobleman who goes by."

"Those times had to be," said my grand-father, as he drew the cork out of his bottle of malmsey.

"Yes, France was like a tree that needed pruning," added Lou Materoun.

And so each one had his say, while La Mie took the chestnuts off the stove and handed them around.

While I had been sitting still in my corner the cat had gone to sleep on my lap and I did not dare to move for fear of waking her.　But my tongue was burning to ask a question; and after they all were quiet, with their mouths full of chestnuts, I ventured to speak.

"If you please, Pascal?" I said.

"Well, little man, what is it?" he answered.

"If you please, Pascal, did you never see dear little Adeline again?"

"Never, child."

He was quiet for so long that I feared that was the end of it. But at last he spoke. "As I told you, I went off to the army of Italy with General Bonaparte—who afterwards became the great Emperor Napoleon. I went through all the wars with him. I followed him through hundreds and hundreds of battles, which were hundreds and hundreds of victories. Under him we conquered Italy, Egypt, Austria, Prussia, Germany, Spain, Russia. We only stopped when there was no more earth to conquer. I ate wheat-bread in Rome and rye-bread in Berlin. I made my bivouac in Vienna and lighted my camp-fire beside the palace walls. I sharpened my sword on the stones at Jaffa. I picked figs in the gardens of Saragoza. I ate Russian horse-ribs roasted in the fire of Moscow. I followed the great Napoleon through everything, and I was with him at the last at the battle of Mont-Saint-Jean. It was then, finding himself betrayed, that he vanished. But he will come again! He surely will come again!

"And as to Adeline, not a day of my life has passed without my thinking of her—though only once I heard of her in the course of all my wars.

"It was in Egypt, on the third of Thermidor, in the year VI. We had just finished killing all those thousands of Mamelukes. The sand was covered with their bodies as far as a man's eyes could see. I was tired out after so much fighting; and while I was resting myself, sitting in the shade of the first step of the highest Pyramid in Egypt, a drummer of our army came up to me. 'If I'm not wrong about it, comrade,' said he, 'you're Pascalet, the son of La Patine?'

"'Oh, yes, that's me, my good Célégrè,' I answered. 'And I'd know you anywhere by the way you speak. How do you happen to be here? And when did you leave Malemort? Tell me what my people are doing there.'

"So Célégrè sat down beside me there on the Pyramid and gave me all the news from home. My mother had given me a brother named Lange, he said; and two years later my father, poor fellow! had died. But I had no need to worry about my mother, Célégrè went on, because the daughter of the old Marquis d'Ambrun, Mademoiselle Adeline—who since had died a nun in the Ursuline Convent at Avignon—had made her a present of the hut at La Garde with a bit of land around it, and of a larger bit of land at Pati, and of a snug little house in the village in the Rue Basse; and with all that property my mother and my little brother lived very comfortably indeed. 'And there's somebody to look after her, too,' Célégrè went on; 'a man in Avignon, a joiner, named Vauclair. It was he who brought out to her the deeds, written by the notary's hand, that made her sure of Mademoiselle Adeline's gifts; and he is as kind to her as if he were her own son. He told me that you and he marched up to Paris together in the Marseilles Battalion, and he thinks the world of you to this day.

" 'What a good fellow he is, that Vauclair! And his wife Lazuli and his boy Clairet are made of just the same good dough! I went to see them as I passed through Avignon; and after I'd said I was from Malemort, and was a neighbour of your mother's, and knew you, they couldn't do too much for me and everything in their house was mine. They made me take breakfast and dinner and supper with them; and all the time they talked about Pascalet, their own dear little Pascalet; and they

cried like children—just as you are doing
now.'

"And it is true," Pascal said, as he rose to
get his glass of malmsey, "that the tears had
come as I listened to all that Célégrè had told
me—but the sands of the desert can drink
many tears."

I think that we all understood how deep
was Pascal's feeling as he said these words.
No one spoke for a minute or more; and then,
of course, the speaker was Lou Materoun.

"There's just one thing, Pascal," said Lou
Materoun, "that I must ask you to clear up
for me. Just now, when you were speaking
about the great Napoleon, you said 'He surely
will come again.' If he's still alive, I'd like to
know what our picture at home means—the
one on which is written: 'The return of Napoleon's ashes'? I always thought that that picture showed how they brought him back from
Saint Helena and buried him in the Invalides,
up at Paris."

"Hold your tongue, chuckleheaded donkey!" answered Pascal, angrily. "Don't you
know that the Bourbons got up that funeral to
make people think he was dead? But he is
not dead. I who speak to you will swear—
and I am ready to put my hand into the fire if

I swear falsely—that within these three years past I have seen him and spoken with him. It is a matter about which there can be no mistake. It happened in broad daylight in my field at Pati—that lies near, you know, to the place they call Cæsar's Camp.

"I had been spading that field to get rid of the couch-grass, and while I was standing resting I saw a strange man coming toward me with a rake on his shoulder. He walked straight into my field, and when he was within ten paces of me he stopped and said: 'Good and brave soldier of the Empire, show me the way to Cæsar's Camp.'

"And as he stood there, plain before me in the sunlight, I knew him—it was the Emperor!

"I was so upset, so dazed, that I did not know which end I was standing on. And all I could say, as I pointed out the way to him, was: 'There—straight ahead.'

"The Emperor turned and left me, crossing from corner to corner of my field. And since that day"—Pascal spoke these words very solemnly—"I have never given a single hoe-stroke or spade-stroke where his footsteps passed! You may go up there, if you like, and you will find in my field a grassy crosswise path. That path marks the footsteps of the great Napoleon. I tell you, he is still alive!"

Old Pascal drained his glass of malmsey; and then, the meeting being over, each man kindled his lantern and La Mie blew out the light.

THE END.